Peg

Praise for

DEATH IN KEW GARDENS

"This is one of my favorite new series. Ashley writes exquisite historical romance and equally marvelous mysteries."

—*The Washington Post*

"Ashley does a fine job portraying urban life among the well-to-do and those who serve them. . . . [An] unusual and well-thought-out plot. Anne Perry fans will find a lot to like."

—*Publishers Weekly*

"The third winning entry in Ashley's Below Stairs mystery series is another beguiling combination of sharply etched characters, an impeccably realized historical setting, and a cleverly conceived plot that makes excellent use of the Victorian fascination with both botany and China, all wrapped up in writing imbued with just the right dash of dry wit." —*Booklist*

"This is a well-researched, well-constructed novel that leaves one curious to read the further adventures of the main characters." —Historical Novel Society

"The first-person intrigue is nicely described and captures history and mystery in a fine presentation that will intrigue and delight genre fans looking for an absorbing, fun read."

—*Midwest Book Review*

Praise for the Below Stairs Mysteries

"A top-notch new series that deftly demonstrates Ashley's mastery of historical mysteries by delivering an impeccably researched setting, a fascinating protagonist with an intriguing past, and lively writing seasoned with just the right measure of dry wit." —*Booklist*

"An exceptional series launch.... Readers will look forward to this fascinating lead's future endeavors."
—*Publishers Weekly* (starred review)

"A smart and suspenseful read, *Death Below Stairs* is a fun series launch that will leave you wanting more." —Bustle

"This mood piece by Ashley is not just a simple murder mystery. There is a sinister plot against the crown and the race is on to save the queen. The characters are a lively, diverse group, which bodes well for future Below Stairs Mysteries, and the thoroughly entertaining cast will keep readers interested until the next escapade. The first installment is a well-crafted Victorian adventure." —RT Book Reviews

"A fun, intriguing mystery with twists and turns makes for a promising new series." —Red Carpet Crash

"A charming new mystery series sure to please!"
—Fresh Fiction

"What a likeable couple our sleuths Kat Holloway and Daniel McAdam make—after you've enjoyed *Death Below Stairs*, make room on your reading calendar for *Scandal Above Stairs*."
—Criminal Element

Titles by Jennifer Ashley

Below Stairs Mysteries

A SOUPÇON OF POISON
(an ebook)

DEATH BELOW STAIRS

SCANDAL ABOVE STAIRS

DEATH IN KEW GARDENS

MURDER IN THE EAST END

The Mackenzies Series

THE MADNESS OF LORD IAN MACKENZIE

LADY ISABELLA'S SCANDALOUS MARRIAGE

THE MANY SINS OF LORD CAMERON

THE DUKE'S PERFECT WIFE

A MACKENZIE FAMILY CHRISTMAS

THE SEDUCTION OF ELLIOT MCBRIDE

THE UNTAMED MACKENZIE
(an ebook)

THE WICKED DEEDS OF DANIEL MACKENZIE

SCANDAL AND THE DUCHESS
(an ebook)

RULES FOR A PROPER GOVERNESS

THE SCANDALOUS MACKENZIES
(an anthology)

THE STOLEN MACKENZIE BRIDE

A MACKENZIE CLAN GATHERING
(an ebook)

A MACKENZIE CLAN CHRISTMAS

A MACKENZIE YULETIDE
(an ebook)

MURDER IN THE
THE
EAST END

Jennifer Ashley

Berkley Prime Crime
New York

BERKLEY PRIME CRIME
Published by Berkley
An imprint of Penguin Random House LLC
penguinrandomhouse.com

Library of Congress Cataloging-in-Publication Data

Names: Ashley, Jennifer, author.
Title: Murder in the East End / Jennifer Ashley.
Description: First edition. | New York: Berkley Prime Crime, 2020. |
Series: Below stairs mysteries; 4
Identifiers: LCCN 2020005046 (print) | LCCN 2020005047
(ebook) | ISBN 9780593099377 (trade paperback) |
ISBN 9780593099384 (ebook)
Subjects: GSAFD: Mystery fiction.
Classification: LCC PS3601.S547 M87 2020 (print) | LCC PS3601.S547
(ebook) | DDC 813/.6—dc23
LC record available at https://lccn.loc.gov/2020005046
LC ebook record available at https://lccn.loc.gov/2020005047

First Edition: August 2020

Printed in the United States of America
1 3 5 7 9 10 8 6 4 2

Cover art by Mark Owen / Arcangel
Cover design by Emily Osborne
Book design by Laura K. Corless

1

February 1882

He's asking for you, Mrs. H."

Ordinarily, these words, spoken by a lad called James, the son of my dear friend, Daniel McAdam, would give me a flutter of pleasant anticipation. I hadn't spoken to Daniel in several long weeks, as he'd been traveling, this time to Ireland.

Tonight, however, Daniel would have to wait. The kitchen of the Mount Street house where I was cook boiled with activity, the oven hot as a blacksmith's forge, as I turned out meats, puddings, and tasty sauces as quickly as my assistant, Tess, and I could make them. The odors of roasted flesh and burned sugar competed with that of boiling vegetables and sautéed fish. I'd recruited Charlie, the boy who tended the fires, to help with peeling and chopping. Maids and footmen streamed to and fro, and Elsie, the scullery maid, washed dishes with the vigor of a sailor swabbing down a deck.

"He is most inconvenient, your father," I called to James as I ladled pan juices over a roasted duck on a platter and arranged boiled new potatoes around it. "Please tell him Mrs. Bywater decided to host a supper ball, of all things, with half a week's notice. A great part of Mayfair is upstairs now, trying to waltz in what's meant to be the parlor. Food must flow, Mrs. Bywater said, as though I am a fish-and-chips man." I slammed the spoon back into the pan and shoved it at Elsie, who fled with it to the scullery.

James took no offense at my brisk words. He sidestepped out of Elsie's way then helped her balance the pan on the way to the sink, to her delight.

"When service is done, he means," James said cheerily over his shoulder. "Anything I can do to help, Mrs. H.?"

He was a lovely young man. Going on seventeen now, James was a good foot taller than he'd been when I'd first met him. I was pleased to see that his coat and trousers covered his long arms and legs, new clothes if I were any judge, or at least sturdy secondhand ones.

I wiped my sleeve over my sweat-streaked face. "Take the other end of this platter, and we'll haul it to the dumbwaiter. And for heaven's sake spill nothing. A day's work, this is."

James lifted his end of the duck's tray robustly, the lad strong, and it nearly tilted out of my hands. I gave him an exasperated look, and he grinned and eased the platter down to my height.

We had the duck safely into the lift at last, and James cranked the ropes to haul it upstairs. I could only hope that the footmen above who retrieved it treated it with care.

James lingered, and so I used him shamelessly. Another pair of hands was not unwelcome.

Tess and I had spent much of yesterday making a large layer cake with icing and spun sugar decorations. I entered the larder, where I'd stored it, and of course found the cake sagging in the middle, the icing and sugar half-melted and broken. My shriek brought Tess running. When she saw the wreck, she stared in dismay, her language burning the air.

I hadn't the heart to admonish her for her curses. Many of the words she used were ones that leapt readily to my mind.

"Never mind," I shouted over her. "We must send something. Help me."

In the next half hour we worked a miracle of sorts. Into the dumbwaiter went a large apple charlotte thrown together from apples I'd cooked down earlier in the day along with ladyfingers left over in the larder. I surrounded this with plates of macaroons for those with daintier appetites and the rhubarb tart I'd made for the staff. It had been meant as a treat after our hard work, but needs must.

Once all the food was gone, Tess and I could not collapse, because the kitchen had to be thoroughly cleaned and organized for the morrow. I'd have to cook for the family and any guests all the next day, not to mention the servants.

James vanished somewhere in the process, but I didn't begrudge him his escape.

As I scrubbed down the work table, removing every bit of flour, grease, grit, and meat juices so I'd have a clean surface tomorrow, one of the footmen bounded into the kitchen, out of breath.

He was new—footmen here tended to come and go. Mrs. Bywater had a penny-pinching nature, and an employer had to pay an extra tax on male servants of any kind, as they were considered a luxury. Therefore, she encouraged the lads to seek employment in other houses once they had a bit of experience, while the maids took on the extra work. Of the footmen who'd been here when I'd first arrived, only Paul remained.

This footman, who went by the name of Hector, ran headlong into the kitchen then stopped short, no doubt remembering my admonishments not to blunder through my territory.

"They're asking for you, Mrs. Holloway," he said, eyes wide. "The upstairs."

I continued to scrub, seeing no reason for excitability. "To do what, precisely? If they wish me to send up more dishes, they will have to wait a few minutes. I'm behindhand."

Hector stared in confusion. I did not think this young man would last long under the firm hand of Mr. Davis, our butler, nor the keen eye of the new housekeeper, Mrs. Redfern.

"I mean they're asking you to come up. Mr. Davis sent me to fetch you."

"Ooh." Tess, her temper restored, looked up from scraping out a bowl that had held pureed potatoes. "I wager they want you to take your bow, Mrs. H."

Cooks generally remained anonymous in the kitchen, which I preferred, but every once in a while were summoned to the dining room, where the master or mistress, or her guests, could thank her for the meal. Or, dress her down for her shortcomings—either could be the case.

I disliked these rare summonses above stairs, preferring to remain in the kitchen to get on with my job. But the mistress decided whether I kept my employment or was turned out, so I sighed, removed my apron, and tried to smooth my hair.

Another reason I disliked being summoned to the dining room was that cooking left me sweaty, grimy, and mussed. I brushed off my sleeves as best I could and straightened my cap.

"Wait." Tess grabbed me, wet her thumb in her mouth, and rubbed at a smudge on my cheek. "There," she proclaimed. "You're perfect. Maybe one of them will give you a vail."

Guests did sometimes hand a servant who pleased them a

coin. These tokens I did not mind—an unmarried woman with a growing daughter cannot turn up her nose at an extra bob or two. But to stand in front of company while they scrutinized me was not to my taste.

Once Tess released me, upstairs I went.

The back stairs emerged in the rear of the house, the door opening to a wide hall leading to the front. The house had once been two, the walls knocked out by a previous owner to create one great mansion.

Guests thronged the house tonight, filling the hall and moving between rooms. Few noticed me appear, and those who did gave me no acknowledgment or even curiosity. A domestic was hardly worth a glance.

Mr. Davis spied me and beckoned me into the dining room. The dining table had been turned into a sideboard, filled with food that guests could take to other parts of the house.

Mr. Davis's dark hair shone with pomade, his hairpiece perfectly aligned, his swallow-tailed coat an example of excellent tailoring. He addressed Mrs. Bywater, who hovered with a cluster of guests near the table, the remains of my feast, including the roast duck, upon it.

"Mrs. Holloway, ma'am," Mr. Davis announced.

Mrs. Bywater, who prided herself on dressing like a prudent matron, wore a plain maroon gown and a sort of bag on her head that was meant to be a turban. Her friends were rather more fashionably dressed, a few in the black or gray of mourning or half-mourning.

"Here is our cook," Mrs. Bywater declared. "Responsible for our excellent meal."

The group around her burst into polite applause. I curtsied, trying to look grateful, hiding my discomfort.

One of the ladies, her gray hair in tight ringlets, lifted a lorgnette to peer at me. "It must be a frightful expense to employ her."

"We are frugal with the household budget." Mrs. Bywater managed to look proud and humble at the same time. "Much can be done with careful planning. Mrs. Holloway is clever with her purchases."

This was the first time my employer had admitted such a thing about me, though I did not take her compliments as they were. I knew she spoke to impress her friends.

"She is very young." The lorgnette flashed as it moved over my person. "I prefer a stout woman with plenty of gray hair. You'd know *she* had experience. This one cannot be much into her twenties."

Mr. Davis radiated silent disapproval, considering it gauche for the mistress to discuss not only expenses, but the staff, especially in front of other staff.

I was young, it was true, especially to be a cook in an elegant Mayfair household. The *Mrs.* appended to my name was a sign of respect given to senior female servants, and if people assumed I had once been married, I said nothing to dissuade them.

A new voice joined the conversation. "Mrs. Holloway is thirty. A fine age, I think."

Lady Cynthia Shires, niece to Mr. Bywater and daughter of an earl, halted near Mrs. Bywater and gave the lorgnette lady a look of frank assessment.

I hid my surprise when she came into view. Cynthia had dressed, uncharacteristically, in a frock more beautiful than any in the room. She had recently come out of mourning for her sister, and her evening gown had plenty of colors to make up for her previous lack of them—a deep pink bodice and a cream silk skirt, which was gathered back into a small train and trimmed with ruched ribbon and cloth roses.

She wore her golden hair in its usual unadorned knot, simple elegance in a room filled with diamond-studded turbans, flower-filled bandeaus, and braids and false curls festooned with feathers.

Cynthia met my gaze, a mischievous twinkle in her eyes. That Cynthia, who preferred to lounge about the house in a man's suit, had donned such a splendid dress meant she was up to something.

A young woman joined Cynthia, sliding her hand into the crook of Cynthia's arm. She was dark-haired and a beauty.

The term *beauty* is bandied about without discretion, in my opinion, when every young lady who makes her bow is termed so, regardless of her true looks, but this woman was an exception.

The lady was about the same age I was, by my guess. Her very dark hair was dressed in curls at the base of her neck, bound with a thin gold chain. Her cream-colored gown was subdued, its bustle small and without the masses of ribbons, embroidery, or appliqué that other ladies wore tonight. It was a ball dress, no doubt, but a tastefully made and subtle one.

"The lobster rissoles were excellent, Mrs. Holloway," the young woman said to me.

I curtsied to her diffidently but did not speak. I should only answer when asked a direct question.

"I have not tasted such splendid food in an age," she continued. "A fine treat."

I nodded my thanks, attempting to keep my eyes averted as a proper servant ought, but I shot her a glance of curiosity. I had no idea who she was, but from the way she hung on Cynthia's arm, the two were close friends.

The lady studied me with openness, but in a far more courteous manner than the lorgnette woman. Another difference between this lovely lady and the others in the room was that she spoke directly to me and used my name.

Mrs. Bywater seemed to think I'd had enough praise for one night. "Thank you, Mrs. Holloway," she said in a tone that meant I was dismissed.

I curtsied to the company, darted a last look at Cynthia's friend, and walked sedately from the room. No scurrying back to my hole. I departed with my head high, dignity in place, accepting the praise for my hard work without false modesty.

I could have wished for a coin or two, however. Compliments are all very well, but shillings and pence are far more welcome.

Not until after midnight did I have the chance to hang up my apron, scrub my hands and face in the scullery sink, don coat and hat, and depart to meet Daniel.

February rain poured outside, rendering the night cold and dank. I pulled on gloves and ducked my head against the spattering drops as I hurried into the street.

Little traffic, foot or carriage, roamed on this wet night, the residents of Mount Street wisely remaining indoors. I too ought to have stayed at home to snatch a few hours of sleep, giving Daniel my apologies when I saw him again.

It was a testimony to my curiosity and my fondness for Daniel that I scurried, head bowed, along South Audley Street toward Grosvenor Chapel. James had told me his father would await me there.

I doubted James meant in the chapel itself, which was shut.

I made my way along a passage that edged the graceful church and ended at a gate to a green.

I hoped Daniel did not wish to have a conversation on the grass. It was dreadfully wet, and I felt a sneeze coming on.

"Kat."

He was behind me. I swung around, dismayed by how lighthearted Daniel's voice rendered me. I told myself this was because I had not seen him in many weeks, and I naturally was glad to see him.

He stood in an open doorway, outlined by light, which proved the chapel was not shut entirely.

"My dear Kat, come in out of the rain," Daniel said, reaching for me. "Next time, tell James you wish me to the devil and stay home."

He caught my hand and pulled me into the lighted space, shutting the door behind us. I found myself in a small room lined with cupboards and robes on hooks—the sacristy, I believed it was called. The room had no stove, but the absence of chill wind and rain came as a relief.

Daniel wore his working clothes—wool coat patched at the elbows, linen shirt, knee breeches shiny with wear, and heavy boots. He'd removed his cap, showing me that his dark brown hair had grown even longer during his absence.

At least he was Daniel tonight, meaning I did not have to pretend I knew him as a City gent, or a pawnbroker's assistant, or whoever else he'd decided to be. He disguised himself whenever he worked for the police, but I preferred him as the deliveryman I'd first met a few years ago, who'd heaved a heavy sack to the kitchen floor and given me a smile I never forgot.

"Such language in a church," I said, disengaging my hand.

"I knew you'd not have asked for me if it hadn't been frightfully important."

"True. I know you have little time to spare." His crooked grin was as self-deprecating as ever.

I shook rain from my skirts. "Well, you'd better tell me what you wish to say. I need to make an early start."

What *I* wished him to say was that he'd missed me. Perhaps he'd kiss me, and I'd go home warm.

I was a bit disappointed, therefore, when Daniel said, "I need you to meet someone."

He crossed the room and opened the far door, sticking his head through and speaking words too quiet for me to discern.

The door opened wider to admit a man I'd never seen before. He was as tall as Daniel and as bulky, but there the resemblance ended. Where Daniel's face was hard and square, this man had narrow cheeks and regular features, so regular they made him quite handsome. His dark hair was neatly trimmed and slicked back from his face, and he had a beard, also neatly trimmed, short and brown.

Instead of a workman's clothes, he wore a dark suit with a dog collar—a white starched strip around his neck that proclaimed him one of the clergy.

"Mrs. Holloway," Daniel said, a coolness entering his tone, "may I present the Reverend Errol Fielding." He paused. "My brother."

I do not know which astonished me more—the fact that Daniel's brother was a clergyman or that Daniel had a brother at all.

Fielding, Daniel had said, not *McAdam*, though Daniel had once told me he'd invented his surname.

Mr. Fielding removed his gloves and held out a hand to me. "I am pleased to meet you, Mrs. Holloway. Daniel has told me about you and your cleverness. Just the person, he said, to help me."

I clasped Mr. Fielding's hand, and he shook mine firmly. He withdrew immediately, not holding on any longer than was appropriate.

I turned to Daniel. "And you thought to consult me on a rainy night in the back of a chapel?"

"My fault," Mr. Fielding said quickly. "I thought you'd be more comfortable meeting two fellows in a church instead of a tavern."

The snug in a tavern would have been more amenable to me, though I admit having to make my way to one alone in the dark and rain might have deterred me. Daniel was acquainted with the vicar of Grosvenor Chapel, who'd given him a place to sleep on more than one occasion, though I saw no evidence of that vicar here tonight.

Daniel let Mr. Fielding apologize without offering explanation or change of expression. This puzzled me, as Daniel usually had a glib word to soften any occasion. The tension with which he regarded his brother told me clearly that Daniel did not like him, or at least did not trust him.

"Perhaps you would prefer to sit, Mrs. Holloway." Mr. Fielding dragged a chair from the corner, a carved wooden one with upholstery on its seat and back. This was the vicar's seat, hardly appropriate for a cook.

"Thank you, but no need. Please, tell me the problem, and perhaps we can solve it and all take some rest this night."

Mr. Fielding gave me a look of surprised respect, and his manner softened. "I apologize for troubling you at all. I came to Daniel with this matter, because he is far and away the most capable man I know. He wished to ask you about it, and thought it would be easier if I explained it myself."

So far, there had been much apologizing and little explaining, but I did not admonish him. I opened my hands and waited for him to begin.

"I have a parish in the East End," Mr. Fielding said. "A small church called All Saints in Shadwell, among the most wretched of society. But as I came from a wretched place myself, I fit there." He flashed me a smile that contained no hint of that dark past. "Daniel and I were raised together, and he tells me you know under what circumstances. We refer to each other as brother, but we were no such thing, though as close as. After the man we called our father died, I eked a living on the streets until I had the fortune to be taken in by a gentleman who'd lost his own son. He raised me and paid for me to be privately tutored, and then managed to get me into Balliol–Oxford–as a charity student, where I studied and took holy orders. Though my foster father is wellborn–the younger son of a marquess, in fact–I am not, and so I doubt I will rise higher than I have, but I will be forever grateful for him."

His speech sounded a bit rehearsed, but perhaps Mr. Fielding was trying to convince me he was respectable. The gentleman who'd taken him in must have been one of rare benevolence to give a boy off the streets an education at his own expense.

"I find that I like being a shepherd–as it were," Mr. Fielding went on. "Helping those who were like myself. Though I am no soft touch–I worked hard to relieve myself from poverty and to show my gratitude to my foster father, and I expect no less of my parishioners. One duty I have taken on, which I do without objection, is to serve on the board of governors of the Foundling Hospital in Brunswick Square."

I knew exactly the place to which Mr. Fielding referred, and a chill went through me.

Years ago, when I'd realized I'd conceived, I'd made myself walk to the formidable gray building that was the Foundling Hospital. It stretched its arms around a vast courtyard, forbidding and confining at the same time. I'd hated the Hospital yet was drawn to it, my young heart terrified I'd have no choice but to leave my child there when I delivered her.

I knew that within the Foundling Hospital's walls, Grace would have been fed, clothed, and taught a trade, one that would keep her from the streets, disgrace, and an early death.

But I'd likely never have seen her again. That was the price a woman paid for depositing her baby on their doorstep. She turned away and left the child, trusting others to do what they could for her.

In the end, I was grateful to the gray brick building and its frowning windows, and the equally gray children I'd seen in the courtyard, dressed all alike, marching along under the guide of a matron or rector. It made me decide to work my fingers to the bone to raise my daughter myself, to never give her up, to hold her in my arms and keep her safe.

No easy task, but I did not regret my choice. Grace, now age eleven, lived with my friends, kind people who forgave me my foolishness and looked after Grace with the wages I sent them.

I did not trust myself to answer Mr. Fielding, so I nodded.

"I was elected to the board a year ago, and it has been uneventful thus far," Mr. Fielding said. "I don't see the children much, but vote on budgets, look over accounts, advise on matters of spiritual education, that sort of thing."

He paused as though waiting for my acknowledgment, and I nodded again. I noticed that he, as had Cynthia's friend earlier this evening, talked *to* me, not at me or around me. I also noticed Daniel's cynical expression, as though he did not believe Mr. Fielding had any business advising on spiritual education.

"Please continue," I prompted when Mr. Fielding's pause extended. "You said your year was uneventful. Has that changed?"

"It has." Mr. Fielding heaved a sigh. "As you might gather, Mrs. Holloway, when I was younger, I was a reprobate, and in many ways still am." His blue eyes took on the twinkle I'd seen when he'd spoken of his past, but the twinkle swiftly died. "But this has distressed me."

"Tell her," Daniel said, his voice hard. "No one is blaming you."

"That is true. There is nothing to blame me *for*." Mr. Fielding gave me a troubled look. "A few children have gone missing from the Foundling Hospital."

My eyes widened in alarm. "Good heavens. Have you informed the police?"

"Not exactly." Mr. Fielding glanced about the small room, as though worried he'd be overheard. "When one of the nurses, a young woman called Nurse Betts, noticed them absent, she reported this to me, as a member of the board, and wanted to go to the police. But it would have to be done discreetly, I knew. The Hospital does not want to be known as a place that loses children. Funding would diminish, certainly. The Hospital was formed by a royal charter, and no one wants to risk that. I convinced Nurse Betts to leave the matter in my hands. I consulted with the director of the Hospital—Lord Russell Hirst—who is in charge of the day-to-day running of it, and another governor, an unctuous bishop called Exley. They forestalled me by telling me the children had been fostered, quietly, though no one has seen them since."

"But you do not believe they were," I said, disquiet touching me. "Or you'd not have consulted Daniel. Why are you certain the children are missing?"

"I was more concerned than panicked." Mr. Fielding sounded apologetic. "But then Nurse Betts disappeared herself. *That* I did report, but the police are useless—they tried to tell me she might simply have gone off on her own. But it is too much of a coincidence for my taste."

"Why come to me?" I directed these words at Daniel, who'd rested a hip on the edge of a table and folded his arms, a most irreverent posture for a sacristy. "I do not like this tale and believe the police ought to search diligently for the nurse as well as the children, but what do you think *I* can do?"

"Ask questions," Daniel said readily. "You are good at making people answer them. Speak to the servants at the Hospital. They likely know much about the comings and goings there."

I threw him a look of exasperation. "I am flattered by your confidence, but I can hardly march into the kitchens of the Foundling Hospital and begin interviewing the cooks and maids. *You'd* find it a much easier task yourself, going to them in your delivery van. I have no doubt you could finagle your way into the firms who supply the Hospital."

Mr. Fielding flashed me a very un-clerical grin. "Daniel has ever been skilled at finagling."

Daniel pretended to ignore him. "I could and possibly will. But people open up to you, Kat. Besides, you have a foundling in your own kitchen, another reason I suggested that Errol speak to you."

"Do I?" I blinked. The kitchen staff had been there before I'd come, except Tess, and I knew she wasn't a foundling. She'd been raised by parents, though not very good ones. I hadn't asked any of the others about their origins, considering it none of my affair.

"Elsie, your scullery maid. She told James," Daniel said. "She was raised at this very Hospital. She can tell you who you can chat with, might even know the missing children and nurse in question."

I would certainly ask her, but I fixed both men with a steely gaze. "I have quite a lot to do, Daniel. I cannot simply leave the kitchen whenever I wish. Food does not cook itself."

I spoke with less conviction than my tone might convey. I

did not like Mr. Fielding's story, as Daniel knew I would not. If Mr. Fielding had been worried about someone fiddling the accounting, I'd have walked home and told them to leave me be, but missing children was a different matter entirely. I knew full well the horrors of London for a lad or lass on his or her own. Having to beg for coin or food would be the least terrible thing that could befall them.

"I will consult with Elsie," I said. "Day after tomorrow I take my day out, and I will see what I can do."

Daniel flashed me the smile that never failed to warm me. "Thank you, Kat."

Mr. Fielding noticed what passed between us with sudden interest. "Ever the charmer, is our Daniel. Do not believe anything he says, Mrs. Holloway. You can take my word as a vicar on that."

"You weren't always a vicar," Daniel said darkly.

Mr. Fielding burst out laughing, an impudent sound that did not go with this solemn place. "That is true. Reprobate, as I said, but I am now respectable and reformed—mostly." His merriment faded. "I truly am concerned, Mrs. Holloway. I'd rest easier knowing these children were well."

The look he gave me was sincere, a kindly one in a handsome face. He claimed Daniel was a charmer, but I saw that this man too could charm, laughing at himself while showing sincerity deep in his eyes.

There was something else in those eyes as well, I'd seen when he'd spoken the name of the missing nurse. A worry that had changed into fear, one that had made him seek Daniel, a fellow survivor from his distant past. I very much wanted to know more about Nurse Betts and what she meant to Mr. Fielding.

* * *

Daniel walked me home. I could have gone perfectly well by myself—after all, I'd arrived on my own—but he led me out into the rain, hand firm on my elbow.

It was not far to Mount Street, but the wind had picked up, and the going became arduous. With some relief, I descended the stairs that led from the street to my kitchen, glad to be out of the wind, though the stairwell was quite dark. Very clean, however. Mrs. Redfern, our new housekeeper, was diligent about sending a maid and a footman out to clear and scrub the steps.

Daniel descended with me, but before I could open the back door, he pulled me to a halt. "I am glad to see you, Kat."

The warmth in his voice was agreeable, but the cold wind was foul, and I'd prefer to speak to him out of the weather.

"Come in and have tea," I said. "I still have a bit left from Mr. Li." A Chinese man I'd done a kindness for had rewarded me with a gift of exquisite leaves directly from China.

Daniel was already shaking his head. "Things to do, and I'm late." He closed in on me under the stairs, which was also agreeable, though I realized he merely wished to not be over-heard.

"You are good to help, and I knew you would be," he said in a low voice. "But have a care with my brother. He has taken a collar and proclaims himself a virtuous man, but his motives are not always clear."

"Yes, I gathered that."

"Did you? All I heard was his smooth tongue trying to convince you he'd reformed."

"My dear Daniel, my head is not easily turned by a handsome gentleman," I said. "He tried too hard to be convincing."

Daniel relaxed. "I know you are no fool, but Errol can be beguiling."

"What intrigues me more is that you have said not one word about him. Nor made any mention you had a brother at all."

Daniel's grin flashed. "Foster brother. There is a saying— *Least said . . . soonest forgotten.*"

"It is *Least said, soonest mended.* You are evading the question."

"I am." Daniel's eyes glittered in the darkness. "I will tell you all about dear brother Errol another time, when we are warmer and cozier, and I am not in such a rush. For now—do not trust him. He has the voice of an angel, but Lucifer was once an angel, remember."

The warning made me shiver—or perhaps it was the wind. "You sound dire."

"Errol was a bad 'un once, and I have no reason to suppose he's changed."

I grew more curious. "How long since you've spoken to him?"

Daniel rubbed his chin. "Ten years? Possibly. I'd hoped it would be longer, but today he too easily found me. Have a care of him, Kat."

He leaned closer and fulfilled my earlier wish by kissing me lightly on the lips. The merest brush, but a spark jumped inside me to ease the cold.

Daniel drew a thick-gloved finger across my cheek. "Good night, Kat." He paused, as though he'd turn and go, then he said, "I missed you."

I could have responded with something sentimental, such as, *I missed you too. Please don't stay away so long again.*

But sentimentality embarrassed me, and I said instead, "You missed my cooking, you mean. If you scrub yourself up,

I might have a scrap to spare you when next you decide to darken my door."

Not rebuffed in the slightest, Daniel released me and laughed. "I missed you indeed. Good night, Kat."

He doffed his cap and dashed up the stairs with an energy unnatural for so late an hour. His laughter floated back to me, rich and deep, warming me in the damp darkness.

I skimmed inside on light feet, through the silent scullery, pots gleaming from Elsie's skill, to find Mrs. Redfern standing squarely in the middle of the kitchen.

"Mrs. Holloway," she greeted me.

I stifled a yelp of surprise then slid out of my coat in pretended nonchalance. "Mrs. Redfern. Have you not gone to bed?"

"I prefer to be the last to retire."

I heard the steel in her voice. Mrs. Redfern had been the housekeeper next door until that household had moved north to Liverpool. Mrs. Redfern, wishing to stay in London, had accepted a post in this house, as we'd had a vacancy.

Mrs. Redfern was efficient, fair, and competent, but like me, she brooked no nonsense. I was used to coming and going somewhat as I pleased—Mr. Davis, while he was curious or disapproving of my unplanned outings, did nothing to stop me. Mrs. Redfern was a bit more exacting.

"I beg your pardon," I said, trying to sound contrite. "I did not realize you'd waited up for me."

"I only wished to bolt the door." Mrs. Redfern moved past me into the scullery and did so, giving the scullery itself a quick glance before reemerging. "I have no intention of being a telltale, Mrs. Holloway, but I happened to notice you returning with Mr. McAdam."

My face warmed, and I busied myself hanging up my coat and dripping hat. "He was good enough to walk me home in the rain, yes."

"More than that, I think. Tess was gleeful you'd slipped out to meet him. She is romantic." Mrs. Redfern's tone indicated *she* would never be so. "Do have a care, Mrs. Holloway. Mr. McAdam is an unsavory sort, and Mr. Davis agrees. Consider that this man asked you to see him on such a night, so late. I speak only as one concerned."

I *had* considered it, and I'd rushed straight into the darkness to find him. Perhaps I was not so impervious to charming gentlemen as I'd claimed to Daniel.

Mrs. Redfern seemed to be waiting for an explanation—or apology perhaps? "His son told me it was important," I said. A truth.

"And was it?"

"I believed it so." I had no intention of regaling her with the full tale.

"I fear that you will come to grief over him," Mrs. Redfern said, her sternness relenting a bit. "If it is ever hinted that you are less than respectable, Mrs. Holloway, you could lose your post, and what would become of you?"

Her concern was real, and she was right. In spite of her rigid manner, I knew Mrs. Redfern spoke out of worry, not admonition. At least, not much admonition.

"No harm done," I said, trying to sound cheerful. "I did go out to speak to Mr. McAdam, but as we were also conversing with a vicar, my virtue was in no danger."

"A vicar?" Mrs. Redfern looked alarmed, as though convinced I was about to elope with Daniel.

"He is a . . . friend . . . of Mr. McAdam's," I said quickly.

"Nothing untoward. The man is on the board of the Foundling Hospital, in fact. Good night, Mrs. Redfern."

She regarded me in grave suspicion but at last gave me a stiff nod. "Good night, Mrs. Holloway."

Mrs. Redfern remained in the middle of the kitchen as I departed for the long climb to my bedchamber. I heard her closing doors behind me, and it grew very dark as she put out the last of the lamps.

I was weary in the morning, but arrived on time at my post to prepare breakfast. Tess, a surprisingly early riser today, had already begun the bread for the day and a pan of sausages and potatoes for the staff.

Mrs. Redfern hurried through on her way to supervise the maids upstairs, the woman fresh and hearty, though she'd retired after I had. She barely glanced at me as she went about her duties, never saying a word about our encounter.

"Morning, Mrs. H."

Lady Cynthia's drawling voice preceded her into the kitchen. She took a seat at the table and reached for a carrot from the bunch Tess chopped. Tess gave her a grin, more comfortable now with Cynthia's impromptu visits.

Cynthia wore trousers, waistcoat, and frock coat, with a cravat loosely tied about her neck. She'd told me once that in dressing in men's clothing, she merely emulated a famous lady novelist from France called George Sand, but as I'd never heard of the woman, the reference meant little to me. Lady Cynthia and I had become friends, growing ever closer—she had been of valuable assistance as I'd looked into problems in the past year, some of which had proved quite perilous.

"Favor to ask," Cynthia said after I returned her greeting. "My friend, Miss Townsend. You met her last night."

I recalled the beautiful young woman who had slipped in next to Cynthia and taken her arm. "The lady who praised my lobster rissoles?"

Cynthia chuckled. "I thought you'd remember her liking your food. She's the one who craves a boon. She's an artist, and a dashed clever one. She wants to paint you, Mrs. H."

3

P aint?" I ceased sorting the mushrooms I'd use in omelets
for the upstairs and gazed at Cynthia in dismay. "*Me?* Are
you certain?"

"I am indeed. She wanted to meet you, which is why I persuaded Auntie to summon you above stairs last evening. I beg
your pardon—I know you prefer to rusticate here, but I couldn't
traipse down with Miss Townsend in all our finery without
some explanation to my aunt. Besides, I knew you were running about ragged. Didn't wish to intrude."

I returned to the mushrooms. "You could have brought her
down a quieter day. This morning, for instance."

Cynthia's face crinkled in amusement. "I enjoy when you
admonish me, Mrs. H. So polite you are, but you make your
feelings known. I have my reasons. I wanted to show Auntie
that Miss Townsend is a quiet-spoken, respectable young
woman, never mind she's an artist. I persuaded Auntie to let
her come to the supper ball, and I turned myself out like a

dressmaker's doll so Auntie's cronies wouldn't be shocked by me."

"You looked beautiful," I said in true admiration. "The gown suited you."

"Ha. Full of pins poking at me—dressmaker had to alter it at the last minute. But my sacrifice was worth it. Worked a dream. Auntie was charmed with Miss Townsend and happy to have her come and paint our servants."

I tossed a shriveled mushroom into my slop bowl and continued sorting the others, the woodsy smell comforting.

"I return to my original question," I said. "Why does Miss Townsend wish to paint me? And how exactly does she mean to?"

Tess had been listening hard while her hands continued with the carrots. "Artists' models are dreadful wicked women, ain't they?" She sounded more eager than appalled.

"My, my, I've shocked you both," Cynthia said cheerfully. "Miss Townsend is a lady through and through, I assure you, from a genteel and quiet family. More respectable than *my* scandalous family, believe me. She paints domestic scenes, in the style of painters like Berthe Morisot or Mary Cassatt."

She waited, but I could not claim to be any more familiar with these ladies than I was with the novelist George Sand. My knowledge of the art world was confined to what I read in the newspapers, or what Mr. Davis read out to me—most was criticism of paintings I doubted I'd have the opportunity to view.

Tess allowed me to hide my ignorance by asking, "Who are *they*? Sound Frenchified to me."

"Miss Cassatt is an American," Cynthia answered. "But yes, she moved to Paris and is Frenchified now, as you say. Miss Morisot—she is more properly Madame Manet, as she is married to the famous artist's brother–is indeed French. Anyway, they paint ladies having tea, or mothers with their children, that sort of thing. Miss Townsend had the great fortune to study with Miss Morisot, for which she will be forever grateful. I'm not as clever about art as Bobby, but I think Miss Townsend is a dashing great painter. She is modest about it, but her daubs are beautiful."

"And now she wishes to paint a cook." I finished with the mushrooms and began to separate herbs from their tangle, the pleasing scents of thyme, dill, and chervil replacing the fresh-turned earth scent of the mushrooms.

"She plans a series of domestic scenes, which will include a cook and maids at work, that sort of thing," Cynthia explained.

I gave her a doubtful look. "I cannot imagine ladies and gentlemen in a rush to buy paintings filled with ordinary servants."

Cynthia shrugged. "Miss Townsend is less worried about selling the paintings than she is making a name for herself. Fame is her ambition, not fortune. Her family is appallingly wealthy, and they indulge her."

How splendid it must be to have a doting family and the money to do anything one pleases. "I don't have much time, as you know. My day out, I am afraid, is already spoken for."

Cynthia understood why. Thursdays, my one full day off, were reserved entirely for my daughter.

"That is no trouble, Mrs. H. Miss Townsend wants to come down to the kitchen, to sit and make sketches. She doesn't expect you to pose or anything like that. You and Tess are to go about your business, she says, and she will be a mouse in the corner with a sketchbook."

I glanced at the nearest corner, which was filled with a coal bucket, shelves of crockery and copper kettles, brooms, and empty crates waiting to be returned to the market.

"It will be cramped, hot, and dirty," I warned. "A lady will never be comfortable here."

"Miss Townsend is quite sturdy. The stories she tells me of places she's lived and things she's done in pursuit of her art would make your skin prickle. It did mine." Cynthia rubbed her arms as though feeling the prickle still. "If it is too much trouble for you, I'll put her off."

Cynthia was a kindhearted young woman. Most ladies of the house would simply lead said artist downstairs and tell them to have at it, without bothering about inconvenience to the staff. Cynthia had paused to give consideration to us.

Also, Cynthia and I had become close in the year that I'd worked in this house, far closer than her aunt was comfortable with. Cynthia thought nothing of coming downstairs to sit in the kitchen while I worked, talking of whatever was on her mind. I was also privy to her comings and goings that her aunt and uncle knew nothing of, and I often let her into the house through the scullery long after she was supposed to have been abed.

"I admit curiosity," I said. "I still cannot imagine any interest in pictures of a cook or a kitchen, but as long as she stays out of the way ..."

Cynthia leapt to her feet, all smiles. "You're a brick, Mrs. H. She'll be thrilled to bits. But quiet." She raised her hands. "Very quiet and unobtrusive. Besides, having Miss Townsend here might distract Auntie from her zeal in trying to marry me off."

"Has she started again?" I asked companionably.

Cynthia gave an inelegant snort. "She has never left off. The fits do ebb but never go away entirely. I sometimes think I should elope with a roué and stymie her efforts." She sighed.

"But then, I'd be shackled to a roué, which I can't imagine would be an improvement on my lot now."

"A lady must choose her husband carefully," I agreed.

"I wish a lady didn't have to bother with a husband at all. Miss Townsend is fiercely *un*married. Perhaps I will emulate her."

But Miss Townsend had money and a family who did not mind what she did. A very different situation from a penniless young woman whose parents and aunt found her an inconvenience.

I could see that Cynthia understood this as well. She made a wry face, gave me a wave, and headed for the door. "Thanks for the trouble, Mrs. H. Tess." She left the kitchen with her usual rapid stride, and disappeared toward the back stairs.

"Fancy, I might be in a picture hanging high on someone's wall." Tess grinned, her knife flying over the carrots. "Won't my friends laugh?"

"Miss Townsend might decide not to use our faces at all," I said. "Or we'll be so small no one will recognize us."

Tess was not bothered. She continued with the carrots, humming a merry tune.

I did hope Miss Townsend did not make us recognizable. I could not imagine the embarrassment of appearing in a painting, no matter how innocuous that painting might be. I preferred anonymity and moving through life in a calm and peaceful manner. Much more comfortable all around.

Not until we'd caught up from the frenzy of breakfast and preparations for the midday meal did I have the chance to speak to Elsie. I moved to the scullery where Elsie clattered pans and dishes in her sink, singing with her usual off-key vigor.

I waited until she spied me in the doorway, not wishing to speak abruptly and startle her into dropping plates. Elsie blinked at me, shook water off her hands, dried them on a towel, and turned to await my orders.

"Mr. McAdam tells me you grew up in the Foundling Hospital," I began, keeping my voice gentle but matter-of-fact.

Elsie gazed at me without worry. "I did." Her forehead creased. "Why'd ya ask?"

I wasn't certain how to broach the subject, not wanting to concern her until I knew whether there was something to be concerned about. "Last night I spoke to a vicar who is on the board of governors there."

Her eyes widened. "A vicar? Has something happened? Is Mabel sick?"

"No, no," I said quickly. "The vicar is a friend of Mr. McAdam's." I decided to keep the fact that Daniel and Mr. Fielding were foster brothers to myself. "He asked me to help him with a matter there, and Mr. McAdam indicated you came from the Hospital. He never mentioned anyone named Mabel."

"Oh." Elsie relaxed. "That's all right then. Mabel is a great friend of mine—she's a bit younger than me, so she's still taking lessons. I took care of her when she first came. The older girls are assigned younger ones to look after, ya see. I thought perhaps one day, she could be a maid here."

She gazed at me in hope, but I had to shake my head. "That is not for me to say, but I can put in a word for her if I think she will suit. Mrs. Bywater, as you know, is particular."

Elsie stopped herself from sharing a disgruntled look with me, but only just.

"What sort of problem? If you don't mind me asking, Mrs. H."

Elsie was young, perhaps seventeen at most, with a pointed face, straight brown hair she wore in a bun, and light brown eyes. She'd already been working here when I'd arrived at the house, but I did not know much about her life before this. She was a cheerful sort, if occasionally excitable, with a terrified scream that could cut with knifelike force. Fortunately, she did not shriek often and spent most of her time humming or singing as she scrubbed.

When Elsie didn't work, she slept. Scullery maids were far down in the servant hierarchy, nearly at the bottom. In many houses she'd double as a kitchen maid, cook's assistant, and even the bootboy. She did not have much time to herself.

"I do not wish to upset you," I said. "But a few children might have gone missing. *Might*," I added emphatically. "They also might be just fine, but taken to another place. A nurse has gone too, perhaps with them."

Elsie watched me in trepidation. "What children?"

Mr. Fielding had told me their names before I'd departed the sacristy for the rainy night. "Three—two boys and a girl. Sam Howes, Joshua Tarr, and Margaret Penny."

Elsie shook her head. "I don't know them. Might have come after me. But maybe Mabel does. I could ask her."

"That would be kind." I had no business demanding Elsie do things for me on her half day out, the only rest allotted her, but this problem bothered me. "I don't want Mabel to get into any trouble, mind. Or you."

Elsie's dimples returned. "Never. Who is the nurse what's gone?"

"Her name is Miss Nell Betts. So the parson told me."

Elsie's faint smile vanished once again. "I do know her. She's been at the Hospital awhile, though she's youngish. Very kind too. I hope nothing is wrong."

"As do I. What do you know about the nurse? Is she likely to have up and gone without telling anyone?"

"Don't think so." Elsie sent me a dubious look. "She's sensible—them as is flighty never last long. Weren't none of us scared of her. Most are fond of Nurse Betts."

"For that lady's sake then, I will try to find her. Could be she had someone in her family to take care of and slipped off to do it."

More doubt. "She has a mum and dad, but never visits them much. They don't get on. Mostly she stayed in on her days off and mended. Liked to sing while she did it."

Nurse Betts sounded a nice, comfortable person, unlikely to snatch a few innocent children and take them away with her. Besides, she'd been the one who'd brought the missing children to Mr. Fielding's attention.

There were any number of reasons a nurse at a children's home would vanish, I had to admit. Some of those reasons were unfortunately troubling.

"Is there anyone at the Foundling Hospital, if I were to go there myself, you suggest I speak to?" I asked. "The vicar wishes me to be discreet—to not upset the matrons or other children. Who could I talk to who would keep a confidence?"

Elsie thought. "There's a cook, Mrs. Compton. She's the best of the lot—maybe she'd speak to you. Maids would know more, but the one on Mabel's ward is sour as can be. Old Miss Nick, we called her, though her name's Bessie."

"Mrs. Compton then." I committed the names she'd given me to memory. "Now to think of a reason to enter the kitchens of the Foundling Hospital," I murmured, half to myself.

"Her ladyship could do it." Elsie's eyes sparkled. "She could pretend to be a charity lady and you could visit with her. Or she could go on a Sunday afternoon to watch Sunday dinner."

I pulled myself out of my ponderings to gaze at her in surprise. "Watch Sunday dinner? How does one watch a dinner?"

"It's a fine thing for ladies and gentlemen, innit? To pay a shilling or tuppence, or whatever it is, to view the foundling boys and girls eating their charity food. All in a row we'd sit, all in our same frocks, happy to have our grub. They'd file in and watch us like we were animals in a menagerie, they would. Talking all about us as they did."

I'd heard of such things—a person could pay to stare at madmen in Bedlam, or at the convicts in Millbank. The directors of the places used the fees they collected to keep said place in funds. Wretched humanity on display. I would have hoped children would be spared.

"I am sorry," I said, a bit awkwardly. "It is a pity you had to endure such things."

Elsie shrugged, but I saw her stiffness. "Was better than starving in the streets, wann't it? The matron could be hard, but we was fed and warm. And now I'm here." She gave the copper pots and her sink full of dishes an almost fond look. "Could do worse, couldn't I?"

I patted her shoulder. "You're a diligent worker and a good girl, Elsie. I can ask Mrs. Bywater to consider making you a downstairs maid, so your hands won't be in dishwater all the livelong day."

Elsie looked alarmed, not grateful. "I like the kitchen, Mrs. Holloway. None bother me here, and you don't mind my singing."

I wondered if she'd learned to sing over her task from kind Nurse Betts. "Truth to tell, I like you down here with me," I said. "But there is no need for you to be a scullery maid forever. You might even become a housekeeper one day. Mrs. Redfern was a tweeny as a girl."

"Was she?" Elsie looked doubtful. Tweenies were maids who looked after upper servants, such as the housekeeper and lady's maid. "Bit haughty now, ain't she?"

Elsie darted a fearful look behind me after the words slipped out, as though Mrs. Redfern might pop up from the slates and overhear, but the kitchen was empty of all but Tess.

"She remembers her origins," I said. "That is why she is fair-minded."

Elsie looked chagrined. "Sorry, Mrs. H."

"Never you mind. We'll keep our opinions between ourselves. Thank you, Elsie."

Elsie gave me an answering curtsy. "Can I get back to my dishes now, ma'am?"

"Of course." I sent her a smile and left her, not wanting to unnerve her any longer. Elsie was a sweet girl, but she could break crockery when agitated.

She'd given me much to think on, I reflected as I returned to my vegetables. Much indeed.

M iss Townsend came down with Lady Cynthia later that afternoon. As the evening before, Miss Townsend dressed modestly, in a trim dress buttoned to her throat, her hair in a simple knot, and wore no jewelry, not even a ring or brooch.

Cynthia introduced her to me and an avid Tess, who scanned Miss Townsend as though hoping she'd do something scandalous on the spot. Miss Townsend gave Tess a little smile, the amusement in her eyes telling me she knew full well how others viewed lady artists.

I led Miss Townsend to the corner, from which I'd moved the empty crates. "I've put a chair for you here, miss," I said, giving it a dust off with my hand. "Not very comfortable, I am afraid."

"Never mind." Miss Townsend turned the smile to me and sat down regally, as though I'd offered her the best chair in a luxurious hotel. "This will do nicely. Thank you, Mrs. Holloway."

She'd brought a satchel, which she set on the floor next to her after withdrawing a rather small sketchbook. I'd seen people of leisure sitting in parks with such books, sketching away at the scenery.

As she flipped to a clean page, I saw that part of the book had already been filled. Faces jumped out at me, one of them Cynthia's, but the pages moved too fast for me to study the pictures. I saw large flowers skim past and ordinary things like chairs and windows, all very lifelike.

"Quite beautiful," I said. "If you don't mind my saying, miss. Very skilled."

Miss Townsend acknowledged this with a small nod. "You are kind. Thank you."

"And she is modest," Cynthia broke in. "Overly so, I'd say. Monsieur Degas praised her work, and he is notoriously hard to please. *And* has little use for the female sex."

I agreed with this difficult-to-please man that Miss Townsend's work—what I could glimpse of it—was indeed worth praise.

"I'll leave you to it," Cynthia said. "Mrs. Holloway's a good sort, so if you have any need, simply ask her. She can provide you with food and drink that tastes of heaven."

"Hardly heaven," I said in mild rebuke.

"Now you are the modest one." Cynthia laughed at me and strode off, calling a greeting to Mr. Davis as she went.

That man entered the kitchen, radiating disapproval. He took in Miss Townsend, who settled herself and quietly took out a pencil, but pinched his lips together and said not a word. He and Mrs. Redfern had been told to expect Miss Townsend's presence, and both had expressed disapprobation.

However, Mr. Davis would never air his grievances in front of a guest. He only gave me a look and glided out again.

Miss Townsend had been sharpening her pencil with a knife, but I saw her flash of eyes that told me she'd taken in Mr. Davis's admonition.

"What do ye want us to do?" Tess asked Miss Townsend in eagerness.

"Nothing at all," Miss Townsend replied. "Go about your business. I will keep out of your way."

Tess looked a bit disappointed, but she returned to her task of rolling out dough for this evening's tarts. She couldn't cease glancing every few seconds at Miss Townsend, especially when that lady's pencil began to whisper across the page.

Miss Townsend proved so unobtrusive, however, that after a time, even Tess forgot she was there. I sautéed pears for the tart, adding in the last of the dried berries in the larder. Soon spring would arrive, and with it, delicate vegetables tasting of sunshine and rain, a promise that winter's hold had loosened.

Not long later, Mrs. Redfern, who'd come into the kitchen to fetch a pot of tea for Mrs. Bywater, glanced out of the high windows.

"It's that Mr. McAdam," she said stiffly. "With a delivery, it seems."

I wished I hadn't raised my head so quickly at the mention of his name. Mrs. Redfern gave me a frown, as though to remind me of her scolding the night before.

"He can't help making deliveries," I said, wiping flour from my hands. "It is his job. I do need the things he brings."

"You do indeed." Mrs. Redfern fixed me with a gaze. "But he should not linger."

"Never mind, Mrs. Redfern. As I told you, I am not rushing to elope with him, or even walk out with him. We are friends."

"Be ever so fine if you did elope," Tess put in, not helping matters. "He's sweet on you, Mrs. H."

"Hush," I said sternly. "Don't talk nonsense."

"Afternoon, Elsie, Tess, Mrs. Redfern." Daniel entered on the heels of this comment, moving with his usual briskness through the scullery, a sack across his shoulders. He lowered the sack to the kitchen floor, making a show of rubbing his back. "Good day, Mrs. Holloway. A bit wet out, and your order of potatoes has nearly done me in. Can I beg a bit of coffee from you before I must face the elements once more?"

His face was damp, his cap dripping water on to my clean floor. Mrs. Redfern humphed and marched out with a teapot and cup on a tray. Daniel grinned after her then turned to me.

"Save any scraps for me, Kat? I mean, Mrs. Holloway."

His dark blue eyes glinted, his smile as charming as ever. He dragged his cap from his head and wrung it out with exaggerated care, making Tess laugh and Elsie giggle.

He cast his gaze about the room as he always did when he entered one, no matter which persona he wore. He spied Miss Townsend in the corner, who had looked up to take us in.

Miss Townsend's eyes widened the smallest bit, and her lips parted. Daniel's eyes likewise widened, but so subtly, one had to know him well to discern it. I also saw his very slight shake of head. Miss Townsend subsided, closing her mouth.

Miss Townsend had recognized Daniel, and he her, I could see clear as day. And neither had expected to find the other on this afternoon, in my kitchen.

4

I alone noticed the silent exchange between Daniel and Miss Townsend. Elsie had returned to her sink, and Tess carried on chopping herbs while she burbled at Daniel.

"Mrs. Holloway made us a lovely meat pie for luncheon. There must be some left. I saw her setting back a slice."

"Yes, indeed." I finished crimping the tart shell for the pears and wiped my hands on the towel again. "It is in the larder. Would you care to step through with me, Mr. McAdam?"

Daniel clapped his cap to his head. "Come to think of it, I must get on. Many more deliveries to make."

"It won't take a moment." I gave him a hard stare. "And you need to warm yourself."

I saw Daniel realize refusing me would be a mistake. He gave me his devil-may-care smile and followed me into the corridor to the next room.

"Leave the door open," Tess called after us. "Or Mrs. Redfern might think you up to something." Her cackle of laughter drifted off.

I marched into the larder and to the shelf where I'd left the slice of meat pie on a plate covered with a bowl. When I turned around, I found Daniel immediately behind me.

"I was teasing you," he said in a low voice. "I never expect you to feed me."

I lifted off the bowl and shoved the pie at him. I'd already laid a fork on the plate in preparation. "You know Miss Townsend," I declared.

Daniel took the plate and lifted the fork. "Yes."

I was surprised. Daniel usually answered my direct questions with evasions, rarely the stark truth.

"In Paris?" I guessed, remembering Cynthia saying Miss Townsend had studied with a French lady artist there.

"Yes."

Again, a straight answer. I waited while Daniel shoved a chunk of pie into his mouth and chewed.

"Were you courting her?"

Daniel gulped down pie, coughing in amazement. "No."

"An important question, you will agree. I will ask another—was it to do with your police business?"

Daniel broke off a second hunk of pie. "Yes."

So many acknowledgments in one afternoon. An unusual thing for Daniel.

"How was Ireland?" I asked abruptly.

Daniel chewed and swallowed before he answered. "Cold. Rainy. Gray and gloomy."

"More police business?"

"Business that is finished." He eyed the pie as though debating whether to continue eating it, then gave in and attacked it with the fork.

"I believe the day has come," I said.

Daniel had just taken another large mouthful. He chewed noisily, eyeing me with a frown. "What day?" he asked when he could.

"You have stated many times that one day, you will tell me all your secrets. I believe that day is at hand."

Daniel's cheeky twinkle vanished, and he regarded me with the quietness he took on when he faced dire situations. "Not yet."

I had not thought he would answer. "Will you at least tell me about Miss Townsend?"

Another hesitation and then a shake of his head. A reluctant one. "I can't. Too soon."

This did not please me either. "I see."

Daniel reached the fork to the last bite. "This pie is delicious, Kat. I thank you for it. Haven't had anything this fine in a while."

"Flattery." I watched him scoop up the crust sopping with gravy and bits of meat and shove it into his mouth.

He watched me watch him chew, swallow, and put the fork back into his mouth to savor the last of its juices.

"Truth." The fork clattered to the plate.

I wasn't certain I liked him looking at me in all seriousness. The cocky assuredness was easier to bear.

"I came with another purpose," he said, dipping a hand into his pocket. "My brother . . . Errol . . . wishes to meet with you again. Tomorrow."

"Tomorrow, I meet with Grace. I'm not certain I will have time for brothers."

"I told him that. He wanted to give you this." Daniel withdrew a piece of card, folded in half. "It is a photo, which includes the nurse and two of the children he is worried about."

The card, when opened, proved to be a frame surrounding a photograph of about twenty people, standing stiffly. Most were children, boys, wearing identical uniforms that the photograph rendered a dark gray. I could see the nubby texture of the cloth—the poor things looked uncomfortable. The boys wore caps, pulled down so far all their faces looked alike, mere paleness peeping from the gray.

On one end of the posed boys stood a man in a suit a little darker than the boys' uniforms. On the right end was a lady in a prim dress with a white collar, a pillbox hat on her head. The picture had been taken outdoors, in a courtyard of some kind, with trees in the background. Not the Foundling Hospital, as far as I could tell, but perhaps in the square beside it. Obviously, this was an outing for the boys, or perhaps a special walk to have their photograph taken.

"This is Nurse Betts," Daniel said, tapping the lady. "The lads are here." He touched a boy nearer the man and one in the exact middle of the row. The photograph had been taken from a little bit above the group, perhaps from steps, and the boys were looking up at the camera.

I could barely discern the two from the rest of them. One looked as though he had blond hair, but I couldn't be certain.

"Not a very helpful means of identifying them," I said. "Which is which?"

"Sam Howes." Daniel pointed to the blond lad. "Joshua Tarr." The other boy.

"No photograph of the little girl?"

"Not that Errol had. I imagine there might be one hanging in the Foundling Hospital." He pushed the photograph gently at me. "You keep that."

His hands were warm against mine, but again, I could not let him distract me.

"I will see what I can do. And do not tell me it is good of me."

The half smile returned. "I would not dream of it." As I slid the photograph into my apron pocket, Daniel sobered again. "I wish you could understand how unhappy it makes me to anger you."

He did look unhappy, deep in his eyes.

"You have no need to please me," I said crisply. "I will tell you what I discover."

"I could meet you–"

"No." I imagined myself sitting in a public house with him, or a tea shop, our heads together, shoulders touching, while we compared notes. "I will send word. Through James."

Daniel quietly held my gaze. "If that is what you wish."

"If I am meant to trust you"–I sounded a bit tart, even to myself–"you must trust me."

"I do." Daniel tried to bring forth his winsome smile and put his hand on his heart. "I do, indeed, Mrs. H."

"Not with everything." I took up the plate, which now held only crumbs, and strode past him and out.

The next morning, I finished the breakfast for the upstairs and the hash of leftover potatoes, sausage, eggs, and cheese for the downstairs, changed into my second-best frock, and went out.

Miss Townsend arrived to sketch as I departed. I gave her what I hoped was a cordial "good morning" as she came into the kitchen, and I left via the other door.

An evening of contemplation and a restless night had made me feel no better. Daniel was an enigma–he always had been.

What he got up to out of my sight was no business of mine, I reminded myself. I knew he helped others and the police, because I'd witnessed him do so. He'd helped *me*. He was not a ne'er-do-well with a lady tucked into every port. At least, I did not think so.

As I found an omnibus and climbed aboard, keeping my skirts well away from my fellow passengers, I knew in my heart I was merely jealous, envious of Miss Townsend because she'd been involved in his police work far from my sight. I wanted to trust Daniel and let him do whatever it was he did, for whomever he did it. But I was at the end of my tether wondering who he truly worked for and why, and why he took on different personas without turning a hair.

Learning he had a brother, even a foster brother, had jolted me from any complacency. I could understand Daniel not telling me what he did for the police, if it was a deep, dark secret he needed to keep so others wouldn't be hurt. But a brother was not part of the secret, was he?

Daniel knew all about me and my past, about my daughter—had known before I'd told him. And yet, I was not to know about his family. Did he have more brothers? Sisters as well? Children of his own besides James? Would he tell me or keep this to himself?

By the time I reached my destination of St. Paul's Church-yard and walked along Cheapside to the lane that held my daughter, I was out of breath and highly irritated.

Grace running down the stairs to meet me at the door eased me a bit. I held her, wishing, wishing I never had to let her go.

"What shall we do today, Mum?" she asked in eagerness.

I had promised to look into the affair of the Foundling Hospital and should make a start, but I hesitated. My time with Grace was too precious to squander.

"I have a mind for a nice walk," I suggested as I tried to decide.

My friend Joanna Millburn, who looked after Grace for me, said, "It's blustery for a walk. Why not a game by the fire?"

The Millburn children had gathered for lessons in the cozy sitting room, presenting a picture of domestic bliss. Mr. Millburn worked as a clerk in the City and was not present, but Mrs. Millburn had taken her place at the window to do the mending and instruct the children at the same time.

Grace was of an age with the older Millburn girl, Jane, both of them eleven. Jane sat at a table doing her lessons, her brother, a year older, next to her. Grace's books stacked in the place next to Jane showed she had joined them while waiting for me.

The younger two, another boy and girl, reposed on the thick hearth rug, the warmest place in the room, picture books and writing slates around them. The girls wore white pinafores, the boys in knickers and gray jackets. The four Millburn children were rosy and healthy, happy in their tiny house.

Grace was happy here too.

This was to have been my life, I thought with a pang, once my husband returned from foreign parts where he sailed. Me in a small house, baking and cooking and looking after Grace. Domestic bliss indeed.

Spending a pleasant morning in a warm room would have appealed to me any other day, Joanne and I chatting while the children played or studied, but today I felt uneasy and restless. Grace shared my restlessness—when I glanced at her, she sent me a look of pleading. She'd been confined too long, the look told me.

"A brisk walk will do us good," I said, deciding. "But Mrs. Millburn is correct about the cold. You must wrap up warm, Grace."

Grace flashed her happiest smile and rushed to fetch her coat. The maid of all work Joanne employed helped her button up, handing Grace a scarf and mittens.

"Thank you, Mum," Grace said as we started down the street, pressed together against the wind. "I'd had enough of lessons."

"You must learn everything you can," I chided her, but today I did so because I felt it my duty. "A woman in this world cannot afford to be ignorant."

"I read and write better than Tom," Grace said with confidence, naming the older boy. "Better at maths too. But I can't have lessons *every* day."

"No," I agreed. "All work and no play, as they say."

"Makes Grace a dull girl." She grinned up at me. "And Mum too. Where shall we go?"

While my heart balked at the idea of taking Grace anywhere near the Foundling Hospital, Mr. Fielding's story had me anxious. Whatever Daniel's old quarrels with him might be, missing children was a serious matter. Knowing about it, I could not simply turn aside.

"Do you mind a great walk? Up along High Holborn, and more?"

"I don't mind at all," Grace said at once. "I'm very sturdy."

She was. I was blessed with a healthy child, but I hardly wanted her in the cold too long.

"We'll take the trains," I said. "It will be warmer."

Grace's eyes lit. She liked the underground trains, though they continued to make me nervous.

We entered the station at the end of Ludgate Hill, and I bought the tickets. Grace hurried along the platform, towing me after her, and we stepped onto the train just before it pulled away.

The train ran into a tunnel, but before I could become too anxious, we emerged to the light of day on Farringdon Road.

I disliked this part of London—Clerkenwell—its streets and lanes made dark by a pall of smoke. Because of the cold weather, even more chimneys exuded smoke these days, coating us all in soot and turning the air to a smelly fug. Houses in this area were homes to working-class families, many of whom labored at the nearby brewery, which also emitted its share of smoke.

I led Grace along Charles Street, which crossed Hatton Garden and turned onto Leather Lane, lively with a market this morning, offering plenty of wares that might hold my interest any other time.

We hurried past the market stalls and made for a tiny artery called Baldwin's Gardens, which led past St. Alban's Church and a school opposite. A more salubrious route, I thought, than taking Grace past the brewery or near Coldbath Fields, a prison that lay too near the Foundling Hospital. A number of indigent men and women lingered near St. Alban's, and I tugged Grace close as we passed.

At the end of Baldwin's Gardens lay Gray's Inn Road, and there I turned north. The fine squares of the men of law at Gray's Inn lined the street, shutting us out from whatever parks and greens they enjoyed behind their high walls.

I knew my way around these streets from the almost-daily

walk I'd done when I'd been with child, my feet carrying me again and again to the place I feared I'd have to leave my baby.

Grace trotted by my side, gazing with interest at a part of London she'd never seen. "Where are we going, Mum?"

"To Brunswick Square," I said, not slowing. I decided she'd know soon enough, so I confessed. "To the Foundling Hospital."

"Why are we going there?"

"Mr. McAdam asked me to."

I did not want to tell her about the missing children, not yet. I was not certain how much it would upset her.

Grace seemed to see nothing sinister in visiting the Hospital, however. I kept a tight hold on her hand as we turned on Guilford Street, and slowed our steps before the gates and long courtyard to the massive gray building that had haunted me for the longest year of my life.

The open space behind the gates teemed with activity. A long line of boys in gray coats marched behind two taller boys. They actually did march, a military-like step that rang on the pavement. The lads' coats were shapeless, caps of gray jammed on their heads.

The boys looked neither right nor left as they paraded across the courtyard. Whether they trained for a parade or simply took morning exercise, I could not say.

Grace watched them avidly, but I tugged her away to the lane that led along the west side of the Hospital. A tall brick wall shielded us from the building, though the upper windows glared down over it.

I scanned the wall for any entrance or stairs that would take us to the servants' area. The times I'd wandered past, many years ago, I'd only glanced through the gates and then rushed on.

"Are we bringing alms to the poor children here?" Grace asked. "Like you do with the beggars in Mount Street?"

I realized I gripped Grace's hand more firmly than necessary. She hadn't complained, but I made myself relax.

"Something like that," I answered. "There." I pointed. "That looks as though it leads to the kitchens."

A small gate, unlocked, opened to a short flight of brick stairs that ended at a dust-covered door, its windows so dark I could not see through them. Taking a chance, I turned the handle, and was rewarded by the door opening easily.

Beyond was a small hallway that stored mops and buckets and a tattered broom evidently meant for the back steps. The ceiling was low, this entry out of the way and unimportant.

The passageway led around a corner to another set of steps, and at the bottom of this, a larger hall opened out. The ceiling was higher here, with stone beams, painted white, holding the immense weight of the building above.

Noise came at us, a cacophony of it. I moved cautiously along . . . and then took a startled step back as a maid with a wide basin of water dashed out of a room immediately in front of me to dive into another across the hall.

A second maid followed with another basin. She caught sight of me, started, and spilled a wave of water down her front before she could right the basin.

"Out of the way, missus," she snarled at me, then disappeared across the hall.

I peeked carefully into the room from which she had departed, finding a large scullery. Three sinks lined the far wall, and three maids in black, sleeves rolled to their elbows, scrubbed like fury at the mountain of dishes beside them.

The maids banged dishes, breaking several as I watched, which they tossed onto a pile of scraps. They never noticed or heard me or Grace look in on them, and I led Grace onward before anyone else could rush in front of us.

The end of the hall opened into a wide room with long tables—a servants' hall, I surmised. Plenty of men and women, young and old, surrounded the tables, busy polishing spoons, mending mounds of clothing, or scrubbing small shoes.

One of the older women, a plump personage with a broad bosom, darned socks with quick efficiency. She glanced up and caught sight of me and Grace.

"She's a bit old for you to shove off on us," the lady said, and chuckled. "What you want, love?"

5

Is Mrs. Compton about?" I asked, giving the name of the cook Elsie had mentioned.

"Not in here, dear," the darning lady said. "She'll be in the kitchen, won't she? Yonder." She pointed a thick finger at a door on the other side of the busy servants' hall. "Won't have time for a chat, I'm thinking."

"I'll just pop in," I said. "May Grace sit with you a moment? Kitchens are dangerous places."

"That they can be. Grace, is it? A lovely name, child. Sit yourself down." The lady dragged a stool from under the table with her foot and patted it. "Sure you're not after leaving her behind, missus?"

Grace sat down, unworried. "My mum just wants to see your kitchen. She's a cook, the best one in the world."

The woman regarded Grace with wide brown eyes. "Well, ain't you a cheeky one? Nice to see a gel what hasn't had all the spirit knocked out of her. Go on." She waved at me with the gray sock.

The others in the room alternately stared at me in curiosity or got on with their work, uninterested. I crossed the room, not without a qualm at leaving Grace behind, and entered the largest kitchen I'd seen in my life.

The vast room ran the length of the building, with tables, stoves, and sinks filling every space, plus shelves upon shelves of crockery, pots, and roasting pans. Cooks and their helpers, male and female, dashed from cupboard to tables to stoves and back, some of them lads and lasses only a little older than Grace. These last were dressed in black or gray, like the boys I'd seen in the courtyard, the girls' dresses covered with white pinafores.

I remained near the door but off to one side, so I would not impede those hurrying in and out.

One of the maids rushing about was the one who'd splashed water on her dress when she'd nearly run into me. "It's you, is it?" she demanded. "I told you—stay out of the way."

"She wants Mrs. Compton." A lanky youth who'd been polishing boots in the servants' hall had followed me. "She's a cook."

"She ain't doing much cooking I can see." She glared at me with angry dark eyes. "Just standing."

"Shut your gob, Bessie, and fetch Mrs. Compton."

Bessie. I recalled Elsie mentioning a maid by that name, and telling me the girls called her Old Miss Nick. I could understand why.

Bessie snapped out a foul word and stomped off. She shouted down the rows, and a woman in an apron that covered her from neck to ankles turned, craning her head to eye me curiously.

The cook appeared in no hurry to leave her table, so I went

to her. I knew how to avoid the assistants swinging platters or pots of food, the knives wielded in wild chopping, the water, grease, and blobs of lettuce and vegetable peels on the floor.

"Can't stop," Mrs. Compton said to me as I halted at the end of her table. She had a nasally voice with an accent that put her from the East End. "Dinner comes too soon. Who are you?"

"My name is Mrs. Holloway." I watched her basting a hen, and my fingers twitched. "Might I suggest a bit of parsley in the broth? Perhaps a pinch of flour to thicken? I find it fills out a thin sauce."

"Do you now?" The woman sneered. "Your man likes that, does he?"

"I am not married," I said primly. "I'm a cook."

The woman threw a doubtful look at my brown frock, which I regularly cleaned and mended. "You don't look like no cook to me. What you doing in my kitchen? If you've come to look over the lads and lasses, that's on Sunday. Unless you're going to adopt one away." She snorted a laugh. "Fat chance. No one wants the poor motherless things."

The last was said with some sympathy. I snatched up a bunch of parsley that had been left to wilt on the end of the table, rolled it into a neat bundle, lifted a knife, and proceeded to slice the parsley. Mrs. Compton looked on with raised brows.

"Elsie told me to speak to you," I said. "Elsie Dodd. She's the scullery maid in my kitchen."

Mrs. Compton's eyes widened. "Elsie? Sweet girl. Out a few years now. She well?"

"She is very well. Likes to sing." I used the knife to scoop up the chopped parsley, and pointedly sprinkled it into the broth in the pan.

"That she does. Well, well. Little Elsie. Why does she want you to speak to me?"

I glanced at the others at the table, hands moving, eyes on their work, but I knew they listened.

"In private, perhaps?"

Another snort. "Do I look as though I've time for a nice chat?"

"We can fix an appointment."

Mrs. Compton banged down her ladle in exasperation, exactly as I'd have done had someone interrupted *me* at my cooking. "What is this about? Be quick and tell me, or go."

"Nurse Betts," I said.

The change on her face was remarkable. Mrs. Compton's expression moved from annoyed curiosity to dismay, to fear.

"This evening," she said. "Come to the back door. I'll be there." She tried to resume her brisk tones. "Now be off with you, unless you want to chop more herbs. A neat job, that."

"Keeps the cut leaves from turning black too fast. Works a dream with basil and mint especially."

Mrs. Compton gave me a nod, more respectful now. "I'll remember that."

"Beg pardon for disturbing you." I backed from the table, Mrs. Compton and her assistants staring at me, and made my careful way out of the kitchen.

When I entered the servants' hall, I saw that Grace had stretched a sock over a darning egg, and was busily stitching it, assisting the lady who'd greeted us.

I announced that we had to depart, but I allowed Grace to finish her part of the task before taking her away. Those at the table were reluctant to see her go—I could not help but be proud of Grace's good manners and natural friendliness.

"You come and visit anytime, Grace," the lady said as we went. "Such a lovely child." This last was directed at me.

The woman smiled as I thanked her, but I saw sadness in

her eyes, sharp and profound. She took the sock back from Grace, admired her work, and said good-bye as I led Grace away.

Outside, the wind took our breaths away, and we hurried along, heads down. When I looked up again, I found we'd emerged into Great Coram Street, named for the founder of the Hospital. A little way along was a tea shop, and I pulled Grace inside, out of the cold.

The shop was mostly empty, as the midday meal had not yet commenced, but a thin young woman brought us tea and a few slices of indifferent bread.

"That was excellently done, Grace," I said as we warmed our hands on the teacups. "Very kind of you to assist. You do Mrs. Millburn credit."

"I always like to help." Grace glanced behind her at the rest of the shop as though not wishing to be overheard. Two women spoke together over a table in the far corner, and the young waitress had retreated to her kitchen.

"Mrs. Shaw—that was the lady who spoke to me—she's an under-housekeeper," Grace said in a near whisper. "She seems very worried about something. Asked me many times why you'd come. I said I supposed to ask about cookery."

I lifted my teacup and sipped the hot drink. "Did she? I hope she did not frighten you."

"Not much frightens me," Grace said with disarming frankness. "When I am anxious, I simply think about what you would do, and I'm not afraid anymore. Do you know what they were worried by?"

I set down my cup, emotion making my fingers weak. I wanted to sweep her into a hug, revel in the compliment she'd tendered me without a second thought.

I debated whether to tell her why I'd gone to the Hospital. I wanted to shelter my daughter from the nastiness of the world, but on the other hand, I did not want her to be ignorant about danger.

"I do not like to distress you," I said in a low voice. "But Mr. McAdam asked me to look into the fact that a few children might have gone missing. They might not be at all, and we are worried for nothing. But you must not say a word about it. I do not wish to raise an alarm until we know for certain what has happened."

Grace's brow puckered, but she looked sympathetic rather than upset. "That would explain Mrs. Shaw's worry. If she is to look after children there, and something happened to them . . . Mr. McAdam was right to ask you about it, Mum. You'll find them."

At that moment—while I did not share her confidence in my skills—I knew that I had made the correct choice to keep Grace with me after she'd been born. My daughter could now sit across from me, daintily chewing bread, never realizing how close she'd come to being one of those children in the gray uniforms she now felt pity for.

It had never occurred to her that I'd have given her up, that she'd be anything but cared for, sitting in a tiny tea shop on a blustery day with the mother who loved her.

I reached across the table and clasped her hand. "You are a sweet girl, my Grace."

Grace smiled in surprised delight. "I love you too, Mum. Now, let us talk of something more pleasant to cheer you up. How is Lady Cynthia? And Lady Bobby? Do they wear trousers *every* day?"

I relaxed and fell into the gossipy chatter I shared with Grace on my day out. I described Cynthia's beautiful gown at her aunt's supper ball and Miss Townsend coming down to the kitchen to sketch us.

"How funny that she wants to paint cooks and maids," Grace said, as amazed as Tess and I had been at the notion. "But you'll be beautiful in the picture, Mum."

"You are very flattering, my darling. She won't be painting me, exactly, but domestics in general. I admit I do not understand it myself."

"She should paint Lady Cynthia then. She is so very pretty."

Grace spoke in all seriousness, and my heart warmed again. I did not know if all mothers were as proud and boastful of their own children, but I certainly was of mine and ever would be.

Grace and I returned to the Millburns', full of tea and bread, but not too full to partake of Joanna's treat of cakes and scones, and more tea, hot and laced with cream.

I thoroughly enjoyed the rest of my afternoon, visiting with Joanna and Grace and the children, gossiping, playing games, absorbing the warmth of the stove in the sitting room.

This was a home, I thought. Outside the day was gray, the wind giving way to a steady rain; inside all was bright and cheerful. The Millburns hadn't much in the way of money, but they had resourcefulness, and goodness in their hearts.

I wanted this with all my might. A place to call my own, with a fire and a cup of tea, my daughter within reach. When I'd been a girl, my mother and I hadn't had much more than a few sticks of furniture in our tiny lodgings and little to eat, but we'd had each other. We'd also had friends who'd drop by for a chat and incidentally bring us a loaf of bread, or the end of a joint from their previous night's supper. The whole street had made sure Mum and I were all right, especially after my dad had dropped off his perch.

So much generosity among those who had little to share. I compared this with Mrs. Bywater's parsimony and her insistence that Cynthia marry so she'd be out from underfoot.

A large and comfortable mansion was all very well, I decided with some smugness, but I preferred a house like this, warm and filled with friends and my daughter.

When Mr. Millburn returned home as we finished tea, my mind substituted Daniel breezing in after a hard day chasing criminals, his laughter lighting the room. He'd buss me on the cheek and swing Grace into his arms, asking me what riches I'd cooked them all for supper. James would be there too, the tall young man with a smile like sunshine.

The vision unnerved me so much it shattered into fragments, leaving Mr. Millburn puzzled that I stared so hard at him.

Time for me to go. I departed with the greatest reluctance, leaving my daughter and this insular warmth for the cold darkness of everyday life.

I had promised to meet Mrs. Compton, so I took an omnibus to Gray's Inn Road, having had enough of underground trains. I alighted in a pelting rain and made my way to the kitchen door of the Foundling Hospital.

A delivery van stood before it, *Hansen's Produce* emblazoned in red and blue on its black side. I tramped down the short flight of stairs and opened the door, happy to find it still unlocked. Above the noise of the bustling scullery and servants' hall beyond, I heard the unmistakable and affable laugh of Daniel McAdam.

I shook rain from my coat as I walked toward the servants' hall, annoyed with the man. If I'd known Daniel had taken my advice to enter the Hospital with the excuse of making deliveries, it might have saved me some trouble.

I reached the servants' hall to find him laughing with Mrs. Shaw, the woman Grace had helped with the darning. Even the sour Bessie gave him a smile.

Daniel broke off when he saw me peeking in the doorway. "Ah, Mrs. . . . Holloway, is it? I deliver to your kitchen."

He sounded proud he remembered me. I gave him a cool nod. "Indeed. Perhaps you should be about your business."

"Now, missus, can't blame a fellow for stopping to pass the time of day when that day is so horrible, can you? Cats and dogs it is out there—cats and dogs. I heard them yowling as they came down."

Every person in the room found this hilarious, especially the delighted young women.

"Mr. . . . McAdam, is it?" I returned. "The man with the impudent tongue."

No one paid me any heed. Daniel held sway here, and an interloping cook from a stately household would not change this.

"She is quite right." Daniel gave me a wink that set off a new gale of laughter around him. "I have been frivolous long enough. Must deliver the rest of my load so I don't lose my post. Pleasant to have met you all."

He waved like a monarch leaving his populace, amidst cries of, "Good night, Mr. McAdam!" "Come again soon, do!" "Have a care of the cold, man." This last from a male servant, as charmed by him as were the ladies.

I backed into the passageway to let him by, and Daniel looked straight at me as he passed. While his smile never wavered, I read in his eyes that he wished to speak to me. He strode along the corridor and out the door with his usual verve, likely expecting me to follow him out.

Mrs. Compton exited the kitchen just after that, bundled in coat and hat to join me.

"I'm sorry about the commotion, Mrs. Holloway," Mrs. Compton said as she led me toward the back door. "The delivery was very late, and the new deliveryman wheedled a cup of tea out of the maids. I'd wanted to slip out without anyone seeing, but it can't be helped now."

"We are both cooks," I said to soothe her. "Not unusual for cooks to have a chat together."

"Well, I hope that is all they see." Mrs. Compton sounded anxious as she bustled me up the stairs and outside, staying close to me as we went out.

The sky was dark as we emerged, the sun setting early in February, spring still many weeks away.

The delivery van had not moved. Daniel lounged at the rear of the vehicle, its back door open. "You ladies are welcome to ride with me," he said cheerily. "Get you out of the weather."

Mrs. Compton halted and gazed at him in disdain. "In a wagon full of potatoes, young man?"

"It's nearly empty." Daniel opened the door wider, releasing the scent of wilting greens and dusty root vegetables. He motioned to a bench that ran the length of the van, a few boxes and bags of produce stacked on the other side. "I'm happy to drive you. Be a boon for me to have two lovely ladies in the back of me wagon."

"I hardly want to be seen climbing into and out of a produce van," Mrs. Compton said huffily. "At my time of life."

"Oh, that time's not so very great, ma'am. And it is raining powerful hard."

Daniel did not exaggerate. My coat was already soaked, and my hat would need much drying and reshaping after this deluge.

Whether Mrs. Compton feared the rain more than someone seeing her in a delivery van, or Daniel had charmed her with his compliments, she at last conceded that sitting inside would be more comfortable than us hurrying through the wet.

I let out a breath of relief as Daniel handed me in and I sat down on the rough bench, out of the wind and rain. A lit lantern hung in the van's corner, its candle flickering through punched tin.

"Comfortable?" Daniel grinned in at us. "Have to make a few more stops around these parts. Mind?"

"We hardly have a choice," I told him coldly. "Thank you for your kindness."

"Not at all, missus. I have the window down for air, and if you want to stop, you just sing out. Door's not locked."

He shut it, leaving us in a stuffy, if chilly, enclosure. The light leaking through the tin lantern spangled our faces, the points of light moving wildly as the van jolted forward.

"Well, this is highly unusual, but I suppose it will have to do," Mrs. Compton said as the lantern settled down into an easy swing. "You asked about Nurse Betts, Mrs. Holloway." Before I could answer, she seized my wrist in a sudden and crushing grip, and her voice took on a fierce note. "You tell me everything you know about her, where she is, and why she went. If you've kidnapped her or harmed her in any way, it won't go well for you."

6

I blinked in surprise and jerked my arm free. "You misunderstand, Mrs. Compton," I said firmly. "I am trying to find Miss Betts. I am concerned about her well-being."

The wagon bumped over a hole, jostling us together. Mrs. Compton let out a sigh as she slumped in her seat, her intensity evaporating.

"Forgive me, Mrs. Holloway, but I've been so worried. I'm certain something terrible has happened. It's not like Nurse Betts to stay long from the Hospital. She's a responsible girl, good with the children."

I kept my tone as gentle as I could. "When did she go?"

"Tuesday last. She took her afternoon out—she doesn't often. Doesn't like to leave the tykes. One is always getting hurt or upset, and she wants to be there for them. But off she goes, and hasn't come back. Her family lives in Camden Town. We weren't alarmed when she didn't return right away, but when the next day came and went, and Mrs. Shaw made inquiries, her mum and dad said she never come home at all." Mrs. Compton swallowed, eyes glistening with tears.

"Did her parents think to go to the police?" I asked, my consternation growing.

Mrs. Compton made a dismissive gesture. "They're the sort what have no trust of the police. They insist *we* know where she is, that she simply don't want to see them, and we're shielding her. How such a sweet young woman comes from such a family, I don't know."

I wondered. The family might have a history with the police that made them reluctant to summon a constable. And if they were resentful of their daughter working at the Hospital, perhaps they themselves had something to do with her disappearance.

I was speculating wildly, but at this point, I had few ideas. Nurse Betts's parents might simply be poor but respectable people who would be embarrassed to have anything to do with the police. Camden was a rather run-down area, but Nurse Betts's family might be the scrupulous sort who guarded their reputations carefully.

"Did she have friends?" I asked. "Or a young man—someone with whom she might have decided to remain?"

"She is a good girl, Mrs. Holloway," Mrs. Compton said stiffly.

I reflected that plenty of "good" young women in this world had run off with young men, leaving their friends stunned and shocked, but I kept this to myself. "I am not implying she was otherwise. But if Nurse Betts was not happy at home, she might have preferred to visit another besides her parents. Or perhaps she went to tend someone ill and isn't able to send word."

Mrs. Compton shook her head. "I have thought much on

this. Nurse Betts simply isn't the sort to not tell a soul where she is. She'd find a way. And she don't have many friends, not outside the Hospital. She loves the lads and lasses, she does, protective of them, like. She'd not stay from them long."

We lapsed into silence. I longed to find a benign explanation for her absence, but I very much feared Nurse Betts was in danger. Coupled with the missing children . . . I imagined her trying to find them or going after them to keep them safe, coming to grief at the hands of their abductors.

"What about the children who have gone?" I asked. "Were they her charges?"

Mrs. Compton snapped her head around and stared at me as though I'd gone mad. "What do you mean? What children?"

"Sam Howes, Joshua Tarr, Margaret Penny."

Her brows went up. "Someone's been telling you tales, Mrs. Holloway. They ain't missing. Adopted, weren't they?"

"Adopted?" I asked in surprise.

"Put into good homes, in any case. Not missing at all."

"Oh." Mr. Fielding had said the director claimed the children had been fostered. Now Mrs. Compton was telling a similar tale. "Never mind then," I said, reserving judgment. "I must have heard wrong."

"You certainly did. Children don't go missing from our Hospital, Mrs. Holloway," Mrs. Compton said sternly. "They are well looked after . . . if a little harshly, in my opinion. Not allowed out of the matrons' or nurses' sights. They're trained up and either taken in by a family or are hired out in service. Or they remain and work at the Hospital. Like Bessie."

I started. "Bessie? The one who shouted at me several times?"

"Mustn't mind her." Mrs. Compton almost smiled. "Her young man was arrested for theft and is currently banged up in Coldbath Fields. Makes her angry, but it's what happens when a young woman takes up with a bad man." Mrs. Compton spoke as though *she* would never make such a disastrous choice.

"Not the case with Nurse Betts?" I asked.

"Gracious, no." Mrs. Compton looked amazed I'd ever think so. "Nurse Betts warned Bessie—we all did. No, the only young man to catch Nurse Betts's interest, and that's been recently, is a highly respectable gent. I've never met him, but I've seen him walking the grounds with her, and I know he's taken her for tea. He's one of the governors—they visit us sometimes. Mrs. Shaw, in fact, is sweet on a governor herself, the daft woman. As though such a highborn fellow will have anything to do with a housekeeper."

"Is he the same governor who took Nurse Betts to tea?" I asked.

"No, no. The fellow Nurse Betts fancies hasn't been on the board long, a year perhaps. Wears a dog collar—you know what I mean. A parson of some sort."

"A parson." I repeated the word slowly, and the van gave a particularly hard jolt.

"A clergyman anyway. As I said, I've not met him, but I asked her about him. She says he's at a parish in the East End. Probably a curate too poor to marry the girl, I'm thinking, but a fine-looking bloke. Dark-haired, with a nice beard, lovely smile. If *he* knew where she was, I have no doubt he'd say."

Daniel made a delivery to a restaurant in King's Cross Road, then obligingly drove Mrs. Compton back to the Foundling Hospital.

I alighted there with her, but Daniel, remaining in his

breezy persona, offered to take me to the nearest Metropolitan station. Mrs. Compton, with a whispered warning to me to have a care of him and go straight into the station, left us.

Daniel went sober as I returned from seeing Mrs. Compton inside. "I'll drive you all the way to Mayfair, Kat. Too nasty a night for you to be running home from the trains."

"There is always an omnibus, or a hansom," I said in a cool tone.

"Difficult to find a hansom in this mess." His grin flashed. "Save you the fare."

"What about your other deliveries? There is still produce in the back."

"Can wait." His chipper manner did not hide the dark glint in his eyes. "I'd rather see you safely home, and you know this. Then I will go visit my brother."

"You heard Mrs. Compton then?" I asked.

"Indeed I did. Another reason I wished to drive you, Kat. To eavesdrop."

So I had gathered. "I'd like to visit Mr. Fielding with you," I said grimly. "He omitted the fact that he and Nurse Betts have been friendly, didn't he? Monday, I will take my half day and go."

"I plan to wring his neck sooner than that. But if he is still alive by Monday, certainly, you may speak to him."

Daniel ended the conversation by helping me once more into the back of the van, which, true, would be warmer and drier than sitting up front with him. He settled me in and closed the door against the wind and rain.

As he drove along Lamb's Conduit Street to Red Lion and so to High Holborn, I had plenty of time to ruminate over the fact that Mr. Fielding had known Nurse Betts well, indeed was walking out with her. I wanted to question him very much indeed.

We made our slow way to Mayfair, and Daniel helped me down in front of the Mount Street house.

"I might come tomorrow night . . . No, make it the next," Daniel said quietly as he steadied me. "That is, if you'll see me."

He spoke almost deferentially, for Daniel. I was still not happy with him for his reticence concerning Miss Townsend—and anything else he refused to tell me. He and his brother had much in common in that regard. But it was not expedient at the moment to refuse him.

"I will receive you," I said, giving him a nod. "If only to discuss this distressing matter."

"Excellent." Daniel smiled and pressed my hands. "Go in and stay warm, Kat."

"Good night." I withdrew quickly from his grasp and turned for the stairs, not trusting myself to say more.

I knew Daniel watched me descend the stairs. I felt him. Only when I shut the door below did I see the van list as he climbed to the seat, and the patient horse clop slowly away.

I ducked through the scullery to find the kitchen awhirl with preparations for supper. Tess gave orders like a sergeant, sending Charlie and Elsie running every which way. The relief in Tess's face when she saw me was stark.

"I'm glad you've come, Mrs. H., no mistake. There's been a devil of a row upstairs, and the mistress changed the menu at the very last minute."

I quickly hung up my sodden hat and coat and reached for my apron. "Did she? Mrs. Bywater knows better than to alter the menu without consulting me. And what row? Goodness, I fear to leave the house."

As I spoke I tied on my apron and looked over the meal Tess was preparing. The fresh fish delivered early this morning was nowhere in sight—instead a cod, covered in salt, had been brought forth, and was now dressed for the frying pan.

"That woman has no taste at all." I hadn't meant to say the words out loud, but they slipped from my tongue. "A fresh turbot in wine sauce would be far better than salted cod with lemon."

Tess snatched up a paper and fluttered it at me. It proved to be the new menu—Tess wouldn't be able to read it well yet, but Mrs. Redfern or Mr. Davis would have told her what it said.

The cod, a salad, and cold potatoes. No pudding.

"Well, I suppose the staff can enjoy the walnut tart," I said. I'd prepared it the night before, ready to warm after the meal. "But I doubt her dinner guests will be impressed with *this* menu."

"Ain't going to be no guests." Tess scowled at the bowl of lettuce she'd torn up. "As I say, a great row. Lady Cynthia has refused to eat with them. She said she'd go out with Lady Roberta and Miss Townsend tonight, and Mrs. Bywater said over her dead body was Lady C. going to gad about in trousers while perfectly good young men she could marry are coming 'round to dinner. So Lady Cynthia said, if she *couldn't* go out, she was locking herself in her bedroom. Mrs. Bywater was screeching at her ever so loud, and even Mr. Bywater raised his voice a time or two. Result—Lady C. is barricaded in her chamber, the guests ain't coming, and the dinner is off."

"Oh dear." My misgivings rose to a frightening height.

Mr. Davis glided in to hear the end of Tess's tirade. "Tess has it right, more or less. Within the last hour. Bloody rude, I say. I've already uncorked the reds—they'll be ruined now."

Tess perked up. "We'll drink 'em, Mr. Davis. Have 'em with Mrs. H.'s tart."

Mr. Davis looked appalled. "You will not, young lady. They want a trained palate, those wines do."

"Then why was Mrs. Bywater wasting them on the insipid gents she wants Lady C. to marry?" Tess asked.

"I wonder the same thing, young lady, but it's not my place to say." Mr. Davis would say plenty to *us*, however. He'd likely go on about it for days.

Mrs. Redfern entered, her color high. "Tess, the correct term of address for Lady Cynthia for you is *her ladyship*. You are not to speak of her in familiar terms, no matter how friendly she is. You're a kitchen assistant, and you'd do well to remember your place."

It spoke of Tess's respect for the new housekeeper that she didn't stick her lip out and snap a retort. She merely scowled and said, "Yes, Mrs. Redfern. Sorry, ma'am."

"Make certain you never say it above stairs, or let it come to Mrs. Bywater's ears that you have. Mrs. Holloway, I am afraid Mrs. Bywater wishes to speak to you."

"Now?" I scanned the kitchen, which was in turmoil, poor Tess trying to cope with entirely new demands at the last moment.

"I am afraid she won't wait. She's unhappy with you for being out past six."

It was twenty minutes past. "The weather," I said quickly. "I could not find a hansom, and—"

"Mr. McAdam happened to pass?" Tess sent me a cheeky look.

Mrs. Redfern's lips pinched. "And make certain there's no mention of *that*. Mrs. Bywater is waiting, Mrs. Holloway—"

Sara, the upstairs maid, darted in, her eyes wide. "No, she's here. She's come down." Sara scurried from the kitchen across to the servants' hall, barely making it inside before we heard the determined click of heels on the slates of the corridor.

"There you are, Mrs. Holloway." Mrs. Bywater sailed in, her imperious glare all for me.

Tess plunked down her knife and dropped into a curtsy, eyes on the floor. Charlie scrunched into a ball by the fire, trying to remain unseen. Elsie, startled by the woman's arrival, dropped a plate from her soapy fingers.

The plate shattered on the floor. Elsie squeezed her hands together, her cheeks going red with mortification as she managed a curtsy. Mrs. Bywater closed her eyes, pained, then opened them to fix her glare on me.

"If I may speak to you." She paused, as though the rest of the staff would instantly clear out of the kitchen, but then swung around, marching rigidly to the servants' hall. I nervously followed. Sara, trapped inside, curtsied hurriedly, mumbling something.

"Sara, please go upstairs and see if you can persuade my wayward niece to open the door," Mrs. Bywater said. "Tell her she'll starve there if she persists."

Sara fled. Mrs. Bywater barely waited for her footsteps to fade before she turned on me.

"Cynthia refused to have a meal with my guests," she announced.

"Tess has told me," I said, trying to sound subdued.

"My niece defies me at every turn. Defies her parents and runs with lewd women—and who knows what else she gets up to? The best thing for her is to marry, but the company she keeps persuades her otherwise. I include *you* in that company, Mrs. Holloway. I have told you on several occasions that you and she have become far too friendly, and I will not have that in my house."

"I know my place, ma'am," I said as deferentially as I could. She had indeed scolded me for my camaraderie with Lady Cynthia not long before this. "I have not spoken to Lady Cynthia very much lately."

"Not true. She scurried down to the kitchen to see you, and she inserted her artist friend among my domestics. Ridiculous. Cynthia will never obey me as long as she has refuge downstairs, a very odd place for her to find it. She's a grown woman and ought to have a household of her own."

Mrs. Bywater began to splutter, losing the thread of her argument. She drew a breath and fixed a steely eye on me.

"To that end, Mrs. Holloway, I am dismissing you. I ought to have done so long ago, but I was persuaded otherwise. But no more." She lifted her chin. "You are to go. I have written to Lord Rankin about this, and no doubt he will agree with me. Lady Cynthia is a trial to him as well."

I gaped at her, the world falling away. The suddenness of her statement, after I'd left today so complacent of my position here, my awareness that I worked to keep Grace, left me breathless. To be cast out, to leave behind the friends I'd made—Tess, Lady Cynthia, Mr. Davis . . . Word would spread, and finding a decent house to work in would be very difficult.

"Please," I heard myself say. I, the dignified and haughty cook, was happy to beg. "I have no intention of encouraging Lady Cynthia to be disobedient—"

Mrs. Bywater raised her hand. "I do not wish to have an argument about it. I will write you a reference, as I have no complaint with your cooking, but you ought to remain below stairs and have nothing to do with those above it."

At this moment I agreed with her. If Cynthia had not come

to the kitchen when I first arrived, thrown herself down at my table, and worried that she'd killed a man with her impetuousness, I would not have been pulled into her world. I'd sensed a soul out of step and unhappy, and had wanted to help.

"Mrs. Bywater—" My voice was faint, trembling.

"I will allow you time to put your things together, but out you go, Mrs. Holloway. I am finished with nose-in-the-air cooks."

She must have sensed my true anguish, because I saw a flash of remorse in her eyes before she hardened once more. Mrs. Bywater opened her mouth as though she wished to continue her tirade, but then she closed it, turned, and stalked out.

Utter silence filled the downstairs as her heels clicked once more on the slate floor and then on the wooden stairs. The door above slammed as she left our domain and returned to her own, the sound as cutting as the cold February wind.

7

My fellow servants, who'd streamed from the kitchen the moment Mrs. Bywater had vanished, immediately surrounded me.

"She can't," Tess began in a near shriek, but Mrs. Redfern cut her off.

"Hush, Tess. I am afraid she can. Sit down, Mrs. Holloway. You look about to fall."

Mr. Davis, rage in his eyes, watched as I collapsed into a chair, then dashed out. I couldn't wonder what he was about, because I felt nothing at all.

Elsie sat down across from me, her eyes round. "Oh, Mrs. Holloway . . ."

"Drink that." Mr. Davis had reappeared and shoved a glass of something pungent under my nose.

I lifted the goblet without thought and swallowed the contents, though I could have wished for a cup of tea. I realized, as the liquid burned its way down my throat and into my stomach, that it was Lord Rankin's best brandy.

"She can't dismiss ya," Tess said with a touch of hysteria. "The master will never stand for it. He likes your cooking. Besides, it's his lordship what says who stays and goes."

Tess had never met Lord Rankin, whose wife had employed me before he'd moved himself to Surrey and invited the Bywaters to run his house and take care of Cynthia, his wife's sister. I had angered Lord Rankin almost from the first day of my employment, and he found Cynthia a nuisance. I held out no hope of assistance from Lord Rankin.

I was numb, and the brandy only made me more so. The others crowded around me in concern but made no declarations about standing by me.

A few months ago, I'd threatened to give notice to Mrs. Bywater over trouble with our last housekeeper, and Mr. Davis had said stoutly he would as well. But this was different. Peace had been restored, a new housekeeper installed. This was a good place with decent pay, and no one was in a rush to leave, including me.

Tess's voice was the lone exception. "I'll go with ya, Mrs. H. I can't stay here without you."

"No." My voice barely worked. "I cannot guarantee the next house would hire you along with me. You'll do fine here with the cook who replaces me."

Tess pulled off her apron and flung it to the floor. "I ain't. I works for *you*, Mrs. Holloway, none other."

I was too weary to admonish her. Too weary to think. Rushing about London in the cold rain hadn't helped, nor did the brandy on top of it. I needed hot tea, a meal, and a good sleep, but I doubted I'd see any of it.

"I must decide what to do." I rose, my legs shaking so hard

I had to clutch the tabletop to remain upright. "Lodging to sort out. Need a place to stay while I consult with my agency."

If they'd continue to have anything to do with me. I was known to be particular, and getting myself dismissed—the reference Mrs. Bywater promised notwithstanding—would not do me well in the agency's eyes.

I might have to accept a lesser post, in a house where I was the only menial. Some cooks were required to do all the kitchen tasks plus those of a scullery maid, including shovel her own coal. I was always so proud of my cooking and my ability to command a high wage that I never even considered such a position.

Pride, went the proverb, *goeth before a fall*. I certainly felt the sting of that fall, under the warmth of the brandy.

"You look unwell, Mrs. Holloway." Mrs. Redfern's voice cut through the buzz in my head. "You should take yourself to bed. The weather was nasty today. Tess, my girl, weeping and cursing does no one any good."

"Makes *me* feel better," Tess growled. "She's right, Mrs. H. You're all pale and flushed at the same time. Come on. To bed with ya."

She put aside her ranting to take me by the arm and lead me out. Mrs. Redfern came with us, and Mr. Davis led the way up the back stairs to open the door at the top.

"You sleep, Mrs. Holloway," he said. "Everything will be well."

I did not believe him. I tried to break away and walk myself to the next set of stairs, to begin the long climb to my chamber, but Tess and Mrs. Redfern stuck by me.

It was well they did. I was so weak by the time we reached the top of the house I might have tumbled down the stairs without them. They led me into my chamber, and Tess helped me out of my damp clothes while Mrs. Redfern turned down the bed.

Somehow, I had on my nightgown, the garment warm from hanging next to the chimney all day. Tess bundled me into bed, tucking me in.

"You have a sleep, Mrs. H. The mistress can't turn you out when you're ill. We won't let her."

The mistress could do anything she pleased, and well I knew it. I'd witnessed servants, even the old and infirm, turned onto the streets for lesser crimes than becoming too close friends to one of the family.

For the moment, I had this bed in the little room I'd come to call my own.

An illusion—none of it belonged to me. I hired out my cooking skills to others, and they gave me room and board and a very small salary in return. Nothing was mine but the talent I had for putting together a meal. If no one valued that, I would be out in the cold indeed.

My own fault. I ought to have put my head down and done my cookery and not interfered with Lord Rankin or Mrs. Bywater, or had anything to do with Lady Cynthia and her friends. I should have kept on with my chopping, basting, and simmering and let the world do what it would.

Even in my stupor I knew I could not have. Had I done nothing, a maid might have been ravished, a poisoner allowed to remain loose, and a kind Chinaman hanged for a crime he did not commit. I could not have stood by and done nothing. It was not my way.

But Grace would pay if I could not keep my posts and do my work. The Millburns were kind, but they had four growing children to care for, and Grace was another mouth to feed.

These troubled thoughts stayed with me as my exhausted and too-cold body took over and plunged me into sleep.

I woke to find Lady Cynthia sitting on the foot of my bed.

At first I thought I was dreaming—I had been lost in a whirl of Grace, Lady Cynthia in her stunning ball gown, and Bobby leaning down in front of the gates of Kew Gardens to hand Grace a coin.

The dreams dissolved as I blinked my hot eyes open, my head aching. The room was dark but for the lone candle on my bureau, the simple light too bright.

"Poor Mrs. H." Cynthia, in a dressing gown, pressed a damp cloth to my head. The cool of it was so soothing I wilted. "This is my fault," Cynthia continued. "But you're not to worry. I'll see to it."

"*My* doing," I croaked. "Your aunt is right."

"She's not—never say so. She's furious with me, and punishing you. Mrs. Redfern told me you were ill, and I said to Auntie that if she turned you out and you took sick and died she'd be forever branded with it. She worries about her reputation among her cold-stick lady friends, so she'll let you recover before she sends you to the pavement."

I floated back to wakefulness. "If you've come to cheer me up, this is hardly the way to go about it."

"Forgive me. I am trying to joke because I'm so bloody angry."

I was too tired to take umbrage or chide her for her language. "The mistress is right. I should not have got above my place."

"Rot that. I should be able to speak to anyone I damn well please, and take a cup of tea with them without my relations condemning me and sacking you. Ridiculous that a man can share his deepest secrets and best malt whisky with his valet, but I can't have a chat with the cook without endangering us both."

"More than having a chat. We have become friends." My voice was weak, but I knew in my heart this was true. "Your aunt warned me months ago that I was becoming too familiar with you, that I should cease. She threatened to dismiss me then, remember?"

"Why shouldn't I be friends with you? Never mind you work in a kitchen and I live off my family and can't afford my own boots. If minds are companionable, the circumstances of the bodies should not signify."

I smiled shakily. "You have been speaking to Mr. Thanos." It sounded like something he would say.

"He talks a lot of sense, does Elgin—I mean, Thanos." Her flush was obvious, even in the darkness. "What shall we do to mend this? I am certain you can find work in any house you like. I can ask about, find a good friend you can cook for who won't mind me popping in to speak with you."

"Not so simple if I am dismissed," I said sadly. "Word gets 'round. I won't be trusted."

"Absolute nonsense. Any road, Rankin won't let you go. You know too much about him and the family scandals to be let out in the world. Auntie misjudges him. But anyone with a title impresses her, including my own scoundrel of a father. Auntie is ecstatic that her husband's sister—my mum—married an earl, never mind dear papa is one step above a confidence trickster."

Not much above, from what I had gathered. Cynthia's father had tricked his way into the earldom—he'd been in line for the title, yes, but a bit further from it than he'd pretended.

"Aristocrats are descended from the worst thugs in history," Cynthia went on. "But apparently, speaking to a cook is a far worse crime than beggaring serfs. So is remaining unmarried." She heaved an aggrieved sigh.

Now we'd come to the crux of the matter. "Your aunt believes I encourage you to remain a spinster," I stated.

"You have nothing to do with my choice, which is what I try to explain to her. If I wish to be a spinster, I should be left to it. But *spinster* is considered such an ugly word. Don't know why. No one thinks *bachelor* a horrible term. But when a woman is a spinster, she is suddenly hideous, shriveled, and unwanted."

Tears glittered on her cheeks. Cynthia was not one to break down, but I could see she'd been pushed to her limit.

I took her hand, ashamed I'd been lying here feeling sorry for myself when she faced her aunt's needling about her unwed state every day. "I agree a woman should not marry simply for the sake of marrying, but seek a man she esteems and respects," I said, my voice a rasp. "But what *will* you do if you don't marry? I ask of practicality, not despair. At one time, you were prepared to go live with Lady Roberta."

"Yes, but Bobby had assumed we'd become lovers. I had to disappoint her, poor gel."

Cynthia spoke lightly, but I remembered she'd been quite upset she'd had to hurt Bobby's feelings, fearing she'd lose her closest friend.

"She has become fond of another, you said."

"Indeed she has." Cynthia's grin flashed. "Miss Townsend."

"Ah." Surprise flickered through my misery, but it explained things. No wonder Miss Townsend was serenely single, no worries about matrimony on her mind.

"Terribly dark secret." Cynthia lowered her voice to a whisper. "Her family mustn't know, in case they cut off the funds. Bobby won't mind if you know though."

"She knows *my* secret." I was feeling a bit better as I lay here—perhaps what I'd needed was rest.

"And respects you the more for it—she said so." Cynthia waved her hand, the damp cloth scattering droplets on my coverlet. "I can't run off with Bobby and interrupt her domestic bliss, but I wish I could go *somewhere*. Driving me mad, living in this house, dodging the gentlemen Auntie tosses at me. I'd sympathize with the poor chaps, but she has a talent for inviting the most insipid, empty-headed young fools imaginable. They've never read a book in their lives. If you mention Michelson's thoughts on the speed of light, they think you're talking about a racehorse."

I didn't know who Michelson was nor much about the speed of light—indeed, I'd had no idea light had a speed—but again I heard the ring of Elgin Thanos in her words.

"I want you to marry Mr. Thanos." The words slipped out before I could stop them—I must have a fever coming on.

Cynthia sprang up, but only to pace. "That's rich, Mrs. H. He's lovely, and a friend, but he'll have no interest in taking a wife who likes to wear trousers. He needs a quiet, sweet young woman who will organize his notes, bring him tea, and make certain his boots match." Her voice faltered, as though she pictured Mr. Thanos with such a young woman.

"You rub along well," I said with conviction. "He admires you so very much, and you admire him. All we must decide upon is how you will live."

Cynthia ceased pacing and gaped at me. "You are serious. If so, you've run mad. My family will never let me marry a penniless academic, one of Greek origin, I might add. I must marry a pale lordling with colorless hair, no chin, and a fortune, whose ancestors were here to greet old William when he decided to sail over from Normandy. Not a man whose grand-father had to flee Constantinople in the night."

"It doesn't matter. We will manage it."

Cynthia's cool hand landed on my forehead. "You are burn-ing up. I knew it. What I wish is that I could live independently, never mind my family. I'd have a nice cottage where I could put my feet up or tramp about in boots and trousers, and you could come cook for me. With your daughter. Wouldn't that be fine?"

It would be. I closed my eyes, imagining it.

I must have slipped into sleep, because the next thing I knew, Cynthia was touching a light kiss to my cheek. "You have a rest, Mrs. H. Tomorrow, we'll think of something. And you will tell me everything you and Mr. McAdam have been getting up to. Elsie let slip you are looking into something at the Foundling Hospital. I won't cease until you admit me to your adventures."

In the morning, my throat was tight, my head aching—the natural consequence of being out too long in the cold and rain—but the fever I'd experienced in bed the previous night had lessened. I only hoped I didn't begin sniffling.

I washed my face and hands and dressed in my work frock, going down to the kitchen. I did not know what to expect, but it was my duty to go, and so I went.

This was Friday morning, and Tess was already working, her cheeks pink but her countenance dour. She had changed her day out to Saturdays earlier this winter—I suspect because Caleb, the constable of this street, had Saturday afternoons off. Therefore Tess was now hunkered over the table, though working without her usual cheer.

Charlie shoveled coal into the stove, brushing his face with the back of his hand and leaving a black streak on it. Elsie, who had no dishes in her sink yet, peeled potatoes while Tess had bacon frying.

Mrs. Redfern, who must have been waiting to see whether I'd come down, rustled in behind me, the keys that hung at her side softly clinking. "Lady Matthew Baird needs a cook, I've heard. She has a house in Brook Street, though she spends a good part of the summer in Lincolnshire. As her cook, you'd travel with her."

I could not take the post then, as I needed to stay in London all year. I'd put up with the heat and stink of the city to be a short omnibus ride from Grace.

"Thank you," I said. "That is kind of you."

"You'll find a place, I have no doubt." She tried to speak reassuringly, but she knew the difficulties I faced.

Tess would not look at me. I had no wish to leave her behind to a new cook's temper and Mrs. Bywater's arbitrariness, but I would do her no favors if I allowed her to leave with me. I could not guarantee that a new mistress would hire a cook and her assistant both.

As I began to don my apron, Mr. Davis appeared. "She says you're not to cook today." The disgust in his tone was deep.

My hands froze in the act of tying the apron's knot. "Pardon?"

"She wants to see how Tess gets on. You are to spend the day putting together your things and searching for a new post."

"I see."

Mr. Davis's cheekbones stained red. "She is a commoner, Mrs. Holloway. Doesn't understand the least thing about running a large household. In Somerset, her servants are a cook who doubles as a charwoman and a person from the village who comes in twice a week to do the gardening."

His derision was acute. Mr. Davis did not believe a home could be run with less than a dozen servants, no matter how few people actually lived in it.

"No doubt she finds it a savings, Mr. Davis." I hung up my apron and fetched my coat and hat, still on their hooks from last night. The hat was dry now, but the straw was misshapen, its ribbon trim rain-blotched.

Tess at last looked up. Her unhappiness tore at me. "Where are ya going?"

"Out." If Mrs. Bywater did not wish me to work, I could spend my time on the problem Daniel had handed me.

"I will come back," I added as Tess gazed at me in anguish. "I promise. I have errands to run."

Tess had tears in her eyes as she bent her head again, but she scowled at Elsie as though daring her to say a word. Elsie remained silent, too reticent to speak.

I climbed the stairs to the street. The rain from the previous day had ceased, but a cold wind blew down the road, stirring last autumn's dead leaves. I buttoned my coat to my chin and trudged around the corner and down South Audley Street on my way to the omnibus.

"Mrs. Holloway!" Lady Cynthia's voice sang out as I reached Curzon Street some minutes later.

I halted and waited as Cynthia caught up to me at a run. She wore boots laced to her knees, which were encased by cuffs of knee breeches nearly hidden by her long coat. She'd dressed more mannishly than usual today, with a scarf wrapped around her throat and a tall hat pulled down over her scraped-back hair. If I had not known better, I would have thought a slim young gentleman chased me down.

Cynthia carried a satchel in her fine-gloved hand. "Where are you off to, Mrs. H.?" Her breath fogged in the cold air.

"The East End. To see a vicar."

"Capital. I'll join you."

I was not certain the East End was the place for Lady Cynthia, no matter that she was dressed convincingly as a male. The toughs there would steal every bit of clothing from any well-clad person, regardless of their sex.

"Where were *you* off to?" I asked, eying the satchel with suspicion.

She swung that article. "Me? Running away from home." Cynthia laughed cheerily. "Let's fetch a hansom, shall we?"

8

There was absolutely no use dissuading Cynthia and sending her back home, and I did not try very hard. Truth to tell, I was grateful of the company today—I would discuss her rash decision later.

"We are going to Shadwell," I informed the cabbie Cynthia had hailed. "A church called All Saints."

The driver, bundled against the cold, never looked at us twice as we settled in. Cynthia did not speak to the driver at all, to my relief. She shoved the satchel, apparently heavy, under the seat, and sat back, arms folded.

The hackney clopped away. Slowly. Traffic was heavy in Piccadilly, and it took a long time to move.

"Have you ever been to the East End?" I asked Cynthia.

"Of course. Bobby likes to slum. Poverty doesn't shock and offend me, Mrs. H. Saddens me, rather. What a shame, that I'm expected to put on frocks that cost the earth while others can barely buy bread."

"Sad, yes, but also dangerous. We are not taking a holiday."

"Do give me some faith that I'm not a frivolous being. I will help you with whatever you are up to, and keep an eye out for new lodgings at the same time."

I did not answer. Cynthia, I'd come to know in the year I'd worked for her family, could be kindhearted and generous, often impulsively so, but not always wise. I agreed her situation was troubling, but a gently born young woman had a terrible time making her way in this world alone. She would need a safe place to stay, a friend to look after her.

As we went, I told Cynthia in a low voice about Mr. Fielding and his worries about Nurse Betts and the children from the Foundling Hospital. I also related what Elsie had told me about the Hospital, my journey there, and what I'd discovered from Mrs. Compton, the cook. Cynthia listened, blue eyes filling with concern.

The hansom traveled the length of Piccadilly, past Leicester Square and to Long Acre, then north to High Holborn and Cheapside, too near where my daughter resided. I gazed longingly at the turning to the Millburns' home, wanting to run to her, but there would be too many questions, too many explanations. I did not want to worry Grace or the Millburns yet about my change in circumstance.

The hansom moved with the many carriages, carts, and vans jammed in the City, all of us traveling under a thick pall of smoke. We passed the grand edifices that made up the financial world of London, through Cornhill and Leadenhall to Aldgate Street, and so to Whitechapel Road.

The cabbie kept up a foul soliloquy the length of the journey about the many vehicles and their incompetent drivers, shouting his disapprobation and being shouted at in return.

At one point our wheels locked with that of a wagon, our driver raising his whip in threat.

The drover, a large man with giant hands, only said, "Steady on, mate," and efficiently maneuvered his horse until the spokes slid from our hub, and the hansom jerked forward once more.

Cynthia looked back around the canopy of the hansom and gave the drover a good-natured wave.

"Whew," she said under her breath. "We'll hire a different man for the journey back."

At the corner of Whitechapel Road stood the church of St. Mary Matfelon, which had once been whitewashed, I've been told, which was why this entire area was known as Whitechapel. Scaffolding covered the building's walls today, as it was being rebuilt after a fire. From there, the cabbie turned south into Shadwell, an area bustling with traffic and shops, warehouses and workhouses. The bulk of the London hospital and medical college weighted down the horizon. Young men dissected unfortunate beings there, learning from the dead how to stitch and dose the living.

Mr. Fielding was vicar of the small church of All Saints on Christian Street, a fitting name for the road. I hadn't been much to the East End and hadn't seen this particular building before, but I liked it at once. It was elegant and devoid of the overly Gothic embellishments renovators seemed to have put on in the last few decades. The exterior was rather plain, with clear glass windows, reminding me of Grosvenor Chapel.

Cynthia handed me down like a gallant swain and tossed the cabbie a coin. He snatched it out of the air and drove sullenly away without looking at us. I wager he'd never realized Lady Cynthia was female.

I had no way of knowing whether Mr. Fielding was even about, and he wasn't expecting me. Cynthia hoisted her satchel, and we went into the churchyard through a tall gate that squeaked.

The iron fence encircled the church, shutting it firmly away from the street beyond it. Urchins in ill-made clothing played some game on the road that involved throwing small rocks, and they jeered at us through the bars. Cynthia glanced at them in curiosity, but I took no notice. If we paid them too much mind, they might start chucking the stones at us.

A path led around the church to a small house I assumed was the vicarage. As it was a Friday, nearing noon by now, any vicar would be at home, consuming his lunch. A housekeeper with a round face and wisps of white hair across her chin began to tartly tell us just that—the vicar was at his meal and wouldn't be disturbed.

"If you've come about his charitable works, I'm afraid you'll have to make an appointment or see him after evensong. He's very busy, is our Mr. Fielding." She said it fondly and proudly.

"Please tell him Mrs. Holloway has come about the matter we spoke of on Tuesday last," I said. "We will wait."

The woman did not look surprised that *I* spoke instead of the gentleman behind me. Church and charitable work was usually the purview of the ladies.

Hurried footsteps sounded behind the housekeeper, and a moment later Mr. Fielding appeared behind her, beaming a smile at us. "Mrs. Holloway." He greeted me as though he'd been looking forward to this meeting all week. "This is indeed a pleasant event."

Mr. Fielding held a napkin but was formally dressed in a suit with a black shirtfront and white collar. "Come in, come in. No matter, Mrs. Hodder. Mrs. Holloway is helping me on business of great importance. Lay a place for her and her friend, if you please."

"A cup of tea will do nicely," I said quickly. "No need for more."

Vicars, especially those of an East End parish, were notoriously poor, their livings meager. I did not wish to eat food the housekeeper might be saving for her supper.

"Just as you like." Mr. Fielding ushered us into a dining room a few feet from the front door. It was a cozy space, barely accommodating a small dining table, a short sideboard, and a corner cupboard.

Mrs. Hodder, with less stiffness, brought out two extra cups and saucers, set them on the table, and lifted a fat white teapot to pour a stream of very dark tea into the cups. She gave us curious glances, but left us to it when Mr. Fielding signaled her to go.

I waited until I heard Mrs. Hodder's footsteps recede from the closed door before I removed my hat and coat and sat down. The housekeeper had not offered to take our wraps, a hint that we should not stay long.

"Who is your quiet friend?" Mr. Fielding asked me, resuming his seat and lifting his teacup. "May I make his acquaintance?"

Cynthia, who'd taken the chair next to mine, swept off her hat and tossed it to a bench under the window. "*Her* acquaintance. Lady Cynthia Shires, at your service, sir."

Mr. Fielding's hand jerked, tea spilling over his wrist. He hastily set down the cup, shaking out his fingers and snatching up his napkin.

"Good Lord." Mr. Fielding peered at Lady Cynthia in delight as he wiped off his hands. "Such an elegant young lady, but wearing the drab clothes we chaps are forced into day after day. What made you take it up?"

"If you must ask, then you will never understand." Cynthia gave him a weary look and sipped her tea.

"Perhaps not. I am very curious—how do you keep from being arrested? But then, you said *Lady* Cynthia, which means an aristocratic connection. Is your father a duke, a marquess, or an earl?"

I answered, somewhat sharply, "An earl. But we have come about urgent business, Mr. Fielding. I suggest you curb your questions for another time."

Mr. Fielding flicked his blue gaze to me. I saw a worry deep in his eyes, which flared and died in the space of an instant. Then his smile spread over his face.

"You do right to admonish me, Mrs. Holloway. This is no time to be frivolous. You must have discovered something important to journey all the way to Shadwell, with only this lady as escort."

"I have." I saw no reason not to dive straight into the matter. "Nurse Betts. You know her. Not only do you know her, but you have been seen several times with her. The cook at the Foundling Hospital believes you have become her beau."

Mr. Fielding's smile died, as did anything good-humored on his face. "Yes, Daniel has already twitted me for this. My fault for believing I'd been discreet."

"It is true then? You are walking out with her?"

Mr. Fielding sagged back into his chair. "Yes, I confess it. I am very fond of Nurse Betts."

And now she was missing. When Mr. Fielding looked at me again, I saw a man in misery.

Cynthia pulled a flask from her pocket, reached across the table, and poured a dollop of pungent whisky into his tea. "Have a sip of that. Will pull you together."

Mr. Fielding hid his start and drank obediently, some color returning to his face.

"Why did you not simply tell me at once?" I asked him as he recovered. "Or Daniel. If you are well acquainted with Nurse Betts, you might help suggesting places to search for her."

"I know." Mr. Fielding drank deeply of the doctored tea, going silent a time as though debating what to reveal. "The truth, dear lady, is that I did not want to tell Daniel. I was afraid he'd chuck me out and not lift a finger if he thought I asked for assistance on my own behalf. Which I did not. I am very worried about those children. And Nell. I never sought Daniel for selfish reasons, but I knew he'd believe I did. My brother has very little faith in me."

His voice held pathos, but I was annoyed he'd concealed the truth from *me* as well.

"From what Mr. McAdam has told me, he has reason to not believe in you," I said.

Mr. Fielding flushed. "In the past, of course he didn't. I was a desperate boy trying to survive in the world. I have reformed, as you can see, but Daniel will always view me as the chap who deserted him after the man we regarded as our father was brutally murdered. Daniel believed we should have stuck together, but I lit out on my own. I regret that now, but at the time, I was mad with grief and fear and pushed Daniel away. I had phenomenal luck, I realize, to be found by a man of great kindness. The least I can do to return that kindness is take care of others."

It was a nice speech, neatly exonerating him but acknowledging his guilt and shame, blaming the tragic circumstances he'd survived. I wondered how often he'd rehearsed it.

"You ought to have told me in any case," I said. "As I say, I can better know where to begin looking for Nurse Betts if I have an idea where she might go. Did she come here to speak to you?"

"Yes, about three weeks ago. When she was not comfortable about the missing children, she sought me out and asked if I could do anything–go to the police, or find out where they'd gone."

Cynthia broke in. "And you, being smitten, agreed."

"*And* I was concerned about the children." Mr. Fielding acknowledged her perception with a nod. "I looked into the matter at once, as I told you, Mrs. Holloway, visiting the Foundling Hospital the next day and speaking to the director–Lord Russell Hirst, a prominent and respectable gentleman. I was told the children in question had been placed in homes. Lord Russell showed me the record."

His fingers tapped the table as he spoke. Not a drumming, but a faint *tap, tap, tap,* as though he never noticed himself doing it.

"Did Lord Russell express surprise at your question?" I asked. "Or simply show you the record?"

"He admitted it had been a swift decision without much discussion–certainly, it hadn't been brought up to the board. He could understand why Nurse Betts and I might think they'd simply disappeared. He was very reassuring."

"Huh." Cynthia's fair brows drew together. "I'm sure he would be. Do you trust him?"

"He is a knight of the realm for his services to philanthropy, and a duke's son." Mr. Fielding closed the hand that had been tapping and forced it to rest. "Which means, I don't know whether I trust him. If I'd been raised differently, I might, but I've seen too much of the world. The more praised a fellow, the more likely he's a rascal."

Cynthia gave a laugh. "I agree with you."

"Then what happened?" I prompted. "Was Nurse Betts happy with your discovery?"

"She was relieved at first. But since I spoke to you and Daniel, I decided to visit these homes and find out if the children were there. They were not."

"Jove." Cynthia leaned forward, arms on the table. "They'd never arrived?"

"I mean the homes did not exist. The addresses did not, anyway. House numbers do not lay on the streets named, and on one of the roads, all the houses have been demolished to put in a large building. I know London very well, but I also consulted a guide to the streets to be certain. The houses were not there."

I did not like this. A director of a children's home lying about what had happened to his charges? Or was the director innocent, also duped into thinking the children had been placed at these addresses?

"Did you confront Lord Russell about this?"

Mr. Fielding shook his head. "I decided it was better to let him believe I was satisfied. Nurse Betts had asked questions at the Hospital, but she told me she started to feel frightened. I must wonder whether she also looked up these addresses or discovered Lord Russell lied. I at last made up my mind to hunt up Daniel and consult him—he's clever at these things."

"Did you decide to consult him before or after Nurse Betts went missing herself?"

Again the hand stretched out, fingers softly tapping. "After. I wanted to ask Nell what she thought of me bringing in my brother, but she didn't turn up at our meeting. When I inquired at the Hospital, the matron for her ward told me she'd gone for her day out and hadn't returned. That was a week and a half ago now."

Whatever he thought about the situation, or Daniel, or me, I saw genuine distress in his eyes. Even the boys and girl who'd vanished, the record of their leaving a lie, didn't worry him like the absence of Nurse Betts. He feared for her.

"How did you meet Nurse Betts?" I asked, gentling my tone. "In the first place, I mean."

"At the Foundling Hospital, of course." The answer was ready. "As a member of the board of governors, I joined them for inspections at the Hospital, meetings with the staff. Nurse Betts was on hand to answer questions. She's a well-spoken lass, and kind. I noticed her kindness. I was struck by it." He turned appealing eyes to us. "You must understand that in my lifetime, both before I was respectable and after I became a vicar, I have encountered the most deplorable people. Those who pretend to be kind usually are scheming to take every penny you have and possibly your life. The exception has been Nurse Betts."

"Ah," Lady Cynthia said. "Love ensued?"

"Not quite." Mr. Fielding's laugh was breathless. "I have never allowed myself to trust enough for that. But I liked her, quite a lot. I first asked her if she'd take a walk with me, and as we strolled, we talked. Talked about many things. I saw her again, and again. For about, let me see, four months, we have been ambling through London's parks and conversing about . . . everything. I've never suggested more to her—what do I have to offer? The living here is not much. She makes a better wage at the Hospital, in fact, and she dotes on the lads and lasses and doesn't wish to leave them. Besides, she is an angel, and I–" Mr. Fielding gave us a self-deprecating smile. "Well, ladies, I am not. The collar notwithstanding." He touched it as though it pinched his throat.

Mr. Fielding might deny falling in love, but the tension in

his voice, his body, spoke the lie. I could see he cared deeply for Nurse Betts, and that fact made me like him better.

"You said you feared she has gone searching for the children herself," I said.

"Yes." His answer was quiet. "She is that sort."

I subsided. Lord Russell had lied about the fostering, or at least his records did. Why? I knew the perils children could face in London, which was why the Foundling Hospital, as grim as it was, existed. The children were safe within its walls. Lonely and afraid, yes, but bodily safe.

If it were no longer the haven it should be, and Nurse Betts discovered this, she might be in grave danger, indeed.

But then, so might Mr. Fielding be. He'd marched into the office of the director and demanded to be told about the missing children. One would have to be terribly unobservant not to notice the connection between Mr. Fielding and Nurse Betts. Mrs. Compton in the kitchen had known, and now feared for her.

Something was going on in the Foundling Hospital, possibly something terrible. It made me sick to think of.

Cynthia must have agreed with me, because her eyes had gone quiet. "I'd say we need to find this Nurse Betts," she said. "The sooner the better."

"I agree, dear lady." Mr. Fielding turned to me, resigned but resolute. "What do you wish me to do?"

Cynthia also looked at me expectantly. It ought to be comical, a vicar and a highborn lady asking a cook to give them orders, but the situation was too dire for amusement.

"Please keep searching for her, Mr. Fielding," I said. "Go where she would have gone, to the places she told you were special, anywhere she mentioned, even in idle conversation. Lady Cynthia and I will also look, and question. I have made a friend of one of the cooks, and I plan to try to speak to some of the maids who work in the wards. They might have seen or noticed something without knowing it."

"Exactly," Cynthia said. "Mrs. H. told me of the peculiar practice of people observing the kiddies at tea or dinner or some such. I'll put on my visit-the-charities gown and go myself. Who knows? Awful people might be using the opportunity to sweep a child away."

Mr. Fielding's expression was far from that of a man of God. I saw rage in his eyes, raw and unyielding.

"If they have, hell will be too good a place for them. I was one of those children once, ladies, without the good fortune of being taken in by a charity. My mother left me on the street as quite a little fellow, and only by the grace of God did I survive. The man Daniel and I called 'Father'—Mr. Carter—only let us into his house because we could work, though he turned out to be a decent enough cove, for a villain. That was short-lived. In a few years, he was dead, and we were out again, avoiding filth any way we could, until I was fortunate, several years later, to be taken in by another. It made us who we are, Daniel and me. Trust me when I say I will do my utmost to find these children and bring whoever might have harmed them to justice."

His eyes flashed, the rage flaring into incandescence.

I wondered if he meant justice in a court of law, or his own sort. I'd seen Daniel's form of justice when he'd gone after bad men.

I took a last sip of the rather indifferent tea and rose. "I too will do my utmost, I assure you, Mr. Fielding. As will Daniel and Lady Cynthia. I think we can agree that this task is very important."

Mr. Fielding had risen to his feet when I did. "It is, my friends. I will leave no stone unturned."

"But have a care," I warned. "They already know of your interest. You might be in danger."

"I don't give a hang for that." Mr. Fielding's handsome expression revealed more of the street boy he'd been and far less of the educated vicar he'd become. "Let them do their worst."

"I like that." Lady Cynthia surged from her chair and fetched her hat. "You can get them banged up and then pray for their souls. The best of both worlds."

Mr. Fielding sent her an impudent grin, looking much like Daniel in that moment. "I agree, dear lady. I agree."

So he is Daniel McAdam's brother," Cynthia said as we settled into another hansom. This cabbie's temper was a bit better, I was relieved to see. "Or as close as."

"Yes. I do not quite know what to make of him."

"Handsome devil." Cynthia adjusted the satchel under the seat and pulled her coat closer against the cold. "Knows it, I wager."

"It is the devil part I worry about. Daniel does not trust him—he acknowledged that."

"Hmm, well. My sister and I, you know, were blood related and brought up by the same parents, and turned out to be very different people. Our brother too."

Cynthia rarely spoke about her brother, who had taken his own life, nor her sister, also deceased. The memories were not comfortable.

I at least had pried out of Mr. Fielding before we left him the addresses the director had given him. He'd declared they wouldn't be useful, and he was likely right, but I was curious.

I felt bold enough to pat Cynthia's hand. "I appreciate your help."

"Not at all." The words rang with sincerity. She truly was kindhearted.

"If you go to the Foundling Hospital to observe the children, you ought to take Mr. Thanos," I said. "It would look more natural for a young woman to go with a young man."

Cynthia's cheeks went bright red. "Thanos? Yes. Yes, I can see that."

"I will ask him," I said.

"Not necessary—"

"Yes," I interrupted. "I will be less likely to stammer and blush, and he will be less likely to turn me down—not because he would not wish to help, but he would be stammering and blushing too, if you asked."

"You are blunt today," Cynthia said with a wan smile. "Is it because I wakened you in the middle of the night?"

"I am practical, is all. I will ask Mr. Thanos and arrange it. Neither of you need to be nervous."

"Very well, then. You shall play go-between, and Mr. Thanos and I will toddle along when you say." She glanced at the buildings going by, Aldgate Street changing to Leadenhall. "Where to now?"

"Home," I said.

"Not a bit of it." Cynthia folded her arms. "I'm not going back there. And neither are you."

9

It wasn't my home, or hers either really, but I gave her a firm look.

"My things are there," I said. "I'll not risk having your aunt chuck them out." The cookery books alone would set me back a long way.

"Or even sell them, knowing her," Cynthia conceded. "But *I* am not crawling home. Auntie will lock me in my chamber and let me out only when I agree to marry. Even then I'll be in chains as I'm led down the aisle."

I cut through her nonsense. "We'll go to Bobby's flat. I know you say there's no room there, but Bobby and Miss Townsend are your friends, and they will help you find somewhere to stay—with another friend perhaps. I will return to Mount Street, pack my things, and move to my old boardinghouse. If they have a place for me."

I faltered at the end. The landlady at my usual boarding-house was a decent sort, but she could not afford to keep a room open on the off chance I'd need it. I'd have to hope for the best or find another house. The Millburns had no space for another body, I already knew.

"Very well," Cynthia said. "Duchess Street, cabbie," she called. "Off Langham Place."

"Yes, missus." The hansom continued at its sedate pace.

"We shall see," Cynthia said. "I very much think Bobby will insist you stay with us. We will all be very cozy."

I'd visited the flat where Lady Roberta Perry dwelled a few times and liked it. The rooms were decorated in a modern style, with furniture in simple lines, a fern-patterned wallpaper, and much greenery about the place. Bobby also had a parlor stove she kept hot and a landlady generous with tea and pastries.

The flat was on the second floor of a house in a small lane called Duchess Street, not far from the grand Langham Hotel, where the important and wealthy stayed. As Cynthia said, it was quite cozy, and of course, crowded.

Bobby was in, welcoming us with aplomb. "Of course you can stay, Cyn. Judith isn't back yet—she's over sketching *your* lot." She grinned at me as she ushered us to seats.

"Mrs. Bywater allowed Miss Townsend to return?" I asked in surprise.

"Auntie's quite taken with her." Cynthia slung her satchel to a table and herself into a low-backed chair, kicking her legs over one of its arms. "Miss Townsend is from a wealthy and prominent family."

"And she wears skirts." Bobby laughed. "How is your daughter, Mrs. H.? Such an adorable gel. Let her be anything she wants when she grows up, eh?"

I warmed at Bobby's praise for Grace. "At the moment, she wants to read and have plenty of bread for tea."

I did not like to dwell on what would become of Grace when she grew older. She was clever and sweet, but she'd have to grub for her living as I did, or be married, and marriage was no guarantee she'd be taken care of. Those were perilous waters. I wished Cynthia's aunt would understand that.

Bobby set out the tea tray her landlady had brought. Cynthia wordlessly produced her flask from her coat, which Bobby took with thanks. I declined any spirits in my tea, but the young ladies imbibed happily.

Bobby wore a suit of fine tweed, which draped well on her rectangular body. The suit was tailor-made, as Cynthia's clothes were. Bobby cropped her hair close, and with her lack of feminine curves—or at least they were well hidden—she easily passed as a gentleman. Cynthia preferred to keep her hair long, and with her flowerlike face, it was more difficult for her to be mistaken for a man. She was less obviously female when she bundled up, as today, but now that she'd unmuffled, she was very evidently a young lady.

Cynthia related our current problem to Bobby as we drank, and Bobby's amusement died in shock and anger.

"Someone's making off with the little tykes? That's monstrous."

"We don't know whether they're making off with them or not," I said. "But something has happened. I assure you, I will do my utmost to make certain the children are well and unharmed."

"Damn and blast. I sit here in this padded flat drinking whisky when little ones might be in trouble," Bobby growled. "Hungry and cold. I hate to think of it."

"It's why we do charity work," Cynthia told her. "Auntie does it so people will think well of her, but at least the time she gives does *some* good. She won't part with a shilling, but she'll help sell bunting and other junk at a jumble sale to raise money."

"That can't do much," Bobby said skeptically. "How does one get on the board of the Foundling Hospital? Sounds more robust."

"I have no idea," I said as Cynthia shrugged. "Mr. Fielding was elected to it, but he is a vicar."

"I imagine you have to contribute a great lot of money, or be in the House of Lords, or some such," Cynthia said.

"Ridiculous." Bobby removed a silver case from her pocket and extracted a cigar. "Do you mind, Mrs. H.?"

"Not at all," I said politely.

"My brother gets them straight from Havana. Soothes my nerves." Bobby handed a cheroot to Cynthia, and soon both ladies were puffing in a practiced way. The room filled with a sweet, pungent, and heavy scent.

A gentle cough interrupted. I had dozed off, as I had done before in Bobby's flat—her chairs were quite comfortable.

Miss Townsend stood in the doorway, clad in a green and gray walking dress with a fetching hat that I itched to examine. She carried a portfolio under one arm, and waved at the smoke-filled room with a gloved hand.

"I thought we agreed no cigars in the sitting room," she said, closing the door and sending Bobby an admonishing look.

Bobby tamped out her cigar, jumped up, and flung open a window, letting in a cold wave of wind. "Didn't realize you'd be back so soon. It will clear out in a trice."

Miss Townsend did not look convinced, but she said nothing more about it as she set down her portfolio and unpinned her hat.

"Cyn and Mrs. H. are staying the night," Bobby announced. "Mrs. H. has been chucked out, and Cynthia has said to hell with it."

"No, they are not." Miss Townsend spoke in a quiet, matter-of-fact way, and we all stared at her.

"I don't mind," Bobby said. "We'll tuck 'em in somewhere."

Miss Townsend patted her hair into place and carefully set her hat on the table. It was a green plush affair, enhanced with a darker green ribbon, small-brimmed with a modestly high crown, and trimmed only with a few gray feathers. Perfect for this weather, and it matched her walking dress precisely.

"No need." Miss Townsend turned to us. "Mrs. Bywater admits she was a bit hasty in dismissing Mrs. Holloway. She will offer her apology upon your return."

While I blinked at her, Cynthia, who'd risen from her chair to put out her cigar, openly gaped, the cigar hanging from stiff fingers. "Auntie said *that*?"

"She did. And she has no idea *you* have left home, Cyn, so nothing will be said when you go back. She will simply believe you were out for the afternoon."

"But I'm not going back." Cynthia stubbed out the cigar and dropped it into a bowl. A wisp of bluish smoke rose from the end that was not quite extinguished. "To be paraded like a prize racehorse, one a bit long in the tooth, before eligible gents? To pretend to be grateful I have suitors, even those poor specimens?"

Miss Townsend sent Cynthia a patient look. "I have persuaded Mrs. Bywater that she should cease the invitations for a time. Let things settle."

Cynthia's eyes widened. "Good Lord. Have you run mad, or has she? Or perhaps it's me who's mad."

"I saw the distress Mrs. Holloway's departure caused the rest of the staff." Miss Townsend addressed me directly, her brown eyes full of sympathy. "I related to Mrs. Bywater a few anecdotes of the turmoil I'd witnessed in my own family's house when a good cook gave notice or retired. How very difficult it was to replace said cook, and the horrors we suffered until a decent one could be found. It gave her pause, I think." Her small smile told me she'd amused herself with Mrs. Bywater.

"That was kind of you," I said, my heart warming. The stiff unhappiness I'd been wrapped in since last night relaxed.

"Not at all. We will pretend I was simply annoyed she'd deprived me of a subject to paint. I have not finished with my sketches of you."

I nodded, though I wasn't certain which was the truth—was she an artist worried about her work, or a young woman who'd seen my anguish and Tess's, and decided to help?

"You worked your charm on Auntie on my behalf as well, didn't you?" Cynthia accused her.

Miss Townsend shrugged. "I might have told her more tales, this time of poorly conceived matches—how a gentleman who professes to be wealthy is revealed to be penniless, *after* he's married the niece and comes knocking on the well-meaning relative's door. How young ladies pushed too hard at respectable gentlemen often flee with *un*respectable ones. A great scandal so easily avoided."

Cynthia began to grin. "You touched her with the right words. Decent of you to stick your neck out."

"You are Bobby's greatest friend." Miss Townsend turned to a decanter of brandy near the window, poured herself a small goblet, and took a ladylike sip. "Naturally, I do not wish to see you unhappy. I can do this small thing and feel benevolent."

She spoke offhandedly, but to me, it had been no small thing, likewise to Cynthia.

"Thank you," I said, gushing a little in my relief. Because of her intervention, I could remain at the Mount Street house, sleep in my solitary bed in the attics, cook what I pleased, and not have to leave Tess and Mr. Davis and dear Elsie. Miss Townsend was a kind young woman, indeed.

Miss Townsend took another sip of brandy. "Not at all. You must admit, Cynthia, it would be a bit crowded here with four."

"I intended to look for lodgings of my own," Cynthia said. "Something modest, obviously."

"Not too many such places for a young lady living alone," Miss Townsend answered with a wry smile. "Dreary boarding-houses, perhaps, and it would be frocks all the time for you, I'm afraid, my dear. No visitors after eight in the evening, and no *male* visitors at all. Oh, the horror."

She lifted Cynthia's not-quite-spent cheroot and took a pull, the end glowing orange. She stubbed it out more completely as she exhaled smoke.

Cynthia shivered and rubbed her arms. "You're a wise woman, Judith, but blast you, you've brought all my ideas tumbling down. You couldn't see your way to convincing Rankin to bestow a large trust on me, for my sister's sake, so I can set up my own household, could you? I'll bring Mrs. H. to cook for me and be utterly respectable all the time. So long as I can do what I damn well please."

Miss Townsend shook her head. "I wish I could advise you. Having a quantity of money would solve many of your problems, but there is the question of *finding* the quantity of money."

"We'll work on that," Bobby said, her tone sincere. "Meanwhile, I'm going to try to find the poor kids missing from the Foundling Hospital."

"Are you?" Miss Townsend gave Bobby a look of surprise. "Excellent. Do let me help."

Cynthia and I returned to Mount Street in another hansom. When I entered the kitchen, my step much lighter than when I'd gone out, Tess flung herself at me, sobbing.

"There now." I patted her as she clung. "I'll not leave you, Tess."

"Never." Tess hugged me more tightly then pulled herself away, wiping her eyes with the back of her hand. "I can't do without you, Mrs. Holloway, and that's the truth of it."

"I'm going nowhere for now." I gave her shoulders a squeeze. "One day you'll do so fine without me, you'll be happy to see the back of me."

"Not blooming likely," Tess muttered.

I told her to return to preparing the evening meal while I went upstairs, changed into my gray work frock, and moved back to the kitchen to tie on my apron.

Tess had made a start on some capons in white sauce, an easy enough meal to prepare without help. The carrots were cut in a neat dice, for which I praised her.

"Elsie peeled them." Tess could be generous about sharing approval. "She's getting to be a dab hand."

"Thank you, Elsie," I called out to her, and Elsie ducked her head, pleased.

I moved to the larder, surprised how happy I was to see it

again. I'd arranged the shelves to my convenience, and knew exactly where to put my hands on ingredients I'd need to make anything I wished.

I filled a basket with fragrant greens and the last of the lemons and returned to the kitchen.

"I'll do a salad. A bit of lemon will go into the dressing, and the rest will do for a lemon tart. The fruit is not pretty enough to display in a bowl but will make good eating. Shriveled, but still sweet."

"Like me granny," Tess said with a grin. "If I had one, that is. You know these things, Mrs. H. I was too scared to make anything more than a chicken with some cream."

"Which you have done very well. I've said time and again that simple cooking is best. Tasty and flavorful without being exotic and strange. People want to know what they're eating."

"I do, anyway." Tess, her sunny outlook restored, threw the lettuce into a bowl of water and shook it hard to remove any dirt. She did this with so much gusto water slopped over onto the table, rushing toward a fresh-baked loaf. I stopped the flow with a towel and gave her an admonishing look. Tess only grinned at me.

"Mrs. Holloway?" The soft voice of Elsie cut through. "Did you find out what's become of the children?"

"Not yet, dear." I didn't want to tell her all that Mr. Fielding had told me until I knew more, not wishing to upset her. "I will continue looking."

"Elsie told me all about it," Tess said. "Dreadful wicked what people do, innit?"

"Tuesday's me half day out," Elsie said. "I'll go 'round and speak to Mabel. She might have seen something."

"Please do not alarm her," I said quickly. "We do not need the entire Hospital panicked if there is a simple explanation."

Elsie shook her head. "I'll just mention it, like. And about Nurse Betts."

"Do not anger anyone, and do not talk too freely. But I would welcome whatever you learn."

Elsie gave me a nod, happy, and returned to her sink.

"I could go with her," Tess began.

"No," I said quickly. Tess was a good soul, but I did not want her running about the Foundling Hospital, questioning the staff in her frank way. She'd lately formed a friendship with the constable who patrolled this street, and was beginning to enjoy interrogating people a little too well.

"I need you here," I extemporized. "I will want plenty of help if I am to remain in Mrs. Bywater's good graces."

"I'm happy she changed her mind," Tess said, retuning to washing and tearing the lettuce. "But I don't know why she did."

"Snobbery." This last from Mr. Davis as he strode in and plunked a bottle of wine onto the table. "That Miss Townsend took tea with her today—Mrs. Bywater insisted I serve. Butter wouldn't melt in the mistress's mouth. She learned all about Miss Townsend's family and was quite impressed. From the conversation, she no doubt believes Miss Townsend the perfect companion for our Lady Cynthia. Will introduce her to the right young gentlemen and all."

Miss Townsend, I was coming to understand, was talented at getting people to do whatever she wished, all without issuing a harsh command. She'd told *me* to go home, and I'd done it. Even Cynthia and Bobby had obeyed her without question. I had to admire her skill.

"She is a kind lady, is Miss Townsend," I said. "She may sit in my kitchen and sketch to her heart's content."

"That's how she knew about the row," Tess said. "When she

came in this morning to do her art, she asked about you, and I told her. She had me spilling all of it. She was most put out. Upstairs she went, and next thing I know, Mrs. Bywater is telling me we have to do a special tea, and she'll have it with Miss Townsend. I'm afraid they et your walnut tart, Mrs. H."

"I made it for eating," I said, my heart light. "No harm done."

Miss Townsend had worked magic, wrapping Mrs. Bywater around her finger. She was welcome to my walnut tart for the good she'd done me.

Why had she? I wondered again. I wanted to know more about Miss Townsend.

"I'm pleased Mrs. Bywater sent for you to come home," Mr. Davis said to me. "I'd miss our chats over the newspaper. As well as your cooking, of course."

Fine words from Mr. Davis. He took up his bottle and marched away, coattails swinging.

"Bet he's sweet on you," Tess said with a grin.

I remembered what our previous housekeeper had hinted about Mr. Davis and doubted it. But I was happy he considered me a friend.

Tess and I finished the meal—I added dried dill to the chicken to give it a bit heartier flavor. We sent it up and were rewarded with plates scraped clean when they came back down, as well as a message from Mr. Bywater, via Mr. Davis, that the meal had been excellent.

I wondered, as we finished up, whether Mrs. Bywater had dared tell her husband she'd tried to sack me.

I sent Tess to bed early, taking over the preparations for the morrow. She'd worked very hard today, entirely my fault for sailing out in a bad temper, and I could help her as she'd aided me.

* * *

The next morning was a busy one, but every morning is so for a cook in a large house. I shopped at the markets and prepared the meals, testing out a new recipe for a soubise—an onion sauce. I served it with pork for luncheon, when Mr. Bywater returned from working half a day in the City, and again the praise came downstairs with Mr. Davis.

Tess had left early for her day out, giving me a kiss on the cheek and a grin as she went, perhaps off to find her constable. I'd met Caleb—he was a perfectly nice lad, and I didn't mind Tess seeing him, as long as there were no goings-on.

I let work take my mind off my worries, though while I labored, I went through all I had learned from Mr. Fielding and Mrs. Compton, trying to lay the pieces of information in neat rows like the beans I sorted.

I took time to send a note to Mr. Thanos, outlining the problem and my idea of him and Lady Cynthia going to the Foundling Hospital to see what sort of people watched the children. I sent it by way of James, who often visited, looking for an opportunity to earn coins. He knew where Mr. Thanos lived and raced off to deliver the message.

Tess returned in time for supper, happy and breezy. She chattered about seeing her brother, and also Caleb.

Once everyone had gone upstairs for bed, I returned to the now-quiet kitchen.

The knock on the back door came a bit earlier than I expected. He'd told me he'd come, but I was never certain exactly what he would do.

It was no cheerful Daniel I admitted through the empty scullery, however, no teasing, no hoping to restore himself to my good graces. His eyes held bleakness, his mouth a grim line.

"What has happened?" I asked as I closed the door against the night.

He responded just as quietly. "I found Nurse Betts."

"Good." I peered at him more closely, and then my heart constricted. "Where?"

"The morgue at Scotland Yard. Someone has beaten her to death."

10

My hand dropped at Daniel's words, falling slackly to my side. "Dear heavens. Are you certain?"

I knew he was, but the words came out before I could stop them. Hope, or perhaps shock, made me blurt the question.

I'd never met Nurse Betts, never spoken to her. I'd only heard what Mrs. Compton the cook, Elsie, and Mr. Fielding had said about her. A kind young woman, a caring one. Both Elsie and Mrs. Compton had told me she doted on the children, and they'd loved her.

Now she was dead, a body cold and gray in a room in which I'd once feared Daniel lay.

"What happened?" I could barely form the question.

Daniel closed and bolted the door and led me by the hand to the silent kitchen. He sat me down then moved to the kettle on the stove where water perpetually heated. Deftly, he filled the teapot and added tea from the caddy on the dresser, then carried the pot and two cups to the table.

He drew out a pocket watch, one far too grand for a scruffy deliveryman to carry, and set it next to the teapot, to time the steeping. Then he sat next to me and laid a hand on mine, no hesitation or fear I'd jerk away from him.

"To answer, I don't know precisely," Daniel said. "I tried to confront my brother about Nurse Betts the night before last, after I left you here. I began to question him, but he used even-song to evade me and then disappeared after the service. I hunted him down again today, only to find that you had gone to interrogate him yesterday morning."

"Lady Cynthia and I did." I hesitated. "He was very fond of Nurse Betts."

Daniel's frown held high skepticism. "I will remind you again that Errol is a raconteur and a liar. He might indeed have had a tendre for Nurse Betts . . . or he might have been using her for some scheme that would benefit him. He was ever the trickster."

"Mr. Fielding is a vicar now," I pointed out. "Sent to school by his benevolent guardian, and given a living to oversee a parish, tend a flock. Wouldn't he have left his villainous days behind him? Or is the benevolent gentleman all an invention?"

"No—I've met him. Lord Alois Symington, a marquess's son, who I gather is a philanthropist, well-known in high circles. But never believe Errol is reformed because he's become one of the clergy. I'm willing to wager he took the collar as part of a long confidence game. My brother might oversee a flock, as you call his parishioners, but he will certainly view them as sheep to be fleeced." He finished with a wry twist of lips.

I shook my head. "You did not see him when he spoke about Nurse Betts."

Daniel clicked his watch closed and poured me a cup of dark tea. "To me, he tried very hard *not* to speak about her."

For a moment, I listened to the soothing sound of tea trickling into my cup. "Does he know she's dead?" I asked when Daniel righted the teapot again.

"Not yet . . ." Daniel started to say more, then shook his head and poured tea for himself.

"If you are worried he killed her, I believe you wrong." I sipped tea, letting the familiar beverage warm my mouth. "Mr. Fielding showed genuine caring when he spoke of her, a great fondness, as I said. He seemed surprised by how much he cared, as though he'd never intended to fall in love."

Daniel made a sound like a snort. "Errol has never fallen in love in his life."

"My point exactly. He was bewildered by his feelings. I am a good judge of character, Daniel."

Daniel set down the pot and sent me the ghost of his usual grin. "I know you are—you have made very trenchant remarks about mine. But I am inclined to agree that Errol did not kill her. I saw her body. Errol is a liar, a cheat, a scoundrel, a swindler . . . but he would never beat someone to death, least of all a young woman. Even as a child, when he had to fight, he'd strike out only until he was free, then he'd run like mad. Errol learned early how to run."

"What did you do in a fight?" I asked in curiosity.

"I usually stayed a bit longer and was a little freer with my fists. Errol took advantage of that and often threw me into a fray so he could flee."

I could imagine it, and the boy Daniel's irritation. "What do the police say?" I asked. "Who do they think did this?"

"They don't much know what to make of things. Nurse Betts was found near a church in Bethnal Green, one of the sergeants told me, by a kind elderly couple—she was alive when they found her but badly hurt. They took her inside their house and sent for a physician, but he could not help her, and she died in the night. They and the physician reported the death to the police—she was taken away to be examined by the coroner."

"The poor thing." My heart ached for her, lying alone and terrified in the street, in wretched pain. "I'm glad the people took her in. At least she was with someone caring when she went."

"Yes." Daniel was somber. "There is a search for whatever brute did it, but not much hope that he'll be found, unless the police are lucky and discover an eyewitness. Good luck to them in Bethnal Green. Inspector McGregor has been put on this case, as it involves the Foundling Hospital. Prominent members of society are on the board there . . ."

We went silent a moment. A hunk of coal fell inside the stove, the *whoosh* of it muffled. The fire was dying, coal breaking down into ash.

"Would you like *me* to tell Mr. Fielding?" I asked. "He might be very angry at you, or not believe you."

"No, I will do it." Daniel regarded me glumly. "I know him well, and know how to break news like this. And I want to see his face when I tell him. He might not have struck the blows himself, but know who did."

"I doubt it. He was very worried about her."

"With good reason, it seems."

I took another sip of tea then wrapped my hands around the hot mug, soaking up its warmth. "Do you believe she was killed because of the children? Because she knew what happened to them?"

"If she was trying to find them, that is very possible."

I shivered, in spite of the tea's heat. "I hate thinking of them lost and alone, perhaps locked away, perhaps worse. Did Mr. Fielding tell you he'd looked for them, that the director gave him false addresses, pretending that was where the children had gone?"

Daniel nodded. "Yes, I wrested that out of him before he disappeared into his church."

"We must find them, Daniel."

"We will." He rested his hand on mine again. "We will."

I withdrew my hand, but gently. "I know you are trying to comfort me, but it will not work, not about this. We cannot wait. Every day they are missing might be one more horrible night for them."

"I know." The hard light returned to Daniel's eyes. "I was like those children once, Kat. I know exactly what they might be enduring."

I regarded him with sympathy. "I am sorry."

"I grew tough. I had to. That is why Carter's death infuriates me so." Deep anger flashed in his eyes. "He gave us a place of safety. We didn't have to fear the night when we lived with him. We could sleep in truth, like children ought. The night he was killed . . ." Daniel let out a breath that held old anger and grief. "I could do absolutely nothing to prevent it."

He'd told me the tale, and I heard his anguish anew. I squeezed his hand. "You were only a child. There was little you could have done—you'd have been killed yourself if you'd tried to defend him."

"I know." Daniel's blue eyes were quiet. "Perhaps what I do now is meant to make up for my helplessness then. I can ensure others stay alive and safe, away from those whose only wish is to kill."

"You do help," I said with conviction.

"Some days, I believe that. Others . . ." Daniel rubbed his eyes with thumb and forefinger. "What I do makes me lie and trick and be every bit the confidence man I say Errol is." His voice went soft as he met my gaze. "And when you look at me in anger, Kat, the person in my life I least want angry with me, I wonder if I can be anything but a liar and deceiver."

My heart gave a jerking beat as he looked at me with his warm eyes. I wasn't certain I understood entirely what he meant. He wasn't lying now—this man sitting with me was the real Daniel, telling me of his past and his worries.

But what *did* I know about him, in truth? Daniel assisted the police, though at the same time claimed he did not work *for* them. He had several residences throughout London, he disappeared entirely at any given time, and he knew how to transform himself into different guises, all of which were believed by the people he put them on for.

What guise did he assume for me?

"When you refuse to tell me who you work for," I began, carefully choosing my words, "it is because you've been forbidden to. Is that not so?"

Surprise flickered in Daniel's eyes. "It is."

"You've been free telling me much else," I conceded. "I am being charitable and assuming the decision to impart information has been taken from you."

"It has." Daniel gave me a nod, but his shoulders held tension. "I don't agree entirely with the decision, but I understand why it has been made."

"I would certainly not be happy if you were sent to prison for telling me. Am I correct it is that dire a thing?"

"Yes." Now the corners of Daniel's mouth twitched. "You are a frightening person, Kat."

"I am an observant person and a thoughtful one. Slicing twenty carrots and ten turnips for a stew is not the most absorbing of activities. One's mind wanders, and one makes connections about many things."

The twitch became a full grin. "I must remember to take up chopping vegetables when I need to ruminate on a problem."

"You make fun, but it is no joke. A repetitive task releases the mind to think."

"I believe you."

I became serious once more. "We must find those children, Daniel."

"We will." He twined his fingers through mine. "I have not been idle. I have ideas, and Errol will help. Because he already has the Foundling Hospital's board and its director trusting him, he will put that trust to use."

"And I will find things out," I promised. "You have the police and Mr. Fielding, but I know servants, and foundlings. And Lady Cynthia."

"Yes, your own forces. Quite formidable they are too. I make no joke—you can go places and speak to people the police cannot, especially policemen as intimidating as McGregor."

"He is clever and persistent," I said, defending him to my surprise. "If wrongheaded some of the time."

"Shall we be a team again?" Daniel lifted our joined hands and turned the hold into a handshake. "Put aside your annoyance with me to find the children and bring Nurse Betts's killer to justice?"

"I think I will have to," I said, withdrawing after we'd shaken on it. "Neither of us can do this alone."

"True." Daniel did not try to reach for me again, and I suppressed a twinge of disappointment. "We should set up a place to meet—all of us, where we can confer. Not here. Mrs. Redfern does not approve of me, and I don't want Errol too near the costly silver Mr. Davis guards."

"Bobby's flat, perhaps. She has offered to help. Though I will not be able to slip away often."

"Thanos's flat is closer," Daniel said.

"Is it? I thought it was in Bloomsbury."

"It was. He's moved to Regent Street, not far from Hanover Square."

I blinked. "Gracious, that's a fine address. Did he come into money?" I felt a frisson of hope. If he had funds, he could propose to Cynthia.

"Unfortunately, no." Daniel shattered my ideas. "A chap from the Polytechnic on Cavendish Square hired him to do lectures. The flat is part of the salary. The man who hired him is quite wealthy, a dilettante, very clever and half runs the Polytechnic, or will, when it opens again."

I'd heard of the Polytechnic, but I knew little about it. I would have to ask Mr. Thanos. "If Mr. Thanos will allow us to invade his flat, it sounds a good place."

Daniel rose but remained next to the table, his expression guarded. "We'll meet there Monday afternoon, then."

Monday was my half day. "Early in the afternoon. The rest of the time, I spend with Grace."

"Of course." Daniel did not move as I stood up, which put me close to him. He regarded me with eyes so very blue, with a hint of gold inside them. "I wish . . ." he began softly.

I waited, but Daniel closed his mouth.

"You wish what?" I prompted.

Daniel lifted his fingers as though he'd trace my cheek, then dropped his hand. "I wish I could be everything you deserve, Mrs. Holloway."

My heart beat a little bit faster. "Our lives are not our own," I said, hearing my regret.

"No. They are not." The distance between us increased, though I wasn't aware of Daniel taking a step away. "But maybe one day, they will be."

"That is my hope."

Daniel smiled at the determination in my voice. "You teach me so much, Kat. You stare down the world and dare it to take anything away from you."

"I've learned to. I've had very little in my life." Now I had Grace. And for her, I'd fight the desert hordes in the Sudan if I had to.

"I've known strong men who despair at less adversity," he said, "while you simply get on with things."

"Despair does no one any good." I tried to sound reasonable. "Best to dispense with it at once."

Daniel's smile broadened. He leaned down and kissed my cheek, his hand finding mine and warming it. "I always feel better for having been with you."

I ought to have given him my usual scoff of "Nonsense" or "Get on with you, daft man," but my emotions were topsy-turvy and the words would not form. He confused me greatly, did Daniel.

"Good night, Kat." Daniel lifted my hand to his lips and kissed my fingers.

Then he turned from me, disappearing into the shadows of the scullery. The door creaked, and he was gone.

The next day was Sunday. Mrs. Bywater had once again invited a slew of guests for tea, including, it turned out, Miss Townsend. Mrs. Bywater sent word down with Mrs. Redfern that I was to create a fine meal to serve twelve.

Mrs. Redfern delivered the news with apology and stood by while I ranted.

"She has no idea at all what it takes to produce such a feast." I snatched a copper pot from the rack and slammed it to the stove. "It is *Sunday*. The markets are closed. If she had told me yesterday, I could have spent the afternoon shopping for what I need."

"The tea was a last-minute idea," Mrs. Redfern said. Her hands rested quietly on her abdomen, but her ever-present keys clinked. "The mistress wishes to introduce Miss Townsend to her friends, and also to her friends' sons, hoping for Miss Townsend's opinion on the young men, and whether they will suit for Lady Cynthia."

"Oh, good heavens," I snapped. "I thought she'd left off all that."

"Mrs. Bywater wishes to consult Miss Townsend before she resumes her matchmaking schemes. Lady Cynthia will not be joining them, in any case."

Indeed, no. Lady Cynthia would put on a frock and go out and do charitable work today, to which Mrs. Bywater had readily agreed. Mr. Thanos had answered my note, again via James, that he would be pleased to escort her.

I banged down another pot. "Even so, she must realize she will drive Lady Cynthia mad, or at least goad her to take some foolish step."

"That's not for us to say." Mrs. Redfern sent me a superior look, but I knew she had plenty of opinions on the subject. I'd heard her tell them to Mr. Davis when she thought no one could hear.

Mrs. Redfern left me and Tess to get on with things. I was studying my notebook, trying to do decide what I could toss together with the ingredients I had on hand, when Lady Cynthia came down to the kitchen to inform me she was going. She'd dressed herself in a slim blue walking dress and a matching jacket trimmed with dark fur. A black hat tip-tilted forward on her head, its brim tastefully small.

"Very fetching," I said in approval. "The blue brings out your eyes."

"Impossible to walk in this dratted skirt." Cynthia kicked, her foot traveling about eight inches before the tight front of the gown arrested it. I saw that she'd donned her man's boots beneath. "I tore the veil from the hat. Could see nothing but spots."

"It is lovely, all the same," I said, speaking the truth.

"Yes, well, I'm off to view the foundlings. Mr. Thanos will join me there. I will tell you all, later."

"There might be little to tell," I said. "Abductors would be mad to try to coerce the children away in the dining hall, under the matrons' sharp eyes."

"One never knows." Cynthia lifted a muffin from a plate where Tess was piling them and took a big bite. "Mmm. Excellent."

The muffins were full of butter that Tess had melted into them. A droplet of gold leaked down Cynthia's chin as she chewed. I thrust out a cloth and caught the butter before it could stain her frock.

"Take this napkin with you, and do have a care."

Cynthia laughed as she snatched the piece of linen from me and wiped her chin. "You're far better than my own mum, Mrs. H. She'd never have noticed."

Cynthia's age and mine were very close, but I was not offended. Her mother, by all reports, was a frivolous and careless woman.

"Off you go," I said.

Cynthia waved at me and departed, taking the scullery stairs to the street. Tess thrust tongs around another muffin on the rack at the stove and transferred muffin to plate.

"Her ladyship is so beautiful this morning," she said in admiration. "Mr. Thanos's eyes will fall out."

"I agree." I turned back to my notebook, wondering how on earth I'd put together a meal for twelve with the few pieces of salt pork I had in the larder. "I didn't like to say so, for fear she'd balk and decide not to see him."

"They're a rum pair," Tess said as she slid another toasted muffin from the rack. "Think they'll ever marry?"

"I would like that, but Mr. Thanos has little money, from what Mr. McAdam tells me. But he has recently been hired to do lectures. Perhaps that will help."

"Nah," Tess said decidedly. "I think you're born rich or you work for the rich, but nothing in between, Mrs. H."

I sighed. "I'm afraid you might have the right of it, Tess."

I produced a meal, if not out of nothing then next to nothing. The soups were relatively effortless—I frequently prepared stock from bones and herbs and had a pot of broth warming every day on the back of the stove. From that I created a clear soup with chives and a heartier soup by adding new potatoes and thickening the broth with a touch of flour and cream.

The meats were more difficult. I had to make do with grinding up the pork plus leftover chicken and stuffing a seasoned mixture of this into pastry dough Tess had made, intended for more tarts.

Every fresh vegetable I could find in the larder we rinsed, sliced, or tore, and made into salads or simply boiled or sautéed with a bit of butter and herbs. I threw sweet pies together from whatever pastry dough was left over plus walnuts in brown sugar with a dash of brandy.

When I hastened from stove to cupboard at one point, I nearly tripped over Miss Townsend, who'd slipped to the corner stool with her sketchbook. She smiled at me serenely and moved her feet.

I had no time to speak to her at the moment, and once the meal was ready, she went upstairs to partake of it.

Cynthia returned from her outing to the Foundling Hospital late that afternoon. She arrived soon after Mrs. Bywater's guests had departed, and I wondered if she had waited to watch them go before venturing inside.

"It was ghastly," she exclaimed, tossing her hat to my flour-strewn table. "I want to adopt the lot of those poor children. Thanos feels the same. I think I've never been more disgusted at my fellow beings than today, Mrs. H. Would like to herd them straight to hell."

11

"Sit down, Cyn." Miss Townsend, who'd descended to us again once tea had finished, rose from her seat and closed her sketchbook. She'd so far never let any of us see what she'd drawn. "I'm sure Mr. Davis could spare you some brandy."

"A cup of tea," I countered.

Cynthia did not answer but fell into a seat at the table. I poured her a cup from a full pot of tea and slid it toward her as she tugged off her gloves.

"'Fraid it will take more than tea to wash the foul taste from my mouth," she declared after she'd gulped a swallow of the hot liquid and dabbed her lips with her fingers. "I think I'd rather have been at my aunt's table, listening to her tell the gentlemen how well I embroider, which is all rot. I can't embroider a stitch."

Miss Townsend answered in her gentle voice, "Consider that if she boasted how well you played the piano, you'd be called to demonstrate. Not many will demand you take out your basket and fall to embroidering while they watch."

"I wouldn't put it past Auntie to suggest it." Cynthia took another pull of tea, letting the beverage and Miss Townsend's quiet teasing calm her.

"I can't tell you all of it," Cynthia said, holding her teacup in a tight clasp. "Not at present. Later, perhaps. I'm over-whelmed by it all at the moment. A sea of children, all dressed alike. Made to sit quietly to eat, no laughing, no conversation. Little automatons shoveling in their Sunday dinner. The spec-tators filed past them, assessing this one or that one. Some came to gauge whether one would do for a scullery maid or bootboy, but others came to watch their favorites. Visit almost every Sunday, these last folks, taking note of what the chil-dren do, how they look." Cynthia closed her hands around her cup so hard I feared the porcelain would break.

"Unsavory," Miss Townsend said, anger in her eyes.

"Not much different than any workhouse," Tess said as she mixed dough for tomorrow's bread. "Or Bedlam. You can go watch the lunatics there for the enjoyment of it. Had a young man once who liked to do that. I told him he was barmy and he should join 'em in there."

"Unsavory is the word." Cynthia shivered. "Thanos and I made the acquaintance of two couples who professed to be quite interested in the children. Suppose they or people like them pick out a child or two on their Sunday outings, and later the director sends them to these people, putting down a false address to make it look as though the kiddies are being fostered or employed. That would explain things neatly."

"It would," I agreed.

"Cor." Tess stirred flour into the yeasty water with vigor.

"Go and arrest these ladies and gents, then. And the director. I'll tell Caleb, and he'll tell his sergeant."

"I'm afraid it will not be so simple," I said, watching Cynthia. I'd rarely seen her this anguished. "The director is a rather highborn man. A lord."

"Son of a peer," Cynthia said. "Not the same as being a peer oneself, of course, but he'll be protected. Lord Russell Hirst is the apple of his ducal father's eye, I happen to know. *What a benevolent gentleman to run the Foundling Hospital*, everyone thinks." She lifted her teacup again. "But truly, no more questions at present. I would enjoy getting roaring drunk." She glanced at the tea and set it down. "Perhaps Bobby will accommodate me."

"She is not at home," Miss Townsend announced. "She must occasionally make the obligatory stop at her family's house to keep her allowance coming. She faced a Sunday dinner of her own today."

"Ooh," Tess said, interested. "Do they make her wear a frock?"

"I believe they've given that up," Miss Townsend answered, amused. "Know it's useless. But if Bobby turns up every so many Sundays, eats at the family table, and behaves herself, they leave her alone."

"If only *my* family would do the same." Cynthia shoved aside the tea, which sloshed over the rim of the cup to its saucer. "But at least they aren't eyeing children arrayed before them to decide which would make a delectable morsel."

My anger and distress surged. Another night was coming, and what would it bring for those children?

"Go upstairs and have a rest," I told Cynthia. I turned to the cupboard and removed the brandy I'd used for the walnut tart, poured her a glass, and set it in front of her. "To help you settle," I said.

Cynthia downed the brandy in one go, wrist stiff, then coughed. "Thank you, Mrs. H. Had you been there, I assure you, you'd be tempted to have a go at the whole bottle."

The next morning, Tess and I worked side by side until luncheon was served upstairs, and then I changed my frock for my half day out. I would meet Daniel and the others at Mr. Thanos's flat first thing and then spend the rest of the afternoon with Grace.

I decided to walk to Regent Street on my own. Lady Cynthia would also be attending the gathering, but I did not want Mrs. Bywater to look out her window and see us strolling chummily down the street, so I left without waiting for her.

I set off north to Grosvenor Square and turned onto Grosvenor Street, intending to head east in a more or less straight line to Regent Street. I hadn't reached the end of Grosvenor Street, however, when a hansom pulled beside me, containing Cynthia in her frock coat and tall hat.

"Get in," she commanded.

"It isn't far," I pointed out.

"Far enough, and I'm not beastly enough to make you walk while I pass you by. Get in."

Lady Cynthia was in a foul temper, I could see, and I obediently scrambled into the hansom. The cabbie at least waited until I'd seated myself before he careened the horse into traffic again.

Cynthia gazed at me with bloodshot eyes, which told me she'd imbibed a bit more last night than the small glass of brandy I'd given her.

"You were right to tell me to sleep, Mrs. H. Except for my blasted headache today, I am far less morose. Ready to take down so-called respectable ladies and gentlemen and shake Lord Russell Hirst until he lets loose the whereabouts of the young things."

"Well said." I patted her arm. "We will prevail."

She gave me a nod. "I believe *you* will, anyway."

Mr. Thanos's new digs were in a large building in Regent Street, near Hanover Square and across from Argyle Place. The ground floor of the house held two shops—one a bookshop with leather-bound tomes on its shelves, the other a store that sold lovely porcelain from the Orient.

A fine address indeed. I wondered, as we descended from the hansom, about this patron from the Polytechnic, who could lend his lecturers such a regal place to live.

A polished paneled door between the shops opened to stairs leading to the flats above. The landlady took us up and into a sumptuous front room with a high ceiling, tall windows, and an ornate fireplace left over from the turn of the last century. The fireplace had been fitted with a coal fender, where a fire burned merrily, the red and orange flames cheerful against the gray day.

Mr. Thanos was taller and slimmer than Daniel, with dark hair he wore swept back from his forehead and warm dark eyes. He approached as his landlady departed, his smile wide as he held out a hand to me.

"Only too glad, Mrs. Holloway. Is this flat not astonishing? A far cry from my two cramped rooms in Bloomsbury. So much more than a scholar can expect, but my benefactor is proving generous."

He babbled the words as he pumped my hand, avoiding looking at Cynthia.

"I am glad to hear it, Mr. Thanos," I said as he finally released me. I believed he deserved a mansion, one in proportion with his vast cleverness.

"Of course, I have not yet begun my lectures, and perhaps when the students fall asleep or throw things at me, he might change his mind."

Mr. Thanos laughed breathily, and I smiled in response, though I doubted he need worry.

"What will you lecture on?" I asked politely. Mathematics, I was certain, or an obscure puzzle in science I would not understand.

"Maxwell's demon," Mr. Thanos answered. "No one can solve the problem, including me, though I have some ideas. But perhaps I can inspire the next great genius to do so."

"Demons?" Mr. Fielding's voice sounded behind me. "I would have thought that *my* field of expertise."

He kept his tone light, but when I turned to him, I saw that Mr. Fielding's face was drawn, the usual roguish look in his eyes absent. His lips were colorless, his stance rigid.

"No, no," Mr. Thanos said quickly. "Not a *real* demon, you understand. A thought experiment. To do with thermodynamics. You see there is a box, with two compartments and a little door–"

"It will keep." Daniel broke through his words. "Another time."

Mr. Thanos looked sheepish. "Ah yes. Of course. My apologies. I find it fascinating, is all."

"You can explain it to me later," Cynthia said, taking his arm and leading him toward the fire. "I'm interested in all this mathematical thinking."

Mr. Fielding watched them go, but where he once might have made a quip, today, he only looked sad. I touched his arm.

"Are you well, Mr. Fielding?"

"Not really." Behind the sorrow in his eyes lay vast fury. "But I will carry on. What else can I do?"

I caught Daniel's glance, and he shook his head, looking grim. It must have been no easy task breaking the news of Nurse Betts's death to Mr. Fielding.

"Miss Townsend might turn up," Cynthia said as she allowed Mr. Thanos to usher her to a chair. "She is interested in our problem and would like to help. She knows ever so many people."

"The more the merrier," Mr. Fielding said. He indicated a chair for me, a plush one that was more fitting for a lady than a cook, and hovered next to me until I sat in it. "Anything that will help me find the bastard who did over my Nell."

"We will find him." I tried to sound confident.

"And when we do," Mr. Fielding told Daniel in a hard voice, "I get him."

"The police will have him," I answered before Daniel could, but the dark anger in Mr. Fielding's expression made my words trail off.

"Mine," Mr. Fielding said with finality.

Daniel did not argue. He gestured to Mr. Thanos. "Elgin, may I introduce my brother, Errol Fielding, vicar of All Saints Church in Shadwell. Errol, Elgin Thanos, a close friend and a genius."

The two men shook hands, Mr. Fielding looking Elgin up and down. "A genius, eh? Don't meet many of those. Vicars, now, a dime a dozen."

Mr. Thanos blinked at him. "Er. Quite. Whisky?"

"Please." Mr. Fielding dropped wearily into the nearest chair.

Mr. Thanos poured out and carried him a glass. "Daniel told me what happened," Mr. Thanos said in a quiet voice. "You have my deepest sympathy."

Mr. Fielding looked startled, then when he realized Mr. Thanos was sincere, gave him a grateful nod. He took the whisky and drank a large swallow.

"Ladies?" Mr. Thanos turned to us. "I'm afraid I have no sherry . . ."

"Thank God for that," Cynthia said. "Oh, sorry, vicar. Coffee if you can scare it up, Thanos. I have a head."

"If there is only coffee I'll have nothing," I said when Mr. Thanos looked inquiringly at me. I did not care for the stuff. "Do not distress yourself. I have drunk plenty of tea this morning to keep me for the afternoon."

"I will inquire with my landlady," Mr. Thanos said. "Won't be a tick."

He all but ran out the door, which Daniel closed behind him.

"Yes, indeed," Mr. Fielding said with dour humor. "We have come to speak of dire events, including children being spirited away and a blameless young woman losing her life, but we must be so very civilized."

"It is no bad thing," I said quickly. "A cup of something keeps one calm, so that a solution to the matter can be rationally discussed."

"Rational. Calm." Mr. Fielding studied the ceiling. "That is the answer—except of course for the brutes who have left being rational and calm far behind."

My heart went out to him in his grief. "Please do not despair, Mr. Fielding."

Mr. Fielding gazed at me with flinty blue eyes, no more politeness in his demeanor. "Why not? What is the bloody use of reforming and taking up a life of virtue if it couldn't save a person as good as Nell?" He drank deeply of whisky, then let his head drop back on the chair and closed his eyes.

Mr. Thanos returned after a few moments, bearing a tray of

cups and two pots. "I found Miss Townsend on the stairs," he announced, standing aside to let her precede him. "Do you know everyone, Miss Townsend?" He glanced at Mr. Fielding.

Mr. Fielding dragged himself from the chair and made a shallow bow to Miss Townsend. "Pleased to meet you." His voice bordered on the ironic. "Now that we are all here, may we have our useless confab? Then I will go hunt a whoreson and gut him."

Miss Townsend did not even blink. "Of course, good sir. I do not blame you your rage. Cynthia and Mr. Thanos will tell us everything they discovered, and then I will help you find your whoreson if you like."

12

Mr. Thanos looked taken aback by Mr. Fielding's state-ments and Miss Townsend's acceptance of them, but Cynthia and Daniel remained unsurprised. Mr. Fielding flicked his eyebrows up, assessing Miss Townsend with new interest.

"Who the devil are you?" he asked.

Cynthia answered for him. "A talented artist with amazing discretion."

"I lived for years among artists in Paris, gentlemen and la-dies alike," Miss Townsend said, gesturing for us to resume our seats. "Little shocks me."

Mr. Fielding only looked her up and down again before he sank back to his chair.

I wondered at Miss Townsend's interest in the problem—was it simple human compassion for those mistreated and threatened, or something more?

Cynthia accepted a mug of coffee Mr. Thanos handed her. There was tea for me, which I waved him from and poured myself.

"I could not speak of this yesterday," Cynthia said. "My apologies, Mrs. Holloway, but it was too much on my mind. I couldn't close my eyes but see the poor souls shoved into the same clothes, made to sit in silence. Not natural."

"Yes, it was quite moving." Mr. Thanos seated himself in front of a desk covered with papers. He slid his spectacles from his pocket and looped them on before he sorted through sheets of foolscap. "I tried to write notes, but I made little progress."

"Begin with names," Daniel suggested. "Who showed the most interest in the children?"

Mr. Thanos skimmed his pages as though he'd find the answer there. Cynthia sank back in her chair and took a long sip of coffee.

"It is not that simple," she said. "Thanos and I joined a long queue of those winding through the Foundling Hospital. A chatty bunch, we found them. Many had come simply to see the place to which they'd donated money—to assure themselves the children were well-fed and cared for, and that it wasn't a doss-house. Others were curious—ladies and gents wondering what it was like to be poor. Others . . ." She faltered.

"Go on," Daniel said. He alone did not sit but stood by a window, looking out. I noted he kept himself to one side of the window, so those below would not see him. "No need to tell us all if it upsets you, Lady Cynthia. Did you discover anything significant?"

Mr. Thanos cleared his throat. "Yes, two parties we met showed much interest in the children, looking them over as though choosing items from a shop."

Mr. Fielding leaned his face on one hand, the picture of weariness. "Names."

"Give him a moment," Daniel growled. "And keep in mind they might have nothing to do with this."

Mr. Fielding lifted his head and gave Daniel a baleful stare. "You know bloody well that most people have no good on their minds. Anyone who would cross London to gaze upon a building full of unfortunate children is already suspect."

"Including Lady Cynthia and me?" Mr. Thanos asked, brows rising.

"Exactly. *You* were there for ulterior purposes. Why not the rest? Anyway, get on with it."

I broke in. "Perhaps, Mr. Fielding, you should not know the names. If you charge around, half-cocked, and bully them, you could undo everything. We are speaking of the safety of three children. Do not let Nurse Betts's death have been in vain."

For a moment I thought Mr. Fielding would leap at me across the delicate table between us, and I abruptly understood why Daniel called him a dangerous man.

In the next instant, Mr. Fielding calmed himself. I watched him deliberately suppress anything violent and give me a forced smile.

"Never fear, Mrs. Holloway. If I hunt up these people, I will be the unctuous vicar, oozing charm. They'll tell me everything I want to know. Possibly many things I don't want to know as well."

"I am sorry to say my brother has a point," Daniel said. "A clergyman can gather information where others would find difficulty."

"Only too easily." Mr. Fielding cast a disparaging gaze at Daniel. "I'm surprised you didn't think of that yourself."

Daniel's flush was slight, but I and Mr. Fielding caught it. Mr. Fielding laughed, a brittle sound. "Oh, so you *have* discovered the convenience of donning a collar and drinking whatever foul liquids are served you to draw out confidences. Only, I went to university and became the real thing, old boy."

"I prefer setting aside my disguises at the end of the day," Daniel said quietly. "I agree you are well placed to help solve this. But you won't be visiting these people alone. You'll take a committee with you—Lady Cynthia, Mr. Thanos, and Miss Townsend."

All of us watched Mr. Fielding, waiting for his reaction.

The flash of wildness I'd seen became even more suppressed. "Yes, I believe you are right. Did you not want to include Mrs. Holloway in our number? To round out our team of utter respectability?"

I answered before Daniel could. "I would set the wrong tone. I am working-class and can be mistaken for no other."

"A working-class, pious soul, trusting the Lord to take her out of her drab existence, might be just the thing," Mr. Fielding said.

I met his gaze with a stern one. "Possibly, but I am not certain I could keep up the lie."

Mr. Fielding's color rose, but his smile remained. "I think you could, with training." The smile turned admiring, more than was proper. "You and I, dear lady, could swallow the world."

I glanced at Daniel, who was rigid with anger, but he kept that anger in check. Buried it a long way beneath a cool façade, one that pretended he didn't care one whit what his brother got up to.

I understood, though I might not if I hadn't seen Mr. Fielding today. If Daniel became protective of me, let on that he cared, Mr. Fielding might find a way to use that caring against him. I'd sensed a rivalry when I'd first seen the two together, one I suspected had begun the long-ago day they'd met in the house of Mr. Carter.

Mr. Thanos was the one who grew indignant on my behalf. "I say, steady on," he said to Mr. Fielding. "Do not insult Mrs. Holloway, who is a dear friend and a good lady. I will not have it in my house."

Mr. Fielding opened his mouth—possibly to make some jibe, such as perhaps Mr. Thanos would be fine if he insulted me on the street. But Mr. Fielding caught the angry gazes of Miss Townsend and Lady Cynthia, took in Daniel's motionless stance, and rose to his feet.

He bowed to me. "You are correct, Mr. Thanos. I am a blackguard, and always have been. Mrs. Holloway has done me nothing but good turns, and I had no call to speak to her in such a base fashion. My apologies, madam."

"I took no offense." I gave him a nod to show my willingness to forget it. "Never mind, Mr. Thanos. You are very kind to speak for me."

The tension in the room eased. Mr. Fielding *did* look contrite, but I believed I had the measure of him.

Miss Townsend applauded with her gloved hands. "You are excellent at dissembling, Mr. Fielding. As am I. I will go with you and help you shake out the truth. Gently, of course."

"Probably best you do come along," Lady Cynthia said to her. "I might not be able to contain my own temper."

"It's settled then," I said. "The four of you will make appointments with these people and visit them. Meanwhile, Daniel and I will confer on what else we can do."

"A sound idea," Mr. Fielding said. "Don't keep us in suspense, good fellow," he said to Mr. Thanos. "Who are we visiting?"

Mr. Thanos, flustered, returned to sorting through his notes. He fished a paper to the top of the stack and read out two names.

They meant absolutely nothing to me. I'd never heard of the people he named and had never encountered their servants, which meant they were not highborn enough or wealthy enough for my agency to send me to them or to their neighbors. Nor did they live in Mayfair, where everyone knew everyone. If they'd been philanthropists, I'd have heard of them somewhere, if only from the newspaper. The world of charitable London was surprisingly small, with many in the same circles sitting on the boards of several different charities.

"I don't know them," Cynthia said, echoing my thoughts.

"I do," Miss Townsend said. "At least, know of them." We turned to her, but somehow, I wasn't very surprised. She was proving to be an unusual young woman.

"Mr. and Mrs. Florey are patrons of the arts," Miss Townsend said. "They've never commissioned me, but have commissioned friends. Not for very much money, but some artists will paint for anyone who pays them in order to make names for themselves. I've never heard the Floreys were unsavory, but as I say, I know little about them. At the do's in which I've encountered them, Mr. Florey drinks moderately, and they leave at a sensible hour." She threw out her hands as though apologizing she could not tell us anything more scandalous. "The other couple I've not heard of at all."

"At least you will have an excuse to visit the art-lovers,"

Daniel told her. "Thanos, you'll have to use your brief acquaintanceship at the Foundling Hospital for the other."

"I'll do that," Cynthia said quickly. "Sometimes being the daughter of an earl has advantages."

Miss Townsend gave her a nod. "Then we should come up with a plan of action."

I rose. "Meanwhile, I have errands to run. I only have a half day today."

"Ah yes." Cynthia got to her feet with me, but said nothing about what those errands would be, keeping my secrets.

"I will see you out," Daniel said to me.

I said my farewells to the others and allowed Daniel to escort me down the stairs and outside, but it seemed he had no intention of leaving me there. He thrust his hands into his coat pockets and began to walk beside me down Regent Street.

"What will you do next?" I asked as we went along in the cold.

"Investigate the death of Nurse Betts. Or at least prod Inspector McGregor to and to tell me everything he finds."

"Is he likely to inform you?"

Daniel adjusted his hat against the wind. "I can make it an order from higher up if I have to. McGregor, though, is a practical man. If he believes I can give him information, he might give me a measure in return."

I was skeptical, knowing the bad-tempered Inspector McGregor, though I also knew he was an intelligent man, not easily misled.

"How safe are Lady Cynthia, Mr. Thanos, and Miss Townsend investigating with Mr. Fielding?" I asked.

Daniel looked pained. "I'd guess safe enough. He is so adamant to discover the connection between Nurse Betts and the missing children that he will consider the three his partners for now. He is good at using people to his own advantage."

"I gathered that."

"Miss Townsend will keep him tamed if the other two cannot," Daniel said with conviction.

"The mysterious Miss Townsend." I knew he'd tell me the circumstances in which he'd known her when he was ready, but could not stop myself needling him a little.

"The secrets are not only mine, but hers," Daniel said. "And those of others. I would take yours to my grave if you commanded me."

I halted, risking the wrath of those who pressed by us. "Now you are making me feel awful. I am twitting you about having integrity, only because my curiosity is piqued." I paused awkwardly. "And, if you must know, my jealousy."

Daniel bent on me a look of amazement. "Jealousy?"

"Of course. The gentleman I care for has spent a sojourn in Paris with a young lady of talent, sense, and rare beauty. And then he can tell me nothing of what went on there."

Daniel's shock began to wear off, and his smile widened. "Not what you are supposing."

I'd learned from Cynthia that Miss Townsend and Bobby had an understanding, but I also knew that some people did not care which sex their lovers happened to be.

"I find nothing amusing in it," I said stiffly.

Daniel linked his arm through mine and pulled me close to him, continuing our walk. "The fact that you worry I had an affaire de coeur with Miss Townsend gives me hope."

"Why should it? Jealousy is a terrible emotion, and a dangerous one." When I'd discovered my husband had been betraying me—for years—I'd been eaten through by rage and resentment. I regretted now the time I'd wasted on that hurt and anguish, though naturally I'd been upset. It had taken me years to realize that time spent on thoughts of my perfidious husband was time squandered.

Daniel continued to look delighted. "I will take it to mean you have feelings for me."

"Of course I have feelings for you. I'd never let you into my kitchen if I did not."

We'd reached Piccadilly Circus. An omnibus creaked to a halt on the other side of the circle, the horses weary, the advertising placards on the wagon bright against the gray weather. I'd have to run to reach it before it started again.

Daniel kept hold of my arm. "You are a fine and wonderful woman, Kat Holloway. Someday, I will make myself worthy of your trust."

I longed to stand and bask in his praise, his smile, the light in his eyes, but the omnibus had already started moving, the wind was sharp, and Grace awaited.

"You do talk a lot of nonsense." I extracted myself from his grip and hurried for the omnibus.

I heard his laughter behind me, before it was swallowed by the rumble of wheels on stone and the rising wind.

I reached the Millburns' house off Cheapside and spent time hugging my daughter. She was full of chatter about her lessons and games she and Jane, Joanna's older daughter, had played.

"Have you found the poor children yet?" she asked me when she had a chance to speak to me alone.

"I'm afraid not," I had to tell her. "But we are looking hard."

"You'll find them." Grace patted my hand. "You and Mr. McAdam and Lady Cynthia."

Her confidence was touching.

Darkness fell early in February, and lamps had been lit by the time I departed, though it was not yet five in the evening. I kissed Grace good-bye, and she made her usual promise to be good until we saw each other again on Thursday.

I walked away with a heavy heart. The days between visits were always so long.

I climbed aboard another omnibus, but I did not take it directly home. I decided, as I was already out, to investigate the addresses the director of the Foundling Hospital had given Mr. Fielding. Mr. Fielding had already done so, of course, with no results, but I could not shake the need to see for myself.

The first was in a lane near High Holborn, not far from Lincoln's Inn Fields. Not the most prosperous of addresses, but if one turned down the correct roads, one could find respectable homes.

I walked along Red Lion Street toward the square of the same name, but the number of the house I looked for did not exist–Mr. Fielding had been quite correct. The numbers ceased long before the one he'd been given.

The next address lay near where High Holborn segued into New Oxford Street. It was too close to St. Giles and Seven Dials for my comfort, near the church of St. Giles-in-the-Fields.

I paused before this church, which had much the same look as the one Mr. Fielding had charge of in the East End–spare lines and a graceful steeple, a refreshing picture of calm in the busy city.

Behind the church sprawled the slum of St. Giles. Reformers and building schemes swept the area from time to time, trying to tame the rookeries, but with limited success.

The address Mr. Fielding investigated must have fallen victim to one of the building schemes. Houses along the street had been cleared away, and a huge new edifice was being erected—a factory or some such. Even at this hour, men crawled over the scaffolding and hammers pounded. The house number Mr. Fielding had given us, 33 Dudley Street, ought to be exactly where the new structure rose.

I stood back and gazed at the building, lanterns swinging from the scaffolding, men shouting at one another as they worked.

"What you want here, missus?"

A large gentleman with a full beard and side whiskers had appeared beside me with unnerving suddenness. He was a belligerent specimen in heavy work boots and thick coat. Lantern light shone on greasy dark hair sticking out from under his cap and an equally greasy beard.

"Just passing," I said, pretending he did not worry me. "What are they building here?"

"Brewery."

"I see." I would have thought London had enough of those already, but ale made money. "Quite a lot of houses pulled down to make way for it."

"Slums." The big man spoke with disgust. "Not worth saving."

"Mmm." I wondered whether the inhabitants of those houses had agreed.

He took a step toward me in a way I didn't like. "Shouldn't be here, missus. Dangerous for a lady."

"As I say, I am only passing." I tried to move around him, but he stepped in front of me, blocking my path. "You will have to move," I said crisply. "I want to go that way." I pointed behind him.

"No, you don't."

Another large man slid off the scaffolding and joined the first. He grinned at me, but it was not a nice smile.

"Best you do what he says and go along," the second man said.

It was actually immaterial whether I went onward or back—either way, I'd have to make my way to Oxford Street to catch another omnibus or find a hansom, if I didn't simply walk all the way home. But I was curious as to why these men did not want me to continue down this street.

"I am trying," I said impatiently. "I want to get to St. Martin's Lane. This is the shortest route." I pointed again.

"Not nowadays," the grinning man said. He had lighter hair than the other, but it too was quite greasy. "Too much building."

I realized the folly of arguing with them. I'd have to return another time and discover the reason they didn't want me down this road. Or I'd tell Daniel, who'd be less conspicuous than I was in this area.

"Very well. Good evening." I gave both men a civil nod, which they did not deserve, and turned to retreat the way I'd come.

I found a third man blocking my way. The blond man, who continued to bare his teeth in a smile, gestured down a lane that opened at my right, a narrow passageway that would take me straight to Seven Dials.

"Off you go, missus."

"I will return to the church, if you please," I said in a hard voice. Though I longed to run, I knew a firm tone and a frown would do me more good among these sorts of toughs.

"You'll go where we say," the large bearded man said, his voice a rumble.

"Bugger that," I snarled and sidestepped the third man to continue my march to the church.

The next instant, the bearded man seized me by the arms from behind and hauled me into the air. "No, ya don't, love. You do what we say, or ya pay the price. That's how it is 'round here."

13

The bearded man's friends brayed with laughter as I kicked and squirmed, frantic to get loose.

The man had hands like bear paws, huge and strong, pinning my arms to my sides. I did not like to think where he'd carry me, or what he and his friends had a mind to do when he did.

Unfortunately for him, I'd grown up on streets where the genteel feared to walk. I'd learned to fight for my life at an early age, not to mention defend myself against my husband when he was in a pique.

I gave a hard kick backward, aiming my boot heel at the vulnerable spot between his legs. My captor flinched, though he blocked my kick with his very hard thigh.

It was enough, however. Before he could recover, I wrenched myself from his grasp, gained my feet, and fled.

I had no choice but to dash down the lane southward, which was exactly where they'd wanted me to go. I heard laughter behind me and then swift and heavy footfalls. They were giving chase.

In those moments I learned what it was to be a fox hunted by a pack of hounds. I prayed I could be as agile as those animals, as my boots slipped and skidded, and my breath came too fast.

But I knew how to run. I'd done it as a child on London's cobblestones and then as a youth, and nowadays long hours on my feet kept me robust.

It was dark here, no gas lamps to light the way, and the pavement came and went. I leapt over broken stones and bodies of sleepers, both human and canine. The smell was ripe.

I came to Seven Dials, the circle with a pillar in its middle, with seven roads radiating from it. I'd heard that this area, once affluent, had become a slum soon after it had been built, nearly two hundred years before.

Things had not much improved in the time between. Seven Dials was the home of gin halls, doss-houses, brothels with courtesans of both sexes, and streetwalkers for every taste. The area contained not only pickpockets but desperate thugs who would knock a person to the ground and steal all they had, right to their undergarments and the shoes on their feet. My dress and coat alone, though secondhand and nowhere near finery, could feed a household for days.

The men from the building site had chased me here deliberately, knowing I would be prey.

I cursed them at the same time I went cold with fear. My only hope was to keep running, to wend my way to a more salubrious part of the city and find a public vehicle to take me back to Mayfair.

A gin house, brightly lit and noisy with music, spilled people into the street. A man who'd stumbled from it drunkenly grabbed my arm.

"Come in and dance with me, missus."

He was only inebriated, not malicious, and I jerked from him. "No, thank you. Good evening to you."

He laughed and doffed his cap. "You come back any day, missus. Ask for old Jim."

His friends jeered at him, and old Jim vanished.

I broke through the crowd but heard my pursuers, who'd not been content with simply driving me off. The gin hall had given me an idea, and as my would-be captors called to one another, searching for me in the growing throng, I ducked into a tavern.

Taverns were slightly more reputable than gin halls, if only just. But while women did not go into the taprooms, we could sit and sip an ale in the snug, as I sometimes did with Daniel.

I nipped through a short passageway beside the taproom to a snug that held only a few people. But it had no windows to the street. A person would have to barge into the tavern and through the hall to find me. If my pursuers hadn't seen me come in, they might give up and drift away.

I realized I was cornered in this shabby room where the whitewash had gone gray, but at least I could catch my breath.

A waitress condescended to look in on me. "What you want?"

"A cup of tea, please," I said as I sat down and took out my handkerchief. "Make certain the water is clean."

"Ooh." She wrinkled her nose at me. "Ain't you the queen?"

She sounded so like Tess I couldn't help a breathless laugh. "The Princess Royal," I said. "Please bring it."

The waitress laughed, a sunnier nature coming forth. She gave me a mock curtsy and wandered off, scooping up dirty mugs on her way.

She brought me tea that was drinkable if bitter, although I wiped the rim of the mug with my handkerchief before lifting cup to mouth.

My hands shook as I tried to sip calmly. The men had frightened me badly, demonstrating how far I was out of my depth. I'd always been proud that, because I'd grown up in Cockney London, I could hold my own. Tonight had reminded me that a young woman with too much confidence could not prevail alone against three hardened men.

As I drank the tea and tried to restore my equilibrium, one point tapped through my fears—why had they not wanted me to continue down that street?

When Mr. Fielding had come to look for the address, had they driven him off too? He'd not mentioned any such thing, but I now realized Mr. Fielding only imparted information he wished to.

A half hour passed as I drank bad tea and speculated, the hot water replenished once by the barmaid. My assailants did not appear, but I knew I could not remain much longer. I had a job to return to, and the later I lingered in Seven Dials, the more dangerous the area would become.

I handed a coin to the barmaid when I rose to leave. "Will you take a peek outside the front door for me?" I asked her. "Tell me whether a very tall gentleman, quite large, with a black beard and thick side whiskers is anywhere about? He has two friends with him, one of them with pale hair."

The barmaid's face screwed up in concern. "Is *that* who you're hiding from? Sounds like you mean Luke Mahoney, you do." She shook her head. "He's a bad, bad man, is Luke."

"So I gather. Will you tell me whether he is about? I do need to go home."

She did not look happy, but she nodded. "Right you are."

The barmaid nipped away, the unkempt hem of her skirt brushing her worn boots. She returned not long later.

"Looks like he's gone," she said. "But I'll slide ya out the back way, in case he's hiding himself and watching. You his new woman?"

I blenched. "Indeed, no."

"I thought ya looked too sensible, but a sensible woman can be a fool about a man, can't she? Don't have nothing to do with the likes of 'im, is my advice. This way."

She took me down a squalid back hall to an even more squalid cubby of a kitchen. Had I seen the kitchen first, I certainly would not have drunk the tea.

From here we went into a noisome passageway that exited to a tiny lane. The barmaid pointed through the inky blackness to a light at the end.

"That's Queen Street. You take it to King Street, which will lead you up toward St. Giles's Church. But go carefully. There's bad people about."

Well I knew. I gave the young woman another shilling to thank her and went on my way. "Ta ever so much," she called after me in a whisper.

I lifted my skirts from whatever filth might be coating the alley and hurried toward the light. It was a lantern, hanging from yet another public house, swinging back and forth in the wind that struck me as I emerged from the narrow walk.

Queen Street led to King, as the barmaid had said, and not long later, I was in Oxford Street, hailing a hansom. I could ill spare the money for a cab, but I was finished with the roads of London and the brutes I might encounter in them.

I went almost eagerly to my warm kitchen that night, and even more eagerly to my bed at the top of the house. I took a long time to drop off, while I studied the ceiling and tried to convince myself I was safe.

The next morning everything was as usual, and I enjoyed slipping back into my routine. Elsie took her half day at noon, hurrying over the dishes so she could depart as soon as they were done.

Tess and I started the pies and bread for the evening meal after Elsie had gone, keeping ourselves warm near the stove with hot cups of tea. Mr. Davis came stalking down the stairs and into the kitchen not long later.

"A vicar's come to call," he said. "And he's asking to speak to *you*, Mrs. Holloway."

"A vicar?" I repeated, though the next instant I realized he must mean Mr. Fielding.

"He said he'd come to you below stairs, with the mistress's permission, but Mrs. Bywater says you may speak to him in the small sitting room on the ground floor." Mr. Davis dropped his imperious tones and took on a look of disbelief. "The mistress has been gotten 'round by that Miss Townsend, no mistake. She'd never have let you have a visitor, not even a vicar, otherwise."

As he spoke I busily peeled off my apron then hurried to the scullery and dashed water over my floury hands.

"Off you go," Tess said, her interest acute. "You'll tell me all about it, won't ya?" she added in a whisper.

Mr. Davis led me upstairs to the smaller of two parlors on the ground floor, where Mrs. Bywater received visitors neither important nor intimate—more prominent guests were taken to the grander sitting room on the first floor. This was a polite room, with restrained furniture in a salmon color, the paneled walls painted white, fitting for a guest of lesser status.

Mrs. Bywater herself sat on a small sofa, looking utterly charmed by Mr. Fielding, who inhabited the wing chair next to it.

Mr. Fielding rose smoothly to his feet as Mr. Davis opened the door and announced, "Mrs. Holloway."

"So good of you to receive me, Mrs. Holloway," Mr. Fielding said before Mrs. Bywater could speak. "And for agreeing to converse with me about the committee for the Foundling Hospital." He regarded me neutrally, waiting for me to go along with whatever rigamarole he'd concocted for Mrs. Bywater.

Mrs. Bywater also rose. "How kind of you to consider contributing, Mrs. Holloway. It speaks well of your character."

I tried to look modest. "The least I could do."

"I came to tell her our latest ideas," Mr. Fielding said, a man happy to find a willing donor for his cause. "Explain our mission, as I promised. There are many details."

His glance at Mrs. Bywater implied that such details would be tedious for the lady of the house, who surely had better things to do. Mrs. Bywater, to my surprise, took his cue.

"I'll leave you to it. Ring when you are ready to leave, Mr. Fielding, and Mr. Davis will see you out."

"Excellent. Thank you." Mr. Fielding would overdo the dithering, I feared, becoming like something from a music hall stage.

Mr. Davis, at his butler best, stood rigidly aside as Mrs. Bywater glided out of the room, then he closed the pocket doors and left me alone with Mr. Fielding.

"Lovely house," he said admiringly, studying the furnishings and elegant bric-a-brac. "Not cluttered up with peacock feathers and preserved flowers under glass and other such rubbish."

I remained in the middle of the room, hands at my sides. "I am pleased you approve," I said coolly. "What did you wish to tell me, Mr. Fielding? Have you set appointments with those Lady Cynthia and Mr. Thanos met at the Foundling Hospital?"

"Not yet. Lady Cynthia agreed she would write to them and be every inch the earl's daughter. We can only wait for their response."

"Then what did you wish to say to me?"

I debated whether to impart what had happened to me the evening before in Seven Dials. The incident might have nothing to do with the Foundling Hospital, except as happening at the address arbitrarily chosen to throw Mr. Fielding off the scent. I also wanted to see if I could pry out of Mr. Fielding whether he had encountered the bullies himself, or had learned more than he'd let on.

Mr. Fielding turned his ingratiating smile upon me, his neatly trimmed beard emphasizing a flash of white teeth.

"I simply wondered if you'd turned up anything else in the awful business. You and Daniel left together yesterday, and he did not return." His smile deepened. "You are rather intimate with him, are you not?"

I drew myself up. "I hope you are not insulting me, Mr. Fielding."

I saw him realize he'd taken the wrong tack. He became instantly contrite. "Forgive me. I put it badly. I meant that you and my brother are great friends. He might tell you anything he'd discovered before he would me. I'm afraid he does not trust me."

I did not soften. "I cannot be surprised. But no. I haven't spoken to Daniel since we parted yesterday afternoon."

"Ah." He looked disappointed. "Then I apologize for annoying you. But what happened to Nell has thrown me all in a flutter." In spite of his light words, I saw a flash of grief in Mr. Fielding's eyes, raw and powerful. "I long to bring her assailants to justice."

I rather thought he wanted to show them the might of his fists, but I kept silent on that matter.

"I am very sorry for her," I said gently. "I too wish to see the villains found."

Mr. Fielding let out a sigh, abandoning his pretense at simple curiosity. "Shall we sit?"

I was not comfortable being seated in the mistress's parlor, but I saw sense in us not standing rigidly in the center of the room. I perched on the edge of the sofa, and Mr. Fielding resumed the wing chair.

He took time to look me over—I imagined he was deciding how to broach whatever subject was truly on his mind.

I'd noted that he did this with every person he met. Took them in and assessed their measure. Only then would he speak, tailoring his words carefully.

"How is Daniel?" he asked as though the question was incidental. "I mean in general. I haven't spoken to him in years, but he seems to have prospered. *Seems*, anyway. He is friendly with the police, which is quite a change. So many a time I witnessed young Daniel speed from the constables."

He chuckled, and I permitted myself a smile. If Mr. Fielding could take the measure of people, so could I—his true purpose today was to fish information from me about Daniel.

"I am afraid I can't tell you much," I said. "Daniel does not confide in me."

Mr. Fielding's brows went up. "Does he not? And yet, he speaks to you in a far more open manner than he ever did anyone. Including me, the man raised as his brother. He is very fond of you, I believe."

"And I am fond of him. But I speak the truth. I know Daniel works as a deliveryman and sometimes assists the police, but that is all." I saw no reason not to impart any further information than Mr. Fielding already seemed to know.

"That statement could cover a multitude of facts. If he's in thick with the police, why spend his days carrying sacks of meal up and down kitchen stairs? He could take an office and put his feet up on a desk. And why would they trust a deliveryman to bring them information?" He shook his head. "Then there's his son. *Daniel McAdam*, with a son. I can scarce credit it."

"These things happen," I said, making my voice uninflected. I kept to myself my feelings about Daniel and the woman who'd borne James. None of my business what Daniel had got up to before I met him, I'd told myself. "Daniel has not imparted much about James's mother. He did not realize he'd fathered a child at all until she sent for him on her deathbed, so I've been told. She'd sent James away, but Daniel managed to find him, and now looks after him."

"Good heavens, what a tale. Very melodramatic." Mr. Fielding watched me closely. "Do you believe him?"

"Of course. Why shouldn't I?"

"Because Daniel is a great liar, my dear. He was a fabulous mimic as a lad, could become anyone he wanted. A chameleon, I called him."

Mr. Fielding's words held a ring of truth, I hated to admit. Daniel took on other guises well, subsuming his true self in them. When I'd first seen him in the suit of a City gent, I'd not recognized him for a moment. If I hadn't met him before that, I'd never have realized the man in front of me was anything but a middle-class banker.

"I see no reason for him to have made up the story of James and his mother," I said.

"Good." He pronounced the word with satisfaction. "Then I am pleased he has taken you into his confidence."

"Are you?" I eyed him. "Why?"

Mr. Fielding leaned back in his chair, the very picture of a relaxed clergyman who'd come to discuss nothing more dangerous than charitable works. "He needs a confidant. Daniel was ever alone. Had few friends, trusted no one."

"I cannot blame him. I have heard a little about his childhood, and I understand why he kept himself to himself."

"Our life was not *all* bad." Mr. Fielding took on a nostalgic look. "Carter was kind to us, in his way. He knew we believed he'd taken us into his house for the worst of reasons, and so at first he left us alone, simply giving us place to sleep and food to eat and not minding if we came and went as we pleased."

"Kind of him, indeed. What was his price?"

Mr. Fielding blinked at me. "Beg pardon?"

I sent him a pitying look. "Unless this man was of angelic disposition, wishing to save all boys from the streets, he must have expected something in return."

"He did," Mr. Fielding conceded. "But what Carter asked was far less disgusting than some would have demanded. He had us run errands, nothing dangerous and none that would get us arrested. Or we'd carry messages to his cronies. We'd find out things for him—no one pays much attention to small boys. Men who thought themselves clever criminals would tell their entire schemes to one another right in front of us and never notice." He chortled in remembrance.

"How long did you live with Mr. Carter?"

"Oh . . . two or so years. That seemed a great while when we were young."

"I know Daniel was fond of him. He told me he was quite broken up when Mr. Carter was killed."

Mr. Fielding's laughter died, his expression darkening in an instant. "It was a cruel thing. Terrible. They didn't even give

Carter a chance to defend himself. Daniel is correct when he said I fled that night. I knew we'd never prevail. If I hadn't gone, and Daniel hadn't hidden himself, we'd not be here now. Those men slaughtered everyone in the house."

He fell silent as more true grief flickered through his eyes. Daniel had told me of the horrors of that event, which Mr. Fielding had likewise witnessed.

After a moment, Mr. Fielding cleared his throat. "And now someone's done for Nell. The Lord seems determined to take away everyone I care for."

"Life has tragedy, Mr. Fielding," I said gently. "And that is the way of it. I do not speak lightly—I have had my share. Most of us do."

"Thank you for reminding me I am a selfish sinner," Mr. Fielding muttered, then he sighed. "You are right, of course. I have been wallowing in self-pity and not thinking straight."

"Of course." I kept my voice quiet. "As you loved her."

"Nothing so sentimental." Mr. Fielding frowned. "Let us say I cared deeply for her."

"It is the same thing."

Mr. Fielding studied me a moment, then his face lost its dour expression. "I believe I understand why Daniel is so taken with you. You are a sensible woman, and kind, but also unrelenting. Daniel must find this irresistible."

"Please, cease speculating about Daniel and me," I said sternly. "We are friends only."

Mr. Fielding's quick smile blossomed. "Ah, well, if I am deluded about my feelings for Nell, then I can't be surprised Daniel is about you. What is holding him back? There is affection, there is friendship—"

I cut him off. "He is a busy man. And I am a busy woman."

"Neither of you would be half so hard-pressed if you joined

forces in holy matrimony." Mr. Fielding peered at me. "Or is it you who is resisting? You have refused his suit?"

"There is no suit." I rose, my annoyance growing. "Now, if you have finished with your interrogation, I must get on with my work."

He was on his feet and beside me in an instant. "Mrs. Holloway, forgive me. I had no wish to offend you, only to know you better. Daniel will not speak to me. Not in a friendly way, I mean, sharing stories from our pasts, our thoughts and hopes, as we once did."

Mr. Fielding took on a morose expression, but I'd seen he could be as much of a chameleon as Daniel.

"Are you truly a vicar?" I asked. "Anyone can purchase a suit and find a collar."

Mr. Fielding's amusement returned. "Yes, dear lady, I am. My name is listed among those who took a degree at Balliol. I did not gain top honors, I am afraid, but I finished. I was also granted the living in Shadwell—those records can be checked."

"Why the clergy?" I asked. "You were allowed into a prestigious university, and you chose to study to be a clergyman?"

"I knew I was not clever enough for maths or the sciences," Mr. Fielding answered readily. "Not certain I could pull off law either, having faced enough severe barristers as a youth for my comfort." He gave me a serene smile. "Have you not considered that in divinity studies, I perhaps found my true calling?"

"No, rather you strike me as a man who seizes opportunities."

The laugh he let out was more genuine. "I am indeed." Mr. Fielding took my hand in a firm grip and shook it. "Thank you for seeing me, Mrs. Holloway."

"Not at all." I withdrew from the clasp immediately. "But

you do not need to come to the house to quiz me for information. If I learn something about Nurse Betts or the children, I will tell you. Or Daniel will."

"I doubt I'll have any news from my brother," Mr. Fielding said, resigned. "Old wounds run deep." He gave me a brief bow. "Good day to you, dear lady."

I gave him a cordial farewell in return and stepped back to let him depart.

As he opened the sitting room's door, he resumed the befuddled expression of a minor vicar dazzled by, and a little wistful about, his visit to a great house of Mayfair. Mr. Davis, ever alert, appeared from the shadows of the back stairs with Mr. Fielding's wraps and escorted him to the door.

Mr. Fielding was as good as Daniel about taking disguises, I mused as I watched him fumble with his coat, allowing Mr. Davis to help him. But Mr. Fielding had subsumed himself far deeper into his part than Daniel did in his, and I wondered if that made Mr. Fielding the more dangerous of the pair.

Elsie returned to the house as Tess and I were readying the evening meal for the table. The scullery sink was full again, as Tess and I had used plenty of bowls and pots to prepare the meal.

Elsie generally had a bright disposition, prone to singing or humming as she worked, but this evening her expression was troubled.

"I'm glad I went home today, Mrs. Holloway," she said as I stacked more crockery on the table next to the sink. "Home" to her meant the Foundling Hospital. "I spoke to Mabel—had a good old chat with her. The maid Bessie has been worse than ever, snarling and grumbling one minute, paying no attention to anything the next. Nearly dropped a basin of water all over a matron, and didn't that get her screeched at?"

"Hmm." I wondered why Bessie was so out of sorts. It could be any reason, but I was growing interested in this surly maid.

"Mrs. Compton is very worried, Mrs. Holloway," Elsie went on. "She sought me out when she learned I'd come for a visit. She's afraid that other children have gone missing now, and asks if you'll come talk to her about it."

14

She is afraid they have?" I repeated, my heart growing heavy at the news. "Does she not know for certain?"

Elsie vigorously scrubbed a patch of sticky oil from a pan. "I asked Mabel. She thinks the two—a boy and a girl—were taken in by a kind family. But that's what they thought about the others." She poured more water she'd heated on the stove into the sink. "It's terrible, Mrs. H. What if something happens to Mabel?" She turned eyes brimming with tears to me.

"Now, don't take on so." I wanted to reassure her, but wasn't certain I could. "I will find out what is happening, I promise you. How old are these children?"

"Eight and nine, Mabel says. Mabel was being sister to the little girl." Elsie wiped her eyes and returned to scrubbing. "She hopes you'll find the villains and kick them in the balls. Exactly what she said."

I had kicked a villain in his bits, or tried to, Monday eve-

ning, when I'd fought off the laboring men. It had been satis-
fying.

"I will," I said stoutly.

Elsie summoned a smile, and I went back to the kitchen. I
could promise many things, I realized, but whether I could
deliver the goods remained to be seen.

I could not slip out and make my way to the Foundling Hospital anytime I wished, however. I had work to do. I knew,
the next day, as I basted the roast and caught the drippings for
the Yorkshire pudding for the midday meal, that I would need
to recruit help.

I found it in the form of Miss Townsend. I'd contemplated
sending for Lady Cynthia, but worried to test Mrs. Bywater's
patience if she caught Cynthia continually descending the
stairs to visit with me.

Miss Townsend had appeared with her sketchbook this
morning and started in, as unobtrusive as ever. Once I'd sent
up luncheon to Mrs. Bywater and the friends she'd invited to
take it with her, I went to Miss Townsend and told her what
Elsie had related to me.

"Perhaps *you* could speak to Mrs. Compton," I suggested. "I
do not know if I will be able to leave the house today."

Miss Townsend glanced about the quiet kitchen, at Tess
across the hall taking her meal, at my work table scrubbed
clean in anticipation of preparing the evening meal.

She closed her sketchbook. "I will tell Mrs. Bywater I am
stealing you for a time," she said. "To show me the markets. I
might paint those too."

I considered, hardly daring to hope Mrs. Bywater would let

me go so easily. "I do need fresh herbs," I said. "Though the best will have already gone."

"Excellent. Meet me outside in twenty minutes."

When I reached the street in my coat and hat, basket over my arm, I gained an understanding of why Daniel had been happy to work with Miss Townsend during their mission in Paris. Miss Townsend arrived at the scullery steps exactly twenty minutes to the second in a closed landau driven by a coachman with a feather in his hat.

"I borrow him from my brother from time to time," Miss Townsend said as I climbed into the opulent vehicle. "Dunstan is happy to drive me about, and he's nicely discreet."

"I should not be riding inside," I said in hesitation, even as the coach jerked forward.

"Please do not distress yourself." The corners of Miss Townsend's mouth creased. "I am a young lady alone—I need a chaperone."

This landau was even finer than the vehicles Lord Rankin had left for Cynthia's family's use. I sank into a plush seat, carpeting soft under my plain boots. Golden wood inlaid with darker flowers and leaves twined along the walls, which had been polished to a sheen.

Miss Townsend looked amused at my discomfort. I decided to enjoy the treat—the landau kept the wind out, and a coal box heated our feet.

"Will you try to speak to the director?" I asked as we rolled along. "While I talk to the cook?"

"Not a bit of it." Miss Townsend studied the passing shops of Oxford Street. "Dunstan will let you off at the Foundling Hospital, and I will proceed to the markets to do my sketching. What sort of herbs do you need?"

While I appreciated Miss Townsend's help, I drew the line at her shopping for produce for me. That took a knack.

"I did not make a list," I explained. "At this time of day, I browse the market and decide what I will cook depending on what I can find that is fresh and appealing. One never knows what special thing a vendor is holding back."

Miss Townsend gave me a conceding nod. "I do that myself, choosing colors or deciding on the composition depending on what I have to hand. Inspiration needs to be allowed to strike. You are an artist yourself, Mrs. Holloway."

"Not at all," I said in surprise. "I can't draw a stroke."

"I've eaten your meals, you know. What you do is high art, nothing less than what any celebrated chef can concoct."

My face warmed, though I was secretly pleased. "Nonsense. It's nothing but a bit of plain cooking."

Miss Townsend laughed at me, and then we journeyed the rest of the way in silence.

Dunstan let me off around the corner from the Foundling Hospital, near the lane that led to the back door. The landau rumbled quietly off, and I went down the stairs and admitted myself to the kitchens.

The halls were as busy as they had been on my last visit. I pressed my basket to my chest to keep from bashing it into the hurrying maids.

I spied Bessie, though she did not see me. She was currently shrieking at another maid, who apparently had made her drop a pile of laundry.

"It's ruined, innit? If I have to wash it all over again, *you're* doing it, don't no matter what."

The other maid dashed away as Bessie began gathering up the linens. I stooped to help.

"Leave it," Bessie growled.

I got a good look at her face as she snarled at me and saw that her eyes were red-lined and puffy. She'd been weeping.

"What is it, Bessie?" I asked as gently as I could.

For my pains, I received a belligerent glare. "I said, leave *off.*" Bessie snatched up the sheets, balling them in her arms, and scuttled down the corridor.

I watched her go, wondering very much. A maid who could go anywhere in the building would be well-placed to assist anyone wanting to spirit children out of the Hospital.

Mrs. Compton stood at her stove when I reached the kitchen, her face red and sweating as she alternately stirred a pot of potatoes and added pinches of salt to a pan of frying meat.

I rescued a box of mushrooms a kitchen maid had nearly dumped on the floor and carried it to Mrs. Compton. "A scattering of these with the pork will flavor it nicely."

"Oh, Mrs. Holloway." Mrs. Compton pressed a greasy hand to her bosom. "I'm glad you've come."

"Elsie told me you were upset." I did not want to mention the missing children here in the midst of the chaos.

Mrs. Compton poked at the searing meat and then the potatoes with the same spoon and beckoned one of her assistants. "Do not let that burn," she instructed, pointing at the sauté pan. "I'll be back in a tick. Put some of these mushrooms in with the pork," she added, taking the box from me and thrusting it at the assistant. "Have someone chop 'em for you."

Mrs. Compton wiped her hands on her apron, leaving dark streaks alongside those already there, and ushered me out of the kitchen.

I caught sight of Mrs. Shaw—the woman who'd entertained Grace while I'd spoken to Mrs. Compton. She looked puzzled when she spied me, but turned to say something to another maid, her voice lost in the din, and seemed to forget about me.

Mrs. Compton led me outside into the cold, not stopping for her coat. We moved into a narrow passageway between buildings, the wind driving straight down it to whip our skirts and the loose tendrils of Mrs. Compton's gray hair.

"I'm very worried, Mrs. Holloway. About the children, as Elsie told you."

"Can you be certain they are gone?" I asked. "Gone in a sinister way, I mean."

"No." Mrs. Compton wrapped her hands in her soiled apron. "I just know the matron said there'd be two less for dinner for the time being. I have to be so careful with my portions, you understand."

I did, indeed. A cook had to measure out and account for every spoonful. If the exact amount of food purchased did not reach the master's dining room table, she could be accused of stealing the difference either to sell or eat herself.

The budget at the Foundling Hospital would be vigilantly controlled. I imagined the extra two helpings would not be distributed among the other children, but the amount of food purchased would simply be cut, until the next children filled the gap.

"Have you asked what happened to them?" I asked.

"I've tried but it ain't easy. I think that Bessie knows something. She's been jumpy all week, especially when the police were here." Mrs. Compton wiped her eyes with the heel of her hand. "The police came to tell us about poor Nurse Betts. A wicked world it is, Mrs. Holloway."

"I agree." I thought of poor Nurse Betts, dying with strangers, and wondered if her family, from whom she was estranged, regretted that estrangement now. Inspector McGregor likely went to speak to them himself. I hoped he'd broken the news kindly. "Did the police have any idea who killed her?" I asked.

"They say not. Nurse Betts had gone to a dreadful area, from what they said. Could have been any villain. It's such a sad thing. She was so fond of the children." Unashamed tears trickled down Mrs. Compton's cheeks.

I put a comforting hand on the woman's arm. "I know. I am so sorry."

"I can't tell you, Mrs. Holloway, that it's a fine thing to have someone believe me that something is going wrong in this place. If you have any powerful friends, make them find those poor tykes, and bring down the villains what did for Nurse Betts."

"I will do my best," I promised her.

The killer might have been any ruffian in the East End who objected to Nurse Betts walking past him or not answering him, or whatever reason he'd decided to be angry with her. London had too many of those toughs, as I'd discovered myself. Then again, I knew that her disappearing and turning up dead could not be a coincidence.

A door banged. Mrs. Compton and I jumped then flattened ourselves against the wall as Bessie herself charged past us, wrapped tightly in a woolen shawl.

"Bessie?" Mrs. Compton called after her. "Where are you off to?"

Bessie threw an angry glance over her shoulder. "It's me day out, innit?" She swung away and kept marching.

"She's got a foul temper, does that one," Mrs. Compton muttered. "In any case, Mrs. Holloway, if you can help, I'd be so grateful."

"I'll do my best, Mrs. Compton." I bid her a hasty good afternoon and started down the passageway after Bessie. I decided to be very curious as to where Bessie was going and didn't want to lose sight of her.

I heard Mrs. Compton retreat, the door thudding as she re-turned to the warmth of the kitchen. I quickened my pace, lis-tening for Bessie's footfalls, but they'd already faded into the distance.

The passage ended at a gate that led to the burial ground, a peaceful stretch of green in the middle of the noisy metropo-lis. A gate rested in the wall on the other side, the only exit Bessie could have taken.

I hastened down the path across the green and out through the gate. A church sat opposite, but I saw a flash of Bessie's faded brown shawl to my right.

I followed her to the main thoroughfare, Gray's Inn Road. She turned south here, moving quickly through the carts and people, past the great edifice of the Royal Free Hospital and darting down another street.

I believed I knew where she headed. The road she'd turned to, Lower Calthorpe Street, led to the prison of Coldbath Fields, also known as the Steel. Her young man was there, Mrs. Compton had told me, banged up for theft.

However, I did not see Bessie as I neared the high walls that surrounded the prison. A gate stood not far from me, guarded by four men, but Bessie was nowhere in sight.

As I continued along Lower Calthorpe Street, skirting the prison, I heard rapid footsteps behind me. Before I could turn, I was slammed forward, straight into the prison's high wall.

"What you doing?" Bessie asked me fiercely, as the rough stone scraped my cheek and tore into my gloves. "Spying on me?"

I wrenched myself from Bessie's hold and spun around, putting my back to the wall and my rigid basket between us. "My dear girl, I am only heading for the train." I kept my voice steady, trying not to let on she'd badly frightened me. "There's a station in Farringdon Road." I pointed to the end of the next street.

"You've been at the Hospital, asking questions, poking your nose in. I heard you mention the police."

She glared at me, backing off and holding her shawl closed with one hand. Her other hand was hidden in the shawl's folds, and I wondered if she had a weapon in it.

"Mrs. Compton was telling me the police had been there about Nurse Betts," I said. "She's been killed."

Bessie's eyes flickered. "I know, and I'm right sorry, but it's nothing to do with *you*."

I glanced at the wall beside me. Behind it lay a prison that, if what I'd read was true, was filled with dreariness. The men were made to march on a treadmill that turned a great wheel all the day long, and to do so in utter silence.

"Your young man is here?" I asked. "Are you allowed to visit him?"

Bessie's eyes filled with sudden and abject terror. She came at me, but in panic, not rage.

"You leave him be," she shouted. "Never you mind about him. He's nothing to do with you. Go on. Run for your train."

The words tumbled out rapidly, becoming incoherent as she yelled them at me. She clearly wanted me away from there, and quickly.

As I opened my mouth to ask her why, a large *boom!* tore through the waning afternoon. A huge cloud of dust and rubble burst upward behind the wall, rising into the wind as Bessie and I gaped. The cloud spread as the bits and pieces of stone reached their apex and then began to pour down on us.

I grabbed Bessie and shoved her into the wall, positioning myself over her as bricks, pebbles, and pieces of mortar rained around us.

Before my eyes, a bottom portion of the prison wall collapsed in a morass of bricks and dust, leaving a hole about three feet in diameter. Behind the opening lay the bodies of men, both guards and convicts, who'd been felled by the explosion, and behind *them* were desperate-eyed prisoners who rushed at the newly formed exit.

Bessie shrieked as the top of the broken wall, too weak to remain in place, toppled forward, burying the prisoners unfortunate enough to have nearly reached freedom.

15

Shouting erupted from guards, convicts, passersby. I heard my own voice join the cries as I rushed into the fray, grabbing for the rocks that covered pathetic limbs. Bessie was screaming, but her hands worked alongside mine, pulling away bricks to reveal bodies of men moaning and struggling for breath. Stones were wrenched away from the other side of the wall as guards and prisoners alike worked to unbury those beneath.

"Jack!" Bessie sobbed. "Jackie!"

She tugged at an arm belonging to a bloody young man, his face coated in gray dust. He was pinned beneath a pile of bricks, unmoving.

I yanked aside the stones on top of him, using my basket to scrape away rubble. Bessie helped me, still crying.

The young man stirred and opened his eyes, which rounded when he saw me and then Bessie.

"Afternoon, love," he said to Bessie, his voice a croak. "The fings you'll do to visit me." His grin broke through the dirt on his face.

I dug away the last of the bricks from him. "Are you all right, young man? Anything broken, do you think? Lie still—don't rise too quickly."

Jack brushed himself off with care, pressing fingers on his arms then legs. "Seem to be whole. Now, Bessie, me dear, don't take on so."

Bessie openly wept in relief and anguish. She and I helped Jack to his feet, and Bessie clung to him. "Thank you, missus," she said to me, her voice hoarse.

"Mrs. Holloway," I answered her. "Now, what has happened?"

"Dunno," Jack said, sounding cheerful. "There I was, heading out to do me shift on the tread, when the wall goes down. Tries to take me with it. Bessie, love, no need for the waterworks, there's a good girl. Others is still down."

He gently pressed Bessie aside and turned to help drag bricks and stones from the fallen. Bessie quickly wiped her tears and assisted him.

As did I. The two of us and Jack shoved aside rubble, lifted men to their feet, steadied them. They were shaking, hurt, some of them badly. Guards had surrounded us, but most were busy uncovering men. A doctor appeared with several assistants, wrapping limbs in bandages or splints. The doctor ordered litters for those unconscious or unable to walk away.

None of the prisoners tried to flee. They were too dazed, too shaken. The able ones helped the unable. If this had been a planned escape, either it had gone horribly wrong or most of these men had not been in on the scheme. They'd been taken unawares—they'd never have gone too near the falling wall if they'd known what would happen.

As I worked through the dust and smoke and falling night, I noticed more men join the effort. Most were police constables, their dark blue uniforms smudges against the gloom. Bessie and her Jack worked tirelessly, and I hoped Jack might be given some leniency in his sentence for his efforts.

At one point, when I straightened up to catch my breath, I saw, through dust and milling constables, Daniel.

He stood about thirty feet from me down the street, on the other side of the break. He wore his workingman's clothes, cap jammed on his head, his face creased with lines of sweat and dust. He finished lifting away stones to free a trapped man then turned and began questioning one of the guards, who was as shaken as the prisoners.

I started to go to him, but checked myself as Daniel turned to a slim gentleman who'd broken through a knot of constables. The man did not have to push his way past the lads—they seemed to melt before him with the air of those deciding they'd rather be doing something elsewhere.

The newcomer wasn't very tall, but he commanded attention. He removed his hat to wipe his dust-coated face, revealing thin graying hair cropped close to his head. He replaced the hat, a bowler like any police inspector might wear, and removed spectacles from his pocket, looping them around his ears.

Mr. Thanos wore spectacles when he needed to read, a fact that embarrassed him, though I thought they made him look scholarly. I had the feeling at times that Mr. Thanos wished the spectacles at the bottom of the sea.

This man wore his spectacles as though daring anyone to mock him. Rather than hiding his eyes, they drew attention to them. Gray, I thought, or light blue, though I could not be certain from this distance.

What I did see was that his eyes were cold. It was like looking at winter. The man's demeanor fortified this appearance, as he stood arrogantly upright, gazing about the ruins as though deriding them and the guards who should have prevented the blast.

Daniel squared his shoulders as the man approached him, as though bracing himself for a daunting encounter.

The man asked a question, a brief one, his mouth barely opening to let out sound. Daniel began to talk, indicating the wall, the rubble, the fallen prisoners. He kept his motions economical, as though knowing his listener would not appreciate dramatic gesticulations.

Another question, even briefer. Daniel shook his head, his hands falling to his sides.

The man's lips tightened. If he'd been cold before, now he became an iceberg. He swept the crowd with his gaze, and when it fell on me, I shivered as though touched by ice.

He snapped his attention back to Daniel but spoke no more. Daniel held himself rigidly until the man swung away and turned that cold gaze on an unfortunate guard.

Daniel didn't slump in relief, but I saw his tension ease. As he turned back to the hurt men, he caught sight of me and halted, his gaze meeting mine.

Daniel stared at me, probably wondering how on earth I'd come to be there. When I took a step toward him, he shook his head and glanced almost imperceptibly at the bespectacled man.

He did not want me near with that man about, that was clear. I understood the warning, if not the reason.

I subsided, admitting to myself that I did not want to be subject to the man's chill gaze. I returned to Bessie and Jack and continued to work, until the guards began herding their charges back into the prison. When I looked up again, Daniel and the man with spectacles had gone.

Jack caught Bessie in a hard embrace and gave her a kiss on the lips. Bessie clung to him, face wet with tears.

"None of that now," a guard said, but good-naturedly. "Come on, Jack. Six months more, and ye can kiss her all ye like."

Jack held Bessie a moment longer then released her with a resigned grin. "Not too long, love." He touched her face, then the guard came to him, and Jack regretfully let Bessie go.

"Look after her, Mrs. Holloway," Jack said, bending his smile on me. "Don't let her do nuffink daft. All right, all right, don't worry," he said to the guard. "I'm a-going back to my palace."

He strode off with the remaining prisoners, leaving Bessie trying to bravely wave a good-bye.

I put my arm through hers. "Come along, my girl. We both need a strong cup of tea."

J ack and me, we've been together forever," Bessie said as we held cups of pleasantly steaming brew. "Seems like it, anyway. Since we was kids."

We sat at the tea shop near the Foundling Hospital, the one to which I'd taken Grace last Thursday. We'd cleaned ourselves the best we could with handkerchiefs and water from a public pump, and I convinced the girl in the tea shop to let us in. She remembered me and grudgingly waved us to a table, plunking a hot teapot and two cups in front of us.

"You were a foundling," I said to Bessie, remembering what Mrs. Compton had mentioned about her. "Was Jack?"

"Jack? Naw." Bessie had laid aside her now-torn shawl, and dark curls framed her face, softening it and showing her prettiness. "But he worked at the Hospital as a lad, doing odd jobs or helping carpenters with repairs to the building—there's always something what needs fixing. Jack and I would sneak into empty rooms and talk, and when we were daring, hold hands. It were innocent. We were children. Then when we got older, and both started working, we thought, might as well get married. Would save up and do it."

I poured out more tea and we took sips of the overly bitter but at least hot liquid. "Then he was sent to prison?"

"Yeah." Bessie held her cup in both hands. "Bet you think I'm going to say he were innocent, and wrongly banged up, but no. Jack did it. Was a fair cop, as they say."

"What exactly did he do?" I added a touch of sugar to my cup, but I doubted it'd cut the musty taste of the cheap tea. "If you don't mind my asking."

"Stole a hammer and some other tools. Daft sod. Well, he wanted to be a carpenter, didn't he? But you have to have tools, or no one will hire you. A man left his box just sitting there, and Jack helped himself. He wasn't a very good criminal, was he, because he got caught five minutes later. But tools is expensive, so Jack got two years in the Steel."

A grim place. A rhyme I'd learned as a child told of the devil getting ideas to improve cells in hell from Coldbath Fields. "His sentence is up in six months, I heard the guard say."

"Yeah. But I think the guv'nor should let him go, for what he did today." She glared, her belligerence returning. "Helping the hurt men and all, guards and prisoners alike. Jack could have run away, but he didn't, did he?"

Her baleful look told me she thought I'd disagree, but I had much sympathy for Jack.

"I too hope that this incident lessens his sentence." My statement surprised but mollified her, and Bessie resumed her

tea. "Now, why were you there, Bessie? You were terribly out of
sorts today. Did you know the explosion would happen?"

Now she looked amazed. "Me? How could I know? Don't
you be putting the finger on me, Mrs. Holloway. I wouldn't
know the first thing about how to break down a wall, and neither would Jack. He's a builder, yeah, but he nails up cornices
or hinges doors, that sort of thing. He wouldn't know nothing
about blowing things up."

"Then why were you so worried today?"

Bessie sighed. She noisily slurped tea, but when she met my
gaze again, the fight had gone out of her.

"I were trying to take a message to him. Nothing that would
get him into trouble, just me telling him I was well and we'd be
together soon. I do that once in a while, and he sends me a message back. Only, I hadn't heard from him in some weeks, and I
started to be afraid."

"That he was ill?"

"Yeah, or even dead. I ain't his wife, so would they tell me if
he were gone? Guard when I went last time wouldn't let me
send a message, just shouted at me to clear off. See, there's a
guard there who's a bit more friendly, who'll say a message for
me or one from Jack in return. I can't read none, or write neither, so it has to be by talking. So we don't say nothing but that
we're well and waiting, or praying for each other. I don't even
want to say I love Jack, because the guard would make fun,
wouldn't he?"

Poor Bessie. My heart burned for her. No wonder she'd
been so disagreeable, knowing the lad she loved was so close,
and yet kept from her by a thick wall and time. Sent to a place
as awful as the Steel for nicking a few carpenter's tools while
he tried to find work.

I would have a word with Daniel about Jack, and he could speak to Inspector McGregor. I vaguely knew that judges had to do with trials and sentencing, not the police, but perhaps the inspector could pass on the fact that Jack was a good lad and didn't deserve such a harsh fate. As disagreeable as Inspector McGregor could be, he was fair.

I set down my cup, remembering what I was about today. "The true reason I went to the Foundling Hospital, Bessie, is to make inquiries about children who have gone missing."

Bessie's head jerked up. "Missing? What children? What you talking about?"

I named them. "And two more lately."

"Oh." Bessie relaxed. "You been misinformed, Mrs. Holloway. They ain't missing—they've been adopted. Least, that's what matron said. Bully for them, I say, if their new home ain't foul."

"They might not have been adopted, or fostered, at all," I said. "The addresses of the places they were supposed to have gone don't exist."

Bessie took this in and understood quickly. She sat up straight. "You sure?"

"I had a look myself. No houses exist at these numbers."

Her eyes were wide. "Where've they gone, then?"

"That is what I am struggling to find out. Do you have any ideas?"

Bessie's forehead wrinkled as she thought. "I asked about little Maggie Penny, when her bed weren't slept in. It's up to me to tidy in the mornings when the kids are having breakfast. They make their own beds, but I smooth out the covers while I'm doing the dusting, so when the matrons come in and inspect, the little ones don't get into trouble. Mrs. Shaw—she's the housekeeper in the wing I do—told me Maggie Penny had been adopted by a good family, and matron said that was right. We pushed her bed to the wall, and it will stay bare until comes the next girl who's old enough for that ward."

"Then nothing struck you as odd?"

"No." Bessie shook her head, curls dancing. "None of them have much in the way of things, but Maggie's little box was empty, her clothes gone. So it must be all right." Bessie's gaze told me she wanted me to agree with her. "If she were snatched by wicked people, her things would still be there, wouldn't they? And the matrons and director would be in a tizzy."

"That is true." This was the first I'd heard that the girl's things had been packed up, which pointed to the fact that her absence had been planned. "But something isn't right. Do you think you can ask Mrs. Shaw, or the other maids, or the matron if they knew anything about Maggie leaving? Without putting the wind up anyone?"

"I can." Bessie looked confident. "I've been passing messages to my bloke for a year and a half with none being the wiser. But shouldn't we send for the police? They're useless most of the time, but maybe they could help."

I shook my head. "My friends have asked me not to. They don't want to bring the law down on the Foundling Hospital and ruin its reputation if nothing is truly wrong."

Then again, the person who'd come to Daniel and me instead of the police was Mr. Fielding. The more I became acquainted with him, the more I realized Mr. Fielding did most things only to benefit himself. But then again, he had truly cared for Nurse Betts and her death had struck him hard. A complex man, was Mr. Fielding.

"If you can keep your eyes open, I would thank you," I said. "And if the police do need to be called in, I certainly won't hesitate to do so."

Bessie regarded me with intelligent eyes. "You're a good woman, Mrs. Holloway, I can see. I don't know much what you can do, but I'll have a butcher's and tell you what I learn."

"Thank you, dear."

She nodded at me, her face dirt-streaked, eyes red from the grit that had fallen around us. We sipped our tea in silence, understanding each other.

When I finally returned home, without my fresh herbs, my basket ruined, Tess took one look at me and barely stifled a shriek.

"What the devil happened to you, Mrs. H.?"

"A wall fell down," I said. "I happened to be near. I'd better go wash up."

They all stared at me—Mrs. Redfern, Mr. Davis, Elsie, little Charlie. I took off my coat, dismayed at the pebbles and dust that rained from it. A gash in the coat's sleeve made me even more unhappy.

"*That* will have to be cleaned and mended," I said with a sigh. "Did Miss Townsend return?"

"No, but she sent that." Tess pointed with the knife she held at a box on a stool, which overflowed with greenery.

The delightful odors assailed me even as I reached it. Dill and thyme, parsley and chervil, chives and spinach, everything perfectly green and crisp, not a wilting stalk in sight.

"Very kind," I said in delight. I lifted a strand of rosemary and slid it under my nose, enjoying the clean fragrance.

"Generous," Mrs. Redfern said. "Those came from a fine garden, if I'm any judge. She's a well-off lady, no mistake."

"Miss Townsend said she could get her hands on a rare Sau-

ternes," Mr. Davis said, a glow in his eyes. "Though Mr. Bywater might balk at the price."

"Lord Rankin might not," I said. "Apply to him."

The glow flared. "Excellent idea, Mrs. Holloway. I'll write to
him at once."

Mr. Davis glided off, a spring in his step. Miss Townsend had
known exactly how to turn him up sweet, I noted. She'd done
the same with Mrs. Bywater and, now with these herbs, me.

"You look a fright, Mrs. Holloway," Mrs. Redfern told me.
She, of course, was as neat as ever, not a hair out of place. "Upstairs with you to wash. Take care you're not seen."

Her advice was good. Mrs. Bywater might once again decide to sack me if she saw me in this state.

When I reached my bedchamber and looked into the small
mirror that rested on the bureau, I winced. Mrs. Redfern had
been right to call me a fright.

My face was red as though I'd been sunburned, streaked with
white dirt and smears of blood. Bessie and I had rubbed the
worst from our faces, but we'd had to make do. My hair had been
mostly protected by my hat, which itself was in a sad state. I
dropped it to the chair—it was the same hat that had been soaked
on my day out, and I definitely needed to clean and retrim it.

I peeled off my gown, also caked with dirt and brick dust. I
hoped it could be salvaged, as I had no spare money for more
clothes. The mistress had given us fabric for new work frocks
on Boxing Day, but as she'd spent little on the coarse material,
I hadn't done anything with mine.

I'd carried up a pitcher of hot water and now sloshed it into
my basin. I contemplated the steam curling from the water
and decided that a quick rinse of hands and face would not be
enough.

I stripped all the way down for a sponge bath, loosening my hair from its pins so I could wipe the dirt out of it. As I watched the sponge move down my damp skin, my dark hair hanging to my hips, I wondered on a sudden if Daniel would like me thus.

My red face warmed, but the prickle of desire didn't embarrass me as it ought. A natural thing, I told myself. Daniel was a handsome man, and kind, with a warm laugh and a fine pair of eyes.

He was also deceitful and as comfortable with trickery as his brother.

But at the same time, I knew Daniel wasn't Mr. Fielding, as much as Mr. Fielding had tried to tell me they were birds of a feather. Mr. Fielding had shown me so far that he used deception for his own gain. Daniel used it to help others—to bring down criminals or find the lost.

Daniel had a gentleness in his eyes that Mr. Fielding lacked. One that made me stand in my room without a stitch, peering into the mirror and imagining Daniel smiling at me. He'd reach a hand to me and pull me close, showing me without words how he felt.

I tried to shove these errant thoughts away, but it was not easy. I'd not had passion in my life for a long time. Before I'd met Daniel I'd thought myself finished with it, too old, a mother and a matron.

Now I pictured Daniel, and desire touched every part of me.

I made myself finish my impromptu bath and dress again.

By the time I reached the kitchen, in clean gray work dress and freshly starched cap, I was restored to my practical self. If I gave way to passion with Daniel, I might end up with another child, and that would be a very silly thing to do.

That child would have Daniel's eyes . . .

The sight of Mr. Davis, in his shirtsleeves, hunched at my table with the newspaper spread before him, cured me of any romantic thoughts. I pushed them aside and went back to work.

Tess was sorting the herbs, delight on her face. "These are ever so nice." She shook out tendrils of dill. "Will make the mushroom sauce so tasty."

"They will indeed," I said. "Why don't you work out how much is needed?"

Tess gaped at me, as this was the first instance I'd implied she could come up with a recipe on her own. She closed her mouth then, resolution in her eyes, and began to assess the amount of mushrooms versus dill.

Mr. Davis turned a page of the evening paper. Every night he read it through carefully before pressing it and taking it upstairs for the master when he came home.

"Is this the wall that fell on you, Mrs. Holloway?" He rested both arms on the newspaper, white shirt protected by sleeve guards.

I bent over his shoulder to see a large story spread across an entire page, complete with a sketch of the broken wall, dust, and unfortunate men staggering from the rubble. The picture contained a guard and wildly gesturing constables. Behind the wall was a hint of the buildings, labeled by the journalist as *The Coldbath Fields House of Correction*.

"Says it was the work of Fenians," Mr. Davis said, then began to read. "'Our correspondent reports that two incendiary devices were placed, one on the north wall between prison grounds and the street, and one on the west side, in Phoenix Street. Nate O'Reilly, a Fenian leader, was spirited away in the confusion, which, the police believe, was the intent of the explosion."'

"Fenians?" I asked breathlessly.

I recalled Daniel in the midst of the chaos—the cold-eyed man asking him a question, and Daniel reluctantly shaking his head.

16

I continued to read over Mr. Davis's shoulder, but the story did not give much more information. The event was so recent I was certain the breathless journalist had scribbled what he could, the artist had dashed off a picture, and both had been shoved into the evening newspaper.

No one had been killed by the blasts, I saw, but a score of men had been severely injured. Except for the man O'Reilly, no other prisoners had escaped.

"Them Fenians are a world of trouble," Tess said as she chopped dill. "Blowing things up, shooting at the queen, hurting anyone who happens to be in the way. To the devil with the lot of them, I say."

"I agree," Mr. Davis said. "They want Ireland to be independent, and it makes 'em desperate. But there's better ways to do it than chucking incendiaries at innocent people."

Mrs. Redfern, who'd paused to take in the tale, joined the

debate about what best to do with the Fenians. The three of them came up with rather bloodthirsty solutions.

I did not participate, the subject being rather close to me. During my first months at this house, a young Irishwoman had been killed, for which I still blamed myself. That incident had led to Daniel and I revealing a Fenian plot against the queen. Daniel had been in Ireland recently, and today, when the prison wall had been felled by the Fenians, he'd been very quick to the fray.

What had Daniel to do with Fenians? I wondered, my heart speeding as I gathered ingredients for the evening meal. Or had he simply happened to be at Scotland Yard this afternoon, and joined the constables in their rush to the prison?

He'd been sent to Scotland at one point, and also to Paris, where he'd worked with Miss Townsend. Daniel disappeared from London frequently, and I did not always know where he'd been sent. I reasoned that all these journeys did not necessarily have to do with unrest in Ireland.

I had once believed Daniel worked for the Foreign Office because of his many journeys out of England, but he'd openly told me I was off the mark.

Perhaps the police held him in a sort of reserve, I pondered, until they needed a man for very dangerous jobs, such as rounding up Fenians or bringing down thieves of stolen antiquities. That would explain why Daniel truly did work as a deliveryman, so he could earn a living while he waited for the police to need him again.

"Mrs. H.!" Tess's cry startled me out of my woolgathering.

I prevented myself just in time from pouring a stream of oil into a bowl of sugar, and I quickly set down the carafe.

"Maybe I should see to the dinner," Tess said, taking on the gentle tone one uses for the infirm. "You've had a shock."

"I am perfectly fine." I redirected the oil to dress the greens I'd torn up and added a splash of vinegar and salt. "You have already done much today."

Tess subsided, but she kept a sharp eye on me as we progressed to the white sauce for the cauliflower, and then the fish in clear butter.

I did not expect Daniel would visit me that night, and he did not. I remained in the kitchen anyway, sipping tea and writing my notes until very late, until I had to give up and turn in.

The next day was my day out, Thursday, but I needed to visit the market—as I hadn't actually done so yesterday—and Tess and I departed for it very early. We stocked up on much produce, bringing home fish and greens I thought the freshest. After we returned, Lady Cynthia came down, accompanying Miss Townsend, who'd arrived once more to resume her drawing.

Lady Cynthia, in a tailored man's suit, plunked herself at the kitchen table, stealing a scrap of dough for the breakfast tarts I'd make with the decent apples I'd found on our shopping expedition.

"Overslept myself," Cynthia said. "Judith's fault." She jerked her head at Miss Townsend, who continued to serenely sketch.

"Did she make ya sit up all night while she drew you?" Tess asked in interest.

"Nothing so tame. She and Bobby invited me to a do in Bloomsbury. Freethinking men and women discussing topics of the day. At least, that's what they told me. Turns out, the freethinking men and women had plenty of whisky, brandy, and wine. Ladies not confined to tea and ratafia."

"I never knew Cynthia was so fond of singing," Miss Townsend said, her eyes on her sketchbook.

"Cynthia never had so much to drink at one time in her life," Cynthia said, stealing another scrap. "My head aches so. But it was a fine thing, to wash away the stench of visiting the ladies and gents we met at the Foundling Hospital. Thanos and I had tea with our pair yesterday."

"Ah," I said. I'd wondered when they'd set up a meeting. "What is your report?"

Only Tess and I and Miss Townsend were in the kitchen at the moment. Charlie was asleep in a corner in the servants' hall; the maids and footmen upstairs were deep into their chores. Mrs. Redfern was upstairs as well, Mr. Davis in his pantry. Elsie splashed in the scullery, but I didn't mind if she heard Lady Cynthia's tale. She had an interest in this too.

"Judith tells me that the Floreys, one of the couples, are quite fine people," Cynthia began. "Just my luck she chooses the upstanding citizens. They apparently are anxious to have children, are getting nowhere, and have decided to adopt a few poor foundlings. They are filled with sympathy and goodness, says Judith."

"That was my impression," Miss Townsend said without ceasing her work.

"Thanos and I met with Mr. and Mrs. Woolner. Agnes and Nelson." Cynthia took a quick sip of tea I'd put before her. "Unsavory people. Thanos has written to the director to keep them far from the Hospital and its children."

I halted in the act of peeling an apple. "Oh dear."

"Quite." Another slurp of tea. "I scarce dare repeat what they said to us. I thought I was inured to vileness, as Bobby and I have slipped into clubs where gentlemen do not withhold their ideas about what women are good for, but I have corrected that misapprehension."

"Nutters, are they?" Tess asked. "You'd be amazed what gets shouted at me on the streets. From gentlemen what should be respectable, no less."

"Some gentlemen believe they only need behave well under certain conditions," Miss Townsend said from her corner. "They show another face when no ladies are present, or when not among gentlemen they need to impress with their uprightness."

Such as a vicar, I added silently. "Is Mr. Thanos very upset?" I asked. *He* was a gentleman in all senses of the word.

"He is indeed. I believe he's taken to his bed." Cynthia's face was wan. "Without repeating the entire sordidness of it, Mr. and Mrs. Woolner keep their married life lively by bringing in others to entertain them both. This may be another man or woman, or another couple—they openly hinted they'd like me and Mr. Thanos to join them. They also expressed interest in those much younger than themselves of either sex." Her hand tightened on her teacup, and I understood her need to imbibe the night before. "They assured us they didn't mean *too* young, but certainly not fully grown. And they assured us they paid the young people well."

"Which makes it acceptable, in their eyes," Miss Townsend added tightly.

I knew full well that girls of thirteen, fourteen, fifteen, and sadly even younger, lads too, plied such a trade on the streets and in bawdy houses. Some of the houses specialized in youngsters. Reformers and the law went through these houses from time to time and shut them down, but they sprang up again as soon as things quieted down. The practice, in all its guises, went on.

I set down the knife I'd lifted, calmly, as though rage did not rush through me. "I believe I will set the police on them." I knew exactly which policeman. Inspector McGregor had no interest in a person's rank or social standing, only that they'd committed a crime.

"I will join you," Miss Townsend said. "If the police balk, I can speak to people who will hurry things along."

Her anger matched mine. Cynthia took another gulp of tea. "I will as well. But as much as we pried, neither Thanos nor I believe the Woolners took the children in question. They would have boasted of it, I think. Nor was there any hint in their home, where we met them, that the children had ever been there. They could have hidden the mites away, of course, or stashed them elsewhere, but we heard no sound, saw no evidence of it. Not that I wouldn't mind the police going through their house and searching. But I also say this because they did not seem to think it would be easy to lure a child from the Foundling Hospital, and in fact, liked that the children were kept there. They enjoy going on a Sunday afternoon and looking at them all, in their drab clothing and strict rules of behavior. The discipline, it seems, excites them." She shuddered.

Tess sent her an incredulous look. "They have to be barmy. Should be locked up in Bedlam. Then ladies and gents can walk through and look at *them*."

Miss Townsend chuckled. "That would indeed be an ironic turn of events. Worry not, Cyn. Their house will be searched, and they'll not touch a child, either from the Hospital or anywhere else." She spoke with conviction.

"Thank heaven for that," Tess breathed. "It's a crime that such dafties live soft, while honest folk grub for their pennies."

Cynthia nodded her agreement.

I gazed speculatively at Miss Townsend. She'd returned to sketching, quite sanguine that she could stop the Woolners from their unsavory practices. Her family was wealthy and prominent, yes, but I wondered at her confidence in her own powers.

"Please tell Mr. Thanos I am sorry he had to meet these people," I said to Cynthia as I returned to the apples. "He has a sensitive nature. Also please accept my apologies that I asked *you* to speak to them."

Cynthia gave me a tremulous smile. "I notice you don't include *me* with Mr. Thanos's sensitivity. But no need to beg my pardon. I volunteered. I imagine that, to catch a criminal, one must encounter all sorts of unsavory people."

"Indeed," I said. "I thank you for your help. You and Miss Townsend both."

Miss Townsend gave me a nod. Cynthia drained her tea. "We are backward, Mr. Thanos and me. He went home to put a cold compress on his head, and I went out and calmed my nerves with strong drink."

Tess laughed at that, but I did not respond. It did not matter, I believed, what each part of a couple did, only that they enjoyed their companionship and deeper feelings.

The conversation had changed something in me, however. A new determination awoke to end this, find the children, and punish whoever had taken them within an inch of their lives. I was only a cook, but I would not stand by while people like the Woolners prowled among children. I would do whatever it took, or order men like Inspector McGregor to go out and stop them.

Cynthia pushed out of her chair. "I'm off to see if Bobby is still alive after our libations last night. You all right here, Judith?"

"I am. And Bobby is well, if a bit groggy and a slugabed." Miss Townsend showed no embarrassment that she knew this.

"She will likely welcome a visit about now. I will finish here and then speak to people about the Woolners."

"Right." Cynthia stretched, her body lithe in the well-fitting clothes. "Tell Auntie I'll be in for supper, Mrs. H." She moved easily into the hall, as though her burden had lessened, and we heard her on the back stairs, her step light.

Once the kitchen had quieted except for Tess's humming and the sound of my paring knife, Miss Townsend closed her notebook.

"Mrs. Holloway, may I speak to you?" She waited, leaving it entirely up to me.

I dropped the last slice of my apple into a bowl, handed the paring knife to Tess, and led Miss Townsend out.

We went to the housekeeper's parlor, which was empty, as Mrs. Redfern was still upstairs. We'd be uninterrupted for a little while at least.

It was nice to have the housekeeper's parlor as a sanctuary again. My cookery books had been restored to the shelves, and the room's air of welcome had returned.

I indicated that Miss Townsend should take the softest chair, while I settled myself on a straight-backed one. She waited for me to sit, then started directly in.

"Mrs. Holloway, I realize you are curious as to how I know Daniel McAdam. He could tell you nothing, but that is not his fault. I am now prepared to enlighten you."

17

I did not want to seem too eager to hear all Miss Townsend had to say, but I imagine my quick intake of breath and twitch of hands betrayed me.

"Mr. McAdam told me the secrets were not his," I said. "I understand." So my mouth spoke, but I burned with curiosity.

"In Paris, two men were secretly and insidiously murdering any gentlemen who had knowledge of weaponry—that is to say, of armaments and of innovations in instruments of battle. Explosives and rifles, that sort of thing."

I nodded, though my understanding of armaments was limited. "Did you find these men?"

"We did indeed. It was difficult, because no one knew exactly who they were, only that those researching and developing improvements to weapons were turning up dead. Obviously murdered—shot or stabbed to death. The killers turned out to be hirelings, who were very good at assassination. Once they were caught and turned over to the French police for trial, I was finished with the business, so I never learned which government they worked for, but it was one that did not want France to advance in terms of weaponry."

I shivered. "Were those killed men of science? Not in the military?"

"You are correct. The gentlemen were involved in study and research, and that research was a deep, deep secret, which meant they were betrayed. Mr. McAdam was recruited to not only flush out the killers but to find the betrayer. I believe he did, in the end. The assassins never made it to the executioner's block—they were found dead in their cells, possibly murdered, possibly slain by their own hands."

I shivered again, harder this time. "I am glad I don't know much about that world."

"As am I." Miss Townsend nodded, her look sincere. "McAdam was sworn to secrecy. I, as a woman, was not told the extent of the secrets." Her eyes twinkled. "I was kept out of much, and so not obligated to sign papers vowing I'd keep my silence. I know little and can tell little." She studied me. "I know that the machinations of the French government are not of much interest to you, Mrs. Holloway, but that Mr. McAdam is."

My face must have been a vivid shade of red. "Am I so foolish?"

"Not at all." Her smile deepened. "I know what strong feelings are—I am no stranger to them. McAdam and I posed as man and wife. We attended the best society events, where those with close ties to the government or vast wealth that funded the research went for entertainment. McAdam reasoned that the assassins learned their secrets from men who liked to boast in social gatherings about what they did, and he proved to be correct. The two assassins posed as wealthy men about town, not taken seriously by anyone, and were highly fashionable and entertaining. It became cachet to be friends with these two. And so they learned where the men of science lived and did their work, infiltrating through their front doors. But Mr. McAdam caught them." She finished with quiet conviction.

I glowed with pride in Daniel and his accomplishments, and at the same time, felt a bit left out. He'd done this far away, in danger when I hadn't known, with this woman as his companion.

I knew, in practical terms, that Miss Townsend was much taken with Bobby and had no feelings for Daniel, but emotions do not always follow logic.

"Mr. McAdam and I stayed in the same hotel, but in separate rooms." Miss Townsend seemed to realize I needed more information. "It is fashionable for a husband and wife to do so, and it suited our purpose. He even let others believe the romantic part of our marriage was over, and we remained married for the convenience of it while seeking pleasure elsewhere. This would explain any lack of passion between us. He is excellent at coming up with stories, is Mr. McAdam."

"He is indeed." I had mixed feelings about that as well. "And did he?" The question came out faintly. "Seek pleasure elsewhere?"

Miss Townsend's brows went up. "Dear me, no. His claim made the assassins like him and relax with him, implying they were birds of a feather. But Mr. McAdam, I believe, had already met a woman he wished to be loyal to."

She smiled so broadly at me that I flushed, uncomfortable. "You cannot mean *me*."

"I can." Miss Townsend nodded. "His Paris sojourn was a few years ago. He told me, when he was awkwardly explaining

that we were together for the purposes of catching the villains
and nothing more, that he was loyal to a woman in London.
One, he said, with beautiful eyes. When I pressed him for details, he laughed and told me you were a cook. Though that
was too small a word for you, he said. You were an amazing
woman who cooked like an angel, too good to be stuffed into
a hot, tiny kitchen."

"Oh." This must have been soon after he'd met me, when I'd
worked for Mrs. Pauling. That kitchen had been cramped, and
Daniel had seen me for the first time in the miniscule cubby,
and smiled at me.

"Did he put you up to telling me this?" I asked. "He knows
I am unhappy with him."

"Indeed, no. I saw your misgivings, and I wanted to assuage
them. As I say, McAdam was officially sworn to secrecy—dire
things heaped upon his head if he breaks that faith, and so
forth. But I was not."

"Poor Daniel," I said. "I must sometimes be a trial to him."

"I doubt that very much." Miss Townsend had a pleasant
laugh. "He feels it keenly, I think, that he must keep things
from you. He hadn't met you yet when he started working for
the men he does, and I think he regrets it now."

"Who *does* he work for?" I thought of the spectacled man
with cold eyes. "The police, I know, but what part of the police?"

Alas, Miss Townsend shook her head. "I have no idea. He
asked for my help in Paris because I am an Englishwoman, I
knew the people whose soirees he needed to attend, and he
found me trustworthy. Easy for me to pretend I'd married a
handsome nobody, to the despair of my family and friends."

"What did your family and friends say to that?" I asked in
true curiosity. "I imagine someone told them."

"They don't pay much attention to what I get up to. By the

time they got word, it was over, and they decided me pretending to be married was just one more madcap thing I would do. An artist is expected to be eccentric." She spoke lightly, but I saw a flash of anger in her eyes, which she quickly hid.

"Thank you for explaining," I said. "It was kind of you."

"Not at all. I noticed your discomfort, and I saw that you are not the sort to pry—at least, not about something concerning your own life."

I suppose that was true.

She'd given me much to think about. I thanked her again, and we returned to the kitchen and to our respective tasks.

After my adventure yesterday, I was content to pay my visit to Grace and stay with her the entire day. I visited with Mrs. Millburn for a time—Jane and Grace had a holiday from lessons while I was there, and the two girls played games together, giggling and arguing and giggling again, like true sisters.

Grace and I then went out for tea, as we liked to, she asking me all about what I'd done since Monday. I did not like to worry her, so I kept what had happened at the prison to myself, though I did tell her about poor Bessie and her chap, and how they sent messages by way of the guard.

I kept Grace close to me while we walked from tea shop to St. Paul's to stroll in the churchyard there, gazing up at the magnificent building. Cynthia's talk of predators had unnerved me greatly, and I imagined eyes on my child as we strolled along. I hated to part from her, but I knew the Millburns were diligent people and would keep her safe.

I returned home in time to prepare the evening meal as usual. Tonight the Bywaters had invited two gentlemen who worked with Mr. Bywater in the City. More suitors for Lady Cynthia, I assumed, and hoped another row did not ensue.

I gave them cod in cream and butter sauce, a stuffed veal roast, a fresh green salad with plenty of Miss Townsend's herbs, slices of ham, rhubarb tartlets, Tess's cauliflower with mushrooms and dill, and finished with my apple tarts served with cream, and a vanilla custard with raspberry jam.

The staff ate the leftovers, and I put my share into a basket.

Tess was busy shoveling in her supper when I breezed out. She only gave me a nod and wink, thinking she knew where I was going.

Her guess would have been wrong. I paused on the street to give the beggars there some scraps, then I walked to Regent Street and Mr. Thanos's flat.

Mr. Thanos was home, but not in bed. He opened his door himself, dressed in a comfortable jacket and slippers, indicating he'd intended to spend the evening indoors.

"Mrs. Holloway!" He beamed in genuine delight. "How wonderful to see you. Is, er . . ." He peered past me. "That is, are you alone?"

"Lady Cynthia did not accompany me, no." I moved past him into the front room. "I hope you are not too disappointed."

"Not at all. That is . . . I am always glad to see *you*, Mrs. Holloway."

I chuckled and set the basket on his table. "I quite understand, Mr. Thanos. You are a man with a warm heart. Lady Cynthia has sought refuge with Lady Roberta and Miss Townsend this evening after spending a meal with her family. She was understandably upset by the conversations you had with the Woolners yesterday."

Mr. Thanos lost his smile. "They were horrible people. I wrote a letter to the governors of the Foundling Hospital about them, begging them to refuse to admit them again. I told Mc-Adam of this, and he went straight to the police."

"Good." I relaxed. While I'd planned to speak to Inspector McGregor myself, he'd pay more attention to Daniel than to me. "But we are no closer to finding the children."

"But if the Woolners know others like themselves . . ."

"Indeed. I hope Inspector McGregor interrogates them. He is very good at interrogation."

"Their actions will have to be proved," Mr. Thanos warned. "Even for McGregor to question them, there must be some evidence."

"Yes, but it is a beginning. Inspector McGregor follows the rules, but he is not intimidated by them. And Daniel follows no rules but his own."

"That is true, very true. It gives me hope."

I unpacked the basket for him, and Mr. Thanos exuded gratitude. I suddenly wished I could cook for him always—he was so pleased with my efforts and also interested in the contents and preparation of each dish.

He invited me to join him, as I had brought plenty, but I was not much hungry tonight, and let Mr. Thanos indulge. He praised the cauliflower with mushrooms and dill, and I explained how Miss Townsend had gifted me with a box of herbs. I'd make plenty of sauces with them before they wilted, and then I'd dry the remainder, keeping me well stocked into summer.

As Mr. Thanos ate, I asked about his new position at the Polytechnic.

"It's rather strange," he said, enjoying the last bites of apple tart. "The Polytechnic, as it had been, is dissolved. Funds depleted. A pity, because so much was developed there. Photography came into its own through the Poly. And many prominent scientists have gone through its doors. But it is difficult to make people understand the importance of science, especially for practical purposes."

"I suppose that is true," I conceded. "If it has dissolved, then how are you to teach?"

"Well, another man, a chap called Quentin Hogg, has bought the building, and intends to start things up again. He's a philanthropist and wants to provide education for poor young men with good minds. I've never met *him*, but the fellow who recruited me, Sir Arthur Maddox, is quite rich. I will begin teaching sometime next year, I believe."

"Meanwhile, they'll put you up here?"

"Indeed."

Very generous. And slightly odd, but Mr. Thanos, who believed in the good in everyone, likely hadn't questioned his fortune. This flat was much more elegant and comfortable than the one he'd inhabited near the British Museum, from what James had told me, and I too would have been loath to turn down fine new lodgings.

I was packing the basket and preparing to leave when a knock came at the door.

"I am popular this evening," Mr. Thanos said. "Ah, speak of the devil and he shall appear."

The visitor was Daniel. Behind him came Mr. Fielding. Neither man looked happy. Though they tried to tame their expressions when they beheld me, I could see that an eruption was imminent.

18

Kat." Daniel stopped in his tracks, clearly taken aback to find me here.

"Mrs. Holloway," Mr. Fielding said in a more deferential tone. "What a pleasant happenstance."

Mr. Fielding tonight did not wear his clergyman's collar. His suit was what I'd call nondescript brown, and he pulled off a cap similar to the one Daniel hung up on Mr. Thanos's coatrack.

"I'm afraid I ate all the food," Mr. Thanos said in his breathless way. "Sit down, do."

"A pity." Mr. Fielding warmed his hands at the fire and then planted himself on a chair and crossed his legs at the ankles. "I would have loved to sample some of Mrs. Holloway's fare."

Daniel shot a glance at me, and I returned it calmly. After we'd gazed at each other a time, Daniel gestured me to a plush armchair then pulled a chair from the table to sit next to me.

"I came to report that I spoke to the police about the Woolners," Daniel said to Mr. Thanos. "Inspector McGregor is not in the office that investigates such things, but . . . he took an interest. That means he will pester the inspectors in charge of looking into immoral acts until they take steps against Mr. and Mrs. Woolner."

"Good," Mr. Thanos said, relieved.

Mr. Fielding sent Daniel a look of approval. "Disgusting creatures. Want to take a cricket bat to them." He looked thoughtful. "Hmm, I could always invite them to my church to discuss mustering a team. Have the equipment handy . . ."

"I have faith in the inspector," Daniel said. "Though he might borrow your cricket bat."

"Please tell me what happens," I broke in. "Even if the police can do nothing, *I* might be able to."

Mr. Fielding raised his brows at me. "How? I believe in your prowess, good lady, but not your fists."

"You misunderstand." I closed said fists on my lap. "I will not have to use violence. I would speak to their servants, and their neighbors' servants, and those employed by the Woolners' more respectable friends. Rumor and tales can do much damage. I believe in discretion most of the time, but there are exceptions."

Mr. Fielding stared at me a moment before he burst out laughing. "Excellent. Between Daniel's inspector and Mrs. Holloway's claque of servants, these monsters will not hold up their heads long."

A crime might have to be proved in a court of law, as Mr. Thanos pointed out, but the pillory of public opinion worked swiftly.

"This is all very well," I said, "but still does not help us find the children."

"As to that." Daniel threw me a hesitant look. "I have James installed in the Foundling Hospital, as an odd-jobs boy. He is keeping a sharp eye out."

He was correct to worry about my reaction. "Are you mad?" I asked in alarm. "He could be hurt if he's caught nosing about, or worse."

"James is no fool and good at dissembling," Daniel said. "Believe me, Kat, I pondered a long time before deciding to let him do this." He winced. "*Let* is the wrong word. James insisted on going, whether I approved or not."

I believed him. Daniel did not have the control over James he would have liked.

"I have my own spy in Bessie," I said. "One of the maids there. But she supposed the children were gone legitimately."

I explained about the children's things being packed up and the housekeeper for Bessie's ward claiming the children had been sent off, nothing mysterious about it. The housekeeper might have been told such things herself, for all I knew. We would have to discover where the lies originated.

"A clever person would make it look as though nothing sordid had happened," Mr. Fielding offered.

"They'd have to corrupt a good number of people at the Hospital in that case," I said.

"And why not?" Mr. Fielding flashed a scowl. He was in a bad temper this evening. "I think the whole lot of them are corrupt."

The odds of every single governor, housekeeper, matron, and maid being corrupt were long, but I understood his point. Anyone employed at the Hospital was in a prime position to give children over to misery in exchange for a fee. It made my blood boil.

"The children *could* have been sent away for legitimate reasons," Daniel said, though his voice held great skepticism. "Though what those reasons are, I could not guess."

"Then why give me false addresses?" Fielding growled. "No, there is evil at work. You know it, Daniel. Or at least, you used to be able to sense it."

Before Daniel could retort, Mr. Thanos sat forward. "We can check the addresses—discover whether something around those places is suspicious."

"Which I did," Mr. Fielding said. "I found nothing."

"As did I," I said. When the three gentlemen broke off and gazed at me in amazed consternation, I went on. "I was curious, so I had a butcher's. That means a look, Mr. Thanos. It was as Mr. Fielding said. On one street, the numbers did not exist. On the other, near Seven Dials, a new building was going up, a brewery. The workers around it chased me off."

Daniel sent me a sharp look. "You haven't mentioned this."

"I haven't had a chance to speak to you since, have I?" I asked. "What with explosions and prisoners being broken out, and me having to get supper for the Bywaters and endless guests brought to gaze at Lady Cynthia."

"What precisely happened at this building site?" Daniel asked me, his voice deceptively calm.

"I've just told you. The builders grew incensed at me for gazing at the scaffolding and ran me off. Sent me scuttling down a lane straight to Seven Dials, which was their intention. A barmaid told me the largest man was called Luke Mahoney."

The name was Irish, and I waited for a flicker of recognition in Daniel's eyes. None came. "Never heard of him. But I can't know every villain in London. There are too damned many."

Mr. Fielding snorted a laugh. "That's the truth."

I decided to keep to myself that Luke and his friends had manhandled and terrorized me. Daniel, and indeed Mr. Thanos, might want to rush out and confront them, and that was not my intention. Luke was huge and belligerent, and who knew how many like himself he could summon? Villains from Seven Dials were not to be taken lightly.

"Whatever their purpose, they certainly did not want me to continue toward St. Martin's Lane," I said. "Were they simply entertaining themselves, or was there something they did not wish me to see? I have not had opportunity to return and look."

"Nor will you," Daniel said in a hard voice. "I will take over investigating that point."

"And me," Mr. Fielding added. "Worry not, Mrs. Holloway. No one will notice us. We were ever good at blending in and finding things out."

"Not if you continue to glare at each other as you have been doing," I said. "You will stand out a mile, not to mention pay little attention to what is around you. I hope you plan to cool off before you go."

Mr. Fielding uncrossed his ankles and sat up on the edge of his chair. "The matter is easily solved. If Daniel throws in with my plan, we'll be great friends again."

"Not the place to discuss it," Daniel said, tight-lipped.

"I believe this an excellent place. Mrs. Holloway and Mr. Thanos can judge. Yes?" Mr. Fielding included both of us in the statement, but his gaze rested on me alone.

"No," Daniel returned.

Mr. Fielding ignored him. "I've come across a man who knew our father, Carter, in the old days. *And* all his enemies, including one called Naismith."

Daniel had told me about Mr. Naismith—he believed Mr. Naismith responsible for the murder of Mr. Carter. Daniel had been trying to get close to Mr. Naismith since a man called Pilcher, a foul specimen, had admitted to working for him.

"And you believe this man you've met can help you find

out whether Mr. Naismith ordered the attack on Mr. Carter?" I asked.

"You have grasped the idea. Daniel seems reluctant."

"Because he will only help for a price," Daniel said in a hard voice. "This gent wants our loyalty. He not only knows about Naismith, but is Naismith's enemy. He'll say anything to gain more soldiers on his side."

"Not soldiers," Mr. Fielding said quickly. "He is not asking us to fight battles."

Daniel threw him a dark look. "He will ensnare you until you are doing what *he* likes, when he likes. All in return for the dubious ability to help us prove Naismith fomented a raid twenty-five years ago."

"This is closer than we've ever come, Danny, my boy. I'd think you'd rush to the man with open arms."

"Daniel is prudent," I ventured. I also wondered if Daniel hesitated because of the jobs he did for the police. He could hardly take up associating with a criminal without Scotland Yard objecting. The bespectacled man's cold gaze told me he'd not be very forgiving.

"Prudent to the point of prissiness," Mr. Fielding said in derision. "My brother used to rush in where angels feared to tread. How the mighty have fallen."

"Exactly," Daniel said. "I learned prudence from the many times I nearly had all my limbs pulled off for my bravado. I will bide my time."

"Very well. I will tell this man I could not convince you. No matter. I'll find out what he knows by myself."

Mr. Thanos had been watching this exchange with a puzzled expression. "Aren't you a vicar, sir?" he asked.

Mr. Fielding turned the derisiveness on Mr. Thanos. "Do

not worry. None of my flock will be harmed by my machinations."

"How do you know?" Mr. Thanos asked.

Mr. Fielding flushed. He started to answer, then spluttered and jumped to his feet. "Lord help me, I'm surrounded by namby-pamby fools. McAdam, if you are not too timorous to join me in Seven Dials, I will hie there myself. I'd prefer not to have to hire fists, as such men can turn on one, but I will if I have to. Of course, I'm used to blokes turning on me."

The bitterness in his words was remarkable. Mr. Fielding had changed from the silver-tongued but good-natured reprobate I'd first met to a hard and vitriolic man.

I rose and put myself in front of him. "Mr. Fielding, I know you are grieving," I said as gently as I could. "But do not let Nurse Betts's trust in you be for nothing. I do believe those in heaven see our actions or know of them somehow. Make her proud of you."

Mr. Fielding regarded me with eyes that held anger—a deep, terrible anger whose short reprieve had been snatched away. Nothing of the vicar was in the man who looked at me now.

"I understand why Daniel is so fascinated by you, Mrs. Holloway." His voice was chillingly quiet. "You reach into a person and tear things forth he doesn't wish to acknowledge." Mr. Fielding stepped closer to me, perhaps a threatening step, but I held my ground. "Nell did not know *me*. She knew a lie, and that lie is very likely why she died. So you cannot placate me by invoking her name."

I studied him a long moment, believing I knew what was inside him. I had no wish to tear it away, whatever he claimed.

"I am sorry," I said softly.

Mr. Fielding made a noise like a growl. He came at me, but it was only to pass me on the way to the door. "For God's sake, McAdam, where did you find this woman? And why the devil did you push her at me?"

Mr. Fielding threw open the door and banged his way into the stairwell, not bothering to slam the door behind him.

Daniel fetched his cap as well as the one Mr. Fielding had left behind. "I'd better go after him. In this mood, he'll pick a fight with a stevedore or a prizefighter and end up on a surgeon's table."

"I agree," I said. "He needs looking after."

Daniel paused to press a kiss to my cheek. "Bless you, Kat."

He was past me and out the door, heading to the stairs. I followed, leaning on the carved newel post at the top of the staircase. "Daniel."

Halfway down the flight, Daniel looked back at me in inquiry.

"Miss Townsend told me about Paris."

"Ah." Daniel's face went through several transformations before he answered. "That both relieves and alarms me. Once I find my brother and nail him somewhere, I will speak to you."

"I will have the kettle on," I promised.

This earned me a grin, then Daniel bolted down the stairs and was gone.

"Good heavens." Mr. Thanos had joined me in the hall. "A cup of tea does sound jolly. I'll have my landlady bring us a pot, then I think you and I should sit very quietly for a time. Daniel and his brother are not easy on the nerves."

"Quite." I steered him inside. "You sit comfortably. I'll fetch the tea, and then we'll have a friendly chat."

I'd tell him about everything Lady Cynthia had said and

done since he'd last seen her, which might assuage some of the moroseness I read in him.

M iss Townsend did not return the next day for more sketching. I scarcely noticed she wasn't there—she always sat so quietly—until I turned to ask her a question and saw she'd not arrived.

Tess noticed when I did. "I wonder if she's done with her drawing," she pondered. "Or if she's found something more interesting to sketch. Why'd someone want to look at a picture of a kitchen, anyway?"

"Perhaps the very wealthy don't know what a kitchen looks like," I offered, only half in jest.

Tess chuckled and returned to beating egg whites for a rhubarb mousse I wanted to try.

The morning wore on uneventfully except that the rhubarb had turned bad and so I made an apple charlotte instead of the mousse. The bowls came down from luncheon quite clean, which I took to mean everyone had liked it.

Mrs. Redfern entered the kitchen to inform me of how many were expected for dinner. "Five," she said. "Lady Cynthia will dine in today, as well as Mr. Bywater's friend, Mr. Thanos, and a vicar called Mr. Fielding."

I dropped the pencil I used to make notes, which fell to the floor and rolled into a crack between the slates.

"Mr. Fielding?" I repeated, trying to hide my agitation.

"Yes, the vicar who called on you," Mrs. Redfern said, as though trying to be helpful. "With the charitable society, wasn't he? I suppose Mrs. Bywater took to him. Or else he is yet another potential match for Lady Cynthia."

She sounded disapproving. Though she thought it high time Cynthia wed, she did not like the way Mrs. Bywater was going about things, and she considered that none but an aristocrat would do for an aristocrat's daughter.

Mr. Fielding had not been in the best of moods last night, and I could not believe he'd suddenly turn agreeable this evening. While I believed Cynthia probably could keep him in order, I worried very much.

"What about Miss Townsend?" I asked. "Was she invited?"

Mrs. Redfern looked surprised. "Not that I know of. Why?"

"It would even the number," I said quickly. "Three ladies, three gentlemen."

"I will suggest it." Mrs. Redfern sounded doubtful. "I will let you know if you need to add one more serving."

"Thank you."

Mrs. Redfern eyed me as though she thought I might run mad at any moment, but she glided away.

I dug my pencil out of the crack and wrote hasty notes about what I should cook, but I could not settle my mind.

What was Mr. Fielding up to? He'd finagled the invitation, I was certain, but why? And why had Mr. Thanos been invited? Mr. Bywater liked him—there was that explanation. But I'd overheard Mrs. Bywater declare he was too poor for Cynthia, no matter how affable Mr. Bywater considered him.

Nonetheless, I put together sole with anchovy sauce for the first course, which would be followed by roast beef and pigeon in a thick gravy, followed by an herb salad and almond custard. The remainder of the apples would go into more tartlets.

With Tess's help, as well as Elsie to assist with apple peeling, we had it finished. I continually moved to the high windows that looked out at the street, waiting to see the arrival of Mr. Thanos and Mr. Fielding.

They came separately, and I wondered if Mr. Fielding was aware Mr. Thanos would also be attending.

As the courses went up, I could not stop my worrying. I wished I could send for Daniel, who might find a reason to take Mr. Fielding away, but I did not know how to find him. James, my trusty go-between, was at the Foundling Hospital.

Nothing for it. After I sent up the roast, I babbled an excuse to Tess and quietly skimmed up the stairs into the main house, making my way soundlessly to the dining room. The double door was closed, but I carefully pried it open a crack and peered inside.

"Extraordinary," I heard Mr. Fielding say. He sounded cheerful, but I detected the sharp irony in his voice. "Do go on, Mr. Thanos. All this mathematics is most riveting."

19

Mr. Thanos flushed. Mr. Fielding was baiting him, and he knew it. Cynthia lifted her goblet of clear wine, the one glass she was allowed at dinner.

"It is riveting to *me*," Cynthia said. "Amazing how numbers can come together and make the world run."

"That is true," Mr. Thanos said. I could see him in my sliver of doorway, and he turned to Cynthia eagerly. "Mr. Maxwell's laws on electromagnetism and thermodynamics really are all we need to know. Equations that are beautiful, elegant, and simple."

"If they are simple, why don't the rest of us understand them?" Mr. Fielding asked in amusement. "I think these fellows invent things simply in order to keep their positions."

"Mathematics can be learned by anyone," Mr. Thanos said in earnestness. "If they take the trouble."

"I concede not all of us are brilliant at it," Cynthia broke in. "But to imply they invent it to stay employed is going a bit far,

Mr. Fielding. Mr. Thanos will be a lecturer at the new Polytechnic, Uncle, did you know? Sir Arthur Maddox is his patron now."

"Is he?" Mrs. Bywater chirped, brightening. "I've been to gatherings with Sir Arthur. He is highly thought of."

"He is indeed," Mr. Thanos said. "Quite generous."

"Congratulations, old chap," Mr. Fielding said, suddenly effusive.

"Excellent news," Mr. Bywater said. "You must give us a tour when the school opens. Now, Mr. Fielding, I can tell you, as a City man, that mathematics is terribly important—we can't count money without it."

"Ah," Mr. Fielding said. "You have a point."

Polite laughter went around the table, and I relaxed a bit. Cynthia would not let Mr. Fielding dominate, as much as Mrs. Bywater seemed to be taken with him.

Mr. Davis blocked my field of vision by leaning to pour more wine into Mr. Fielding's glass. He moved to the other side of the table to pour for Mr. Thanos. When Mr. Davis straightened, his gaze went straight to mine.

He said nothing, did not betray me by any movement of his body. But he looked at me, his disapproval vast.

I withdrew and returned to the kitchen, easier in my mind. Mr. Fielding, a chameleon indeed, had chosen to mind his manners tonight, for whatever reason.

The next morning, after breakfast had been served, Cynthia strolled into the kitchen. It was Tess's day out, she already gone, so I had a stretch of hard work ahead of me. As I rolled out crusts for meat pies I'd make of yesterday's roast, Cynthia sat down at my table and smiled at me.

"I think last night went well," she announced.

"Oh?" I pretended to know nothing about it. "The gentlemen behaved themselves?"

"Not really. At least, Thanos did, but he can't help himself. Mr. Fielding, on the other hand, decided to twist my aunt around his finger."

"Why do you say that?" I asked in some concern.

"Mr. Fielding has Auntie convinced he has the patronage of a wealthy man. Which he does, I suppose. He told the story of being taken in and raised by this august personage, Lord Alois Symington, the son of a marquess." Cynthia looked pained. "Auntie is ever one to admire a title."

Mr. Bywater's sister, Cynthia's mother, had married an earl. I wondered sometimes if that wasn't what had made Mr. Bywater attractive to Mrs. Bywater. She seemed rather uninterested in him in day-to-day life, and they had no children, implying no intimate connection.

"I do believe Auntie has the notion that Mr. Fielding will propose to me," Cynthia said.

I ceased rolling, stretched nearly the entire width of the table. "You will not let him."

Cynthia's eyes danced with merriment. "Hardly. Imagine me, a vicar's wife in the East End. I don't mind helping the downtrodden, but I *would* mind having to be the upright, straitlaced lady pandering to stuffy matrons so they might give a few bob to the said downtrodden. If ever I put on a pair of trousers, the entire parish would be disgraced."

I straightened up and continued rolling the pastry. "I believe your aunt concludes that when you are married, you will be content to leave off the trousers."

"Yes, when I have a husband and children to look after, I'll forget about my silliness. That is the notion. Why on earth would I want the freedoms of a man if I could stay home and devote all my time to one instead?"

"A good marriage, to a good gentleman, would not be so bad," I said.

Her eyes held cynicism. "Good gentlemen are few and far between, from what I can perceive." Cynthia sat back, but instead of turning morose, she retained a lively glint in her eyes.

"What have you been up to?" I asked, suspicions rising.

"Not much." Cynthia clamped down on her spreading smile but couldn't quite contain it.

"Very well, keep your secrets," I said, as though I did not care one way or the other.

"Not so much secrets as . . . plans. But nothing I can say at the moment. Thanos tells me you visited him, and Fielding and McAdam nearly came to blows."

"Nothing so dramatic." I cut the dough into fourths, folded them, and laid them into pans, telling her what had transpired as I worked.

"Interesting," Cynthia said when I'd finished. "My sister and I were rivals of a sort. Nothing nearly as volatile as those two, but she was always the darling, while I was the awkward older Shires girl—what was to be done with me? Em made a good marriage while I was the hanger-on. I loved my sister to pieces, but it was frustrating at the same time."

I remembered the tension between the two, and Cynthia's restless unhappiness.

"I am not sure how much love exists between Daniel and Mr. Fielding." I pricked the crusts with a fork. "Certainly, there is no trust."

"Can't really blame them. Probably raised to *not* trust each other. They lived pretty desperately from what I gather."

"Indeed." Daniel tended to only briefly touch upon his hard times as a child. I wondered if there had been more between Daniel and Mr. Fielding than boys vying for the attention of Mr. Carter. Or whether Mr. Carter had pitted them against each other to see which would prevail.

Daniel spoke of Mr. Carter as kindhearted, but admitted the man had been a criminal, bringing Daniel and Mr. Fielding to live with him so he could train them to also be criminals. Mr. Fielding had later found a true benefactor in Lord Alois Symington, or so he said, and had he lorded that over Daniel? This Symington hadn't been bothered to take Daniel in, and I wondered why not. Did Mr. Fielding simply not mention to Symington that he had a brother in need of help?

I changed the subject. "What has become of Miss Townsend? She has not been here to sketch these last two days. Is she finished?"

Cynthia shrugged. "Haven't seen her. Bobby says she sometimes goes off to paint, and woe betide the person foolish enough to disturb her. Judith travels where she pleases, does what she pleases. How lovely that must be." She trailed off wistfully.

I laid down the fork and began to crimp the crusts. "She is quite efficient, isn't she? Always turning up at the strategic moment, with the right thing to say to make people like her. Sending me the herbs was a master stroke. I'll forgive her anything for that."

Cynthia toyed with the handle of the fork I'd set on the table. "She is what Auntie wishes me to be, a beautiful and accomplished woman with a natural generosity. If Miss Townsend were the marrying sort, she'd be perfect in Auntie's eyes."

"But even she is dependent on her family's goodwill," I said.

"More or less. She has a wise head on her shoulders, does Judith. I have no doubt she's put money by so she'll have her own income if her family gave her the elbow."

"How long have you known her?" My curiosity about this woman had stirred the moment I met her, and I could not seem to satisfy it.

"I haven't– She and Bobby grew up together. Or at least near each other. Judith is a little older than me and ran in slightly different circles." She flicked her finger over the end of the fork's handle, making the fork jump. "Lucky her."

"Perhaps *you* could be an artist," I suggested, wanting to soothe her. "Then you could run in her circles and find a patron."

Cynthia wrinkled her forehead, then she began to laugh. "One has to actually be able to draw or paint to make a living at it. Or sculpt, or write, or compose music, or anything of that nature. I'm rather washed-up, myself."

Any other day, she might say this gloomily, but she continued to be in fine spirits. Spending the evening with Mr. Thanos had agreed with her.

Cynthia sprang up, finished with the conversation. "If I encounter Miss Townsend, I'll tell her you're worried about her. But I suspect she's going at it with brush and oils. I'm meeting Thanos in Bedford Square today. We're going to visit the museum and talk about what to do next to find the kiddies. They can't have vanished into smoke."

But they could have, I knew, my heart heavy. Children of the streets so easily sickened and died. If they survived it was by becoming harder than the men and women around them, which was exactly what Daniel and Mr. Fielding had done.

Bessie's assertion that the children's things had been packed and vanished with them both confused and worried me. This spoke not of an opportunistic snatching of children as they strayed, but of something cold-bloodedly planned.

I did not like it at all.

I could do nothing about the search today, however. I'd have to leave it to Cynthia and Mr. Thanos, Daniel and Mr. Fielding, Bessie and James. Tess was out, so I had to do double the work, which I did without grudging, as Tess worked hard to let me have my day and a half out every week.

Tess returned later that evening, her good spirits in place. Her brother was doing well, she was happy to report, and this week she'd saved a few extra pence to give him. Tess's wages were meager, but she was a generous young woman, happy to share them.

The next day was Sunday, and we were run off our feet cooking a large meal for Mrs. Bywater and her guests. Lady Cynthia slipped out after luncheon and returned late. She'd spent the day with Bobby, she told me, but there'd been no sign of Mis Townsend. Even Bobby was growing worried.

I tucked these facts into the back of my mind, as I continued to work and went wearily to bed, dropping off as soon as I pulled up the covers.

On Monday, I planned to take part of my afternoon out and visit Bobby to quiz her about where Miss Townsend liked to do her painting. I could have a look around for her before I went to see Grace. I kept in mind that Cynthia had said Miss Townsend would not be pleased to be interrupted if she was working, but I'd only peek in to reassure myself she was well.

Before I could leave that afternoon, however, Daniel came into the kitchen at a fast pace, the draft of the door gusting cold wind through the scullery.

"Come with us, Kat. Please. I need you."

Daniel never stormed in, especially not during the day

when Elsie, Charlie, and Tess were in the kitchen, Mr. Davis
pausing to glare at him. And he never called me Kat in front of
the others.

"Good heavens. Whatever is the matter?"

Daniel's clothes were windblown, his eyes wide with pleading. "I have my brother in a coach, the coachman charged with
not letting him out. I told him it would take only a few seconds
to bring you. We must go."

"I haven't changed my frock." I wore my gray working
dress, my cook's cap still pinned to my hair.

"No time, I'm afraid. Cover up with your coat—no one will
mind. Please come."

Never had Daniel spoken to me like this, his urgency clear.
He moved in impatience while I debated.

"Very well." I plucked off my cap and apron and snatched
my coat from a hook.

I did not insist on an explanation as Daniel dashed up the
stairs, me close behind him. I knew he'd never stop to tell me.

The coach was plain and black, likely hired for the occasion. I recognized the coachman—a cabbie called Lewis, who
was Daniel's friend. I wondered if Lewis had changed jobs or
whether he drove both hansoms and hired carriages.

Mr. Fielding sat in the backward-facing seat in the coach,
scowling as I climbed in. Daniel took the seat next to me,
highly improper of him, but there wasn't much point in perfect manners at the moment.

"Tell me now," I said as Daniel slammed the door and the
coach jerked forward. "Where are we going?"

"The Foundling Hospital." Daniel sent a stern look to Mr.
Fielding. "You are coming along in the hope that you can keep
him coolheaded."

"A vain hope," Mr. Fielding snapped. "We discovered the reason the ruffian swine of Seven Dials did not want you down that road, Mrs. Holloway. Because if you'd continued, you might have found the bawdy house specializing in children that Luke and his friends help stock. I'm guessing Nell found it too, and that is why she was killed. I'm off to turn the director upside down and shake him by the heels until he spits out answers. That is, if I don't murder him outright."

20

Gone was the Mr. Fielding who, no matter how bitter he became, managed to be glib and sardonic. This man was grim and furious, and I did not blame him.

"Did you summon the police?" I demanded. If they hadn't, I would.

"Yes." Daniel's word held finality. "Inspector McGregor and many constables are storming the premises of the bawdy house as we speak. Errol is convinced the Foundling Hospital has been furnishing the house with children, and I decided I'd better go with him to keep him from setting fire to anyone."

"Daniel believes *you* will calm me and not let me kill every bastard responsible," Mr. Fielding said, eyes flashing. "He is wrong."

"What about the children?" I asked. "If constables are storming the building, what happens to them?"

"I admit, I don't know," Daniel said. "They won't be hurt, Kat. Inspector McGregor will see to that."

"*I'll* see to it," I said with conviction. "I too want to speak to the director. Mr. Fielding, please leave him alone long enough for me to question him."

Mr. Fielding barked a laugh, not a nice one. "Do your worst, Mrs. Holloway. Did you bring one of your meat cleavers?"

I did not smile. "I do not believe violence will be necessary."

"Won't it?" The highborn tones Mr. Fielding had taken on from his schooling slipped away, and the man of London's backstreets emerged. "I say we give his arse a right kicking, . and then shake him until he spills all his rot."

"I understand your agitation, but we must question him first."

Daniel shot me a look and shook his head, but I remained firm. There was something not quite right in all this, something that did not come together precisely. A discussion with the director would be in everyone's interest.

Mr. Fielding bent a fierce glare on me. "Do you *truly* understand, Mrs. Holloway? Or Kat, if I may call you so. Do you know what it is to be small and scared, overpowered no matter how much you fight? Knowing you'll never see your friends again? Locked away so men can put their filthy hands on you whenever they like? And you're too small to fight 'em off, as much as you try?" He broke off, his bitterness vast. "The whole lot of them should be strung up by their balls. Even worse are the madams and procuring gents who pander to them."

"Oh." I swallowed. "I am sorry, Mr. Fielding. I did not realize."

"Of course you didn't. Why would I want you to? Do you know how I was rescued from that life? The piece of excrement with me one night was an enemy of Carter's. I'd managed to smuggle a knife into the room, and I stabbed the bastard with it, but not hard enough. I was a tiny chap, and he was beating me to nothing when Carter and his bullies broke in and killed him. I laughed. Fell down, I was laughing so hard. Carter had compassion in him—somewhere—and he liked that I was cheering on his lads. Carter took me home with him. At first I assumed I was out of the frying pan and into the fire, but no. Thank God. Daniel was already living with Carter, and was healthy and happy. He explained to me that Carter was a decent chap, not that I believed him at first. But I learned."

The Lord had certainly been looking out for Mr. Fielding that night, I decided, if in an unusual way.

"I am so sorry," I repeated. I had no words of comfort. I knew, that again, but for the grace of God and a mother who'd worked her fingers to the bone to keep me fed, I could have ended up like him. So Daniel could have, and if not for my dear friends and my own determination, so might Grace.

"Don't bleat compassion for any them, Kat," Mr. Fielding went on. "If I break the director's neck, do not try to stop me. I admire you, and I don't want to do you harm."

I held on to my patient tone. "I agree that if the director had anything to do with the bawdy house, he should be speedily punished. But we must first find out. Beating down an innocent man is not the thing, Mr. Fielding."

"Not the thing." Mr. Fielding's voice was acrid. "Not the *thing*, is it? Where did you find this woman, Daniel?"

"I brought her along for a reason," Daniel answered dryly. "She can keep a cool head, even in dire situations."

I had no idea why he had *that* notion. I thought myself a most volatile person when upset. When I'd feared Daniel had been blown up on the river in Cornwall, I'd screamed and run straight at the water, a futile thing to do. Another time when I'd thought him deceased, I'd not been able to think, barely to see, until I discovered whether he was well. I knew that if anything happened to Grace, I'd be too hysterical to ever be calm again.

Daniel gave me a look of quiet assurance, believing in me. I hoped I would not disappoint him.

The current director, Lord Russell Hirst, did not live at the Foundling Hospital itself, but in a small house around the corner on Brunswick Square. He was not on the board of governors himself, as I understood, but did what the governors, when they met, suggested.

The footman's cool look told us Lord Russell would not be happy to be roused from his dinner. From the sounds coming from the dining room, Lord Russell was entertaining. I heard female laughter, and also male, but nothing that suggested anything untoward. The peerage invited people to dine not simply for the pleasure of it, but to court influence and raise funds for projects.

Mr. Fielding barely waited until the footman said his polite, "I will inquire, sir," before pushing his way into the house.

Daniel took Mr. Fielding by the arm and shoved him into a drawing room. I followed, after advising the alarmed footman, in tone that required obedience, that he ought to fetch his master at once.

The drawing room was small but pleasant, with plush armchairs and tables covered with objets d'art. Nothing overdone or ostentatious, only photographs in silver frames, pretty boxes, and a small collection of glass paperweights.

I worried Mr. Fielding might pick up the paperweights from their arrangement and smash them to the floor, but he only paced restlessly.

When the door opened to admit two men, one small limbed with a trim brown beard, one rather gangly with gray hair and pince-nez, Mr. Fielding swung on them.

"We found them, damn and blast you," he said, not bothering to keep his voice down. "What the magistrates do won't be bad enough for the likes of you." He addressed the small man, calling him names so foul I'd never repeat them.

Daniel stepped between him and the gentlemen. "Enough." His voice held command.

Mr. Fielding closed his mouth, but he remained tense, as though ready to spring on the director at any moment. Though Mr. Fielding wore his collar today, he was a less clerical-looking gentleman I'd never seen.

"We *might* have found them," I corrected Mr. Fielding. "Or found where they might be. I do believe you had better come clean, your lordship." I addressed the small, bearded man, assuming him to be Lord Russell. "Is the Foundling Hospital sending children to bawdy houses?"

"*What?*" Lord Russell's jaw dropped, and he turned a gaze on me that must have made the serfs of the Russells of old fall to their knees. "What are you talking about, young woman? A bawdy house?" He spat the words with all the disgust of a man having to lift a dead rat.

The other man looked as aghast. "Who the devil *are* you? And you?" He pinned Daniel with a horrified gaze.

"I am Mrs. Holloway," I answered, keeping my voice steady. "Mr. McAdam is Mr. Fielding's brother. They discovered a house near Seven Dials that deals in the vile practice of providing children for the depraved. We believe one of your staff, Nurse Betts, discovered it as well, and was killed for that knowledge. She was looking for the children who have gone missing from the Foundling Hospital. Five of them now."

"Missing?" Lord Russell spluttered. He glared at Mr. Fielding. "They are not missing. I've told you. They were adopted. I gave you the addresses of the people they were adopted to.

They went to respectable homes, to be raised and trained to a trade. Not the trade you are speaking about now." His lip curled.

"The addresses were false," Mr. Fielding stated before I could speak. "We looked. They aren't there." He tried to get around Daniel, who again put himself in the way.

"The children aren't there?" The gentleman with pince-nez sounded vastly confused. "Russell? What is this?"

"Yes, why don't you explain?" Mr. Fielding snarled. "Daniel, Mrs. Holloway—this man is Bishop Exley, another of the board of governors. No doubt he would like to know exactly what you've done, Hirst."

"Nothing," Lord Russell began.

"The *buildings* aren't there," I said. "The addresses do not exist. Who were these people who adopted the children? I assume you interviewed them."

"*I* didn't." Lord Russell stabbed at his chest with his forefinger. "The rest of the governors did. Or so I should hope. Is that not true, Exley?"

The bishop peered nearsightedly through his pince-nez at me. "This is the first I am hearing of this. Are you certain, young woman?"

"I was given the information and put it into the ledger," Lord Russell spluttered. "As I do all transactions involving the Hospital. I record it, as does the treasurer."

Mr. Fielding growled. "*I* am a governor, and I heard nothing about it."

"Then there must be some hideous mistake." Lord Russell's rather ruddy face lost color. He looked about for a place to sit down, but saw me standing, and clutched the back of a chair. A gentleman did not sit in the presence of a lady.

I pushed past both Daniel and Mr. Fielding and took his

arm. "Rest yourself, your lordship. Shall I ring for some tea? Or a brandy?"

"No, thank you." Lord Russell squared his shoulders, but he did plunk down on the sofa I steered him to. "Who did you say you were?"

"It is not important. Perhaps Mr. Fielding could look at the ledgers, and check what the treasurer has written. It might be as simple as a mistake—the wrong house numbers recorded."

When I said, "Mr. Fielding," I of course meant I wanted Daniel to look at them. However, I knew Lord Russell would be more comfortable turning the books over to a governor, and in fact, it might be his duty to give a governor whatever records he asked for.

At my glare, Mr. Fielding sent Lord Russell a curt nod. "Yes, fetch the ledgers for me, old chap."

Lord Russell, appearing weaker by the moment, sent me an appealing look. "If you will ring, madam . . ."

I'd already moved toward the bellpull in anticipation. I gave it a hearty yank and returned to Lord Russel's side, Daniel and I forming a protective wall around him. Mr. Fielding stood like a stone, arms folded. Prizefighters stood thus, waiting for their bouts to begin.

The footman who'd admitted us returned in a matter of seconds. Lord Russell instructed him to fetch his secretary, and the lad departed.

We heard footsteps before any of us could speak again, and a reedy man, clean-shaven but with thin sideburns, entered. He must have been one of the dinner guests on the other side of the hall, and looked surprised to see Mr. Fielding. He was Lord Russell's secretary, apparently, and Lord Russell sent him off for the ledgers.

We waited in silence. Mr. Fielding had turned to the fireplace, obviously not happy with me or Daniel. I was relieved to see he remained far from the paperweights.

Daniel watched Lord Russell. His stance was nonchalant, but I knew Daniel well and realized Lord Russell would not leave this room without Daniel's permission.

The secretary returned, three large books in his thin arms, staggering a little under their weight. Daniel stepped to assist him, but Mr. Fielding snatched the top ledger of the pile and spread it open on a table. "Show me."

Lord Russell rose and went to him, turning pages with shaking hands. "There." He pointed to a scrawl that listed the addresses Mr. Fielding and I had both investigated. "And the governors' notes."

A list of numbers and letters filled the rest of the page. Mr. Fielding pushed the ledger impatiently aside. "I can't make heads or tails of this."

"Which is why you will take them to study at your leisure," I said. I closed the book and handed it to Daniel, who'd stood silently by.

"Oh dear," Bishop Exley began. "We cannot allow you to—"

"Of course you can," I said firmly. "Mr. Fielding is a governor."

"I'll have to advise the other governors of this," Exley said in disapproval.

"Best that you do," Mr. Fielding said. "If they have anything to do with this, I'll have them. You too, Hirst."

The secretary looked shocked and Lord Russell, resigned. "If you find any evidence of foul dealings, Mr. Fielding, I will be happy to report it."

"You bloody well will." Mr. Fielding snatched up the remaining two ledgers and strode from the room. Daniel followed, nodding once at the stunned secretary and the spluttering Exley as he passed them.

I regarded Lord Russell in some pity. "Consider my suggestion of tea, your lordship. You have had a shock. I hope that my friends are wrong, but I believe something untoward has happened here."

"Yes." Lord Russell looked dazed. "And if it has, my name will be worth nothing. I believe your suggestion of brandy the better one."

M r. Fielding's rage had not subsided by the time Daniel assisted me once more into the carriage.

"What good are books?" he snarled at Daniel as the coach pulled away. "I don't believe Hirst for a moment—a man can look deathly shocked when his sins are found out. Even if he didn't know, I want to go through the governors one at a time until I find the ringleader. Anyone who had knowledge of this will feel my fists."

I shared with him his need to punish the offenders, but I thought we ought to be certain where the blame fell first. "These ledgers might tell us exactly what happened."

"Maybe, but they are beyond me," Mr. Fielding said. "I say we make the treasurer eat them until he deciphers them for us."

Daniel gave him a quelling look. "The governors are made up of peers of the realm, bishops, and other notable gentlemen. How they elected *you* to join them would puzzle me if I didn't know you. But if you punch a peer in the face, you'll only get yourself arrested."

"I am not afraid of toffee-nosed aristos," Mr. Fielding snarled.

"Ledgers can tell tales," Daniel said. "I know you can't read them, and neither can I, but I know a chap who'll likely be able to."

"Mr. Thanos," I said at once.

"Exactly."

Mr. Fielding opened his mouth, derision on his face, then he nodded. "You're right. He's a bloody genius. Even I can see that."

He settled into silence as we made our way back to Regent Street, too slowly for my comfort. It was Monday, and cold, but all of London seemed to want to be out this afternoon.

Mr. Thanos was in, fortunately, and he began an eager welcome before he caught our expressions.

"What has happened?" he asked.

Daniel began to explain. I stepped out to ask the landlady for a pot of tea for us all, and when I returned, Mr. Thanos was already bent over the books at his desk.

The landlady came with a tea tray, and I took it from her and sent her off, busying myself pouring out cups while Mr. Thanos read. Mr. Fielding paced, his fists balled. Daniel took a cup of tea from me with a soft word of thanks.

Mr. Thanos glanced up when I set a cup by his side. He seemed to recall we were in the room with him and turned a puzzled expression to Daniel.

"Why did you want me to look at these?"

Mr. Fielding drew a breath to angrily retort, but Daniel cut in. "To tell us what they mean, of course. What they say about decisions the Foundling Hospital has made."

Mr. Thanos removed his spectacles, still puzzled. "But it's plain as day." He spread his fingers indicating the page open before him.

"Not to us," Daniel said with a patient smile. "What have you found?"

"Well, if they were hiding great secrets, they did it poorly," Mr. Thanos said. "Any accountant, or at least someone proficient in numbers, would see it. Plain as pikestaff."

"For God's sake," Mr. Fielding muttered.

"See what, my friend?" Daniel asked, keeping his voice genial.

"That whoever keeps these books is claiming great success in placing children in good homes." He tapped his page. "This person then puts the word out that with more contributions, the Hospital can presumably do the same again." He indicated a second ledger. "He records those additional donations *here*." When we said nothing, Mr. Thanos regarded us in perplexity. "Do you not see? There is a swindle going on—whether it has to do with bawdy houses, there is no telling from these notes. Someone is claiming great success in helping the children, and then squeezing more contributions out of willing donors because of that success. But the additional contributions never reach the Hospital. The records don't match. Whoever is receiving the money is pocketing it for himself."

21

Neither Daniel nor I bothered to ask whether Mr. Thanos was certain. He would be.

"Bloody hell." Mr. Fielding ceased pacing, his face mottled. "Are you telling me some of the governors are placing the children in brothels, patting themselves on the back, and eagerly asking for more funding from generous donors?"

"And then keeping the money for themselves," Daniel finished grimly.

"That's horrible," I said. "They're procurers, worse than. We must stop them."

"We will." Daniel's expression held a severity that meant whoever he set his sights on was in grave danger.

"I know the treasurer," Mr. Fielding said, frowning. "I always thought him a meek little straitlaced man. Would faint if untoward behavior was mentioned. Strange."

"Why is it strange?" I demanded hotly. "It's awful. Criminal."

"Because I am usually good at assessing a man's character. Or a woman's. Have to be, don't I?"

"As a vicar?" Mr. Thanos asked, bewildered.

"He means as a confidence man," Daniel broke in, voice dry. "Tricksters learn their marks quickly, and then decide their strategy for duping them." He turned to Mr. Fielding. "I'm surprised you didn't tumble that there was fraud going on. You usually have a nose for it."

"I agree. And here, I'd thought—" Mr. Fielding broke off, as though realizing we stared at him.

"Here, you thought you could swindle *them*?" Daniel asked without surprise. "Of course. Why else would you convince them to elect you to the board of governors? How did you plan to do it? You once told me you helped look over the accounts. Why, so you could fiddle them?"

"I never had the chance to." Mr. Fielding's response was bitter. "The books were guarded like the crown jewels. Now I know why. It took the fear of horrific scandal to convince Russell to turn them over to us at all."

"What about Nurse Betts?" Daniel asked. "Did you take up with her to find a way to skim from the funds?"

"Daniel," I admonished. The jab was unkind, though probably not inaccurate.

"At first." Mr. Fielding drooped as he admitted this. "I was trying to discover how the whole charity was run. In places like the Hospital, money is often lost between funders and the staff who actually spends the cash. If I latched onto the free-floating brass, who'd be the wiser? I wouldn't be taking money from the children, you understand. Just the sundry funds that went into budgets that were never spent."

"And then you fell in love with Nurse Betts," I said gently, before Daniel could make another remark.

Mr. Fielding dropped into a chair by the fire. "I did. So help me God, I did."

He spoke as a man surprised he'd experienced a softer emotion, surprised he could feel such grief. I sent Mr. Fielding a look of sympathy, and Daniel closed his mouth, understanding in his eyes.

Mr. Thanos cleared his throat. "But look here—there's no mention in these books of bawdy houses at all. Some of this is in code, which I will need to break, but the words I *can* read make note of a farm. Nothing about brothels, I am happy to say."

"*Farm* might be their word for brothel," Mr. Fielding said. "Can't bring themselves to name it."

"Possibly," Mr. Thanos had to concede.

Daniel took up his cap. "Keep going through the books, Thanos. I will double your regular fee if you can do it by morning. Kat and I are going to find out whether those children were truly in that house in Seven Dials."

Mr. Thanos nodded and turned back to his desk, already absorbed in the problem.

Mr. Fielding heaved himself from the chair. "I am going with you. The children will trust a clergyman." He gave Daniel an encompassing glance. "*You* look like something that crawled from the dustbin."

I thought Daniel rather handsome in his work clothes with his hair awry, but I understood. A collar indicated a level of morality—not always an accurate gauge, of course, but it was human nature to believe so. A reason, I thought, Mr. Fielding had bothered to become a cleric in the first place.

Daniel took us not to Dudley Street where I'd encountered the builders, but to the church of St. Giles-in-the-Fields. The children found in the bawdy house had been taken there, he said, and now were under the watchful eye of the vicar and a few constables.

Six children sat on benches in the vestry house next to the church, warming their feet and drinking tea.

I expected to find dejected, forlorn, and wasted beings, but instead I saw six very different young people. The youngest, who could not have been more than eight or so, drank her tea with determination, as though expecting it to be taken from her at any moment.

Two older girls in their teens who looked much alike huddled together. The three boys ranged from a lad of ten, the youngest, to fifteen, the oldest, who was tall and wore a haughty sneer. The youngest boy sat cross-legged on the bench, peering at us with interest, while the middle boy drank his tea with supreme indifference.

The similarity they shared was their shell, either of defiance or blankness, behind which each had withdrawn. The world had betrayed these children. Instead of letting them enjoy innocence, it had immersed them in vileness, used by people who, in a fair world, should have protected them.

I could not stop the tears that stung my eyes. Daniel took my hand, his grip strong, he no less moved.

When Mr. Fielding walked into the room, he changed. His hard and angry expression dissolved, and he took on a look of kindness I'd never seen in him before.

I knew that part of his transformation was to become a man who would reassure the children. I also knew he possessed true compassion for them. He'd been these lads, and he understood.

Mr. Fielding scraped a chair from the wall and sat down but did not try to go near the children, nor did he take on a look of condescension. He simply observed them with his no-nonsense gaze.

"Which of you are from the Foundling Hospital?" he asked once he had their attention. "And you can tell me plainly if you like—do you want to go back there?"

The children stared at him. The smallest girl, after darting him a glance, went back to her tea—I would do everything in my power to make certain she never had to worry about anything again.

The oldest boy glared defiance, but it was the middle boy, who was about twelve, who spoke up. "Ain't no foundling, guv. Me mum and dad kept me, damn my luck. I left 'em. Couldn't stick it."

Mr. Fielding raised his brows. "If you tell me you were in that nunnery by choice, lad, I won't believe you."

"Who would be? But I didn't come from no Foundling Hospital, and neither did them. They was on the streets, same as me."

I stepped forward. I could not speak as matter-of-factly as Mr. Fielding, my voice barely working at all. "Were there any other children there?"

The lad shook his head. "Naw. Just us. At least since I been. I don't know how long." His bravado faltered the slightest bit.

"No, missus." One of the older girls raised her head. "We been a year. She gets us off the streets, lasses and lads with nowhere to go. Says we can have a good meal. Then we can't never leave."

"Of course she'd say that," Mr. Fielding said. "Coldhearted bitches know exactly how to pretend to be sweet, eh?"

The two younger boys grinned. The lad who'd been speaking to us said, "Ya shouldn't use words like that, vicar."

"Why not? It is only the truth. She'll be banged up for this, mark my words."

The boy shook his head. "She won't. She'll give a back-hander to the magistrate and be let off. She done it before. She'll move somewhere else, open another house. Maybe look for us again."

The sisters fearfully clung to each other at his pronounce-ment. Mr. Fielding kept his gaze on the boy. "Not this time, lad. I'll make certain of it."

The grim finality with which he spoke reassured *me* at least. I had no doubt Mr. Fielding, and Daniel with him, as well as Inspector McGregor, would make certain this madam and anyone working in the house were given their just deserts.

The older girl raised her head again. "Where do we go now?"

I wished I had an answer for her. The Foundling Hospital took in babies at risk for death in poverty, not older children. Besides, if someone at the Foundling Hospital was spiriting children away and collecting money for it, how could I be cer-tain they'd be safe there?

"We'll find a place," I said with confidence I did not feel.

The boy snorted. "No, ya won't. Reformers come for me be-fore, and I legged it. Not going back to a workhouse."

The fifteen-year-old boy lost his sneer and looked haunted. "Never. I'll take me chances on me own. I'm big enough to fight now." Tall, perhaps, but he was spindly.

If these children were not taken in by a workhouse—a fate I'd wish on no one—then they would be on the streets again, prey to those who hunted them. There had to be something we could do, and I was already beginning to have ideas on that score.

But the question remained: If these children hadn't come from the Foundling Hospital—where were the foundlings?

Nurse Betts had been looking for them. I had as well, and had run into the bullies at the building site.

"Do any of you know a fellow called Luke Mahoney?" I asked.

All of them stiffened. The middle lad spoke up again. "Aye, we know 'im. In thick with the missus, ain't he? He fetches and carries for her, beats down those who won't pay, and stays on the lookout for the coppers."

That explained why he'd blocked my way to the bawdy house. He'd worried that I, a respectable-looking lady who might have been a missionary or a member of the Salvation Army, or some such, would discover the nasty secret he was shielding.

Daniel came out of his silence to ask the next question. "Do you know where Luke lives?"

"Oh aye," the oldest boy said. "But you don't want to go after him, guv. He'll kill you as easy as look at you. Don't matter you have a woman with ya. He'll do her too."

Mr. Fielding's face went blank. I knew he was convinced Luke's hand had struck down Nurse Betts, never mind she was found far from here. He would not be sparing with the man, and I, having had the pleasure of meeting Luke, wouldn't dissuade him.

"Tell us anyway," Daniel said.

"A lane off Great White Lion Street," the lad said with a shrug. "Just ask. Everyone knows 'im."

I remembered the barmaid at the tavern I'd stepped into, who'd readily recognized the description. Luke must be dangerous indeed to cow the inhabitants of Seven Dials.

I turned to the constables, who had remained unobtrusively in the back of the room, making more tea and letting us speak.

"May they stay here?" I asked. "For a time?"

The constable who answered was a good-natured lad. "Not up to me, ma'am. But for as long as the vicar of this church will let them sit, they're welcome."

"He'll send us to the workhouse," the voluble boy said. "Vicars always do. It's their duty, innit?"

"Not all vicars, lad." Mr. Fielding rose. "They can be transported to *my* church, Constable—All Saints in Shadwell. Tell your sergeant. They'll find a billet there. I can't say my housekeeper is a soft woman, but she's got a good heart. See that they arrive," he told the constable sternly. "All of them."

"Have to talk to the sergeant and the vicar," the constable said. "But seems like we can do that." The other constable nodded, mug of tea at his lips.

"And then *you'll* send us to a workhouse," the boy said. "No thanks, guv."

"You're an impudent fellow," Mr. Fielding said. "I believe we'll get on. No workhouses, lad, I promise you this. You simply stay with me in my house with too many rooms—all of them small—until we decide what is to be done with you."

None of the children looked optimistic, or elated, and I could not blame them.

But I also knew Mr. Fielding would look after them, in his own way. Feed them and give them a safe roof to lodge under, in any case. I did not think Mr. Fielding's views on raising children would be recommended, but he understood what they'd suffered, and would make certain that these lads and lasses did not lose by it.

"Yes, go to Mr. Fielding," I urged them. "He will not let you come to harm. And I'll drop by and make you fine things to eat. I'm a cook."

They eyed me dubiously, and again, I could not blame them. They'd learned to trust no one.

"Deliver them, Constable," Mr. Fielding said. "I am depending on you."

The constable stood straighter, recognizing a voice of authority. "Yes, sir."

I gave the children a smile as we filed out, but none returned it. They had been subjected to terrible things by terrible people, and it would be a long time before they found comfort.

I managed to remain stoic until we reached the carriage, but there I slumped against the seat and let my tears come.

Daniel's arms went around me. "I'm so sorry, Kat."

"It isn't *me* you should be sorry for." I sank into Daniel's warmth, too grateful for it to push him away. "I wish I had vast riches—I'd build an enormous house for those mites and give them everything they ever wanted."

"I know. As would I."

The trouble was, I knew no one with vast wealth. I had no idea how much money Daniel had, if any. Mr. Fielding was a vicar of a poor parish—he could keep the children awhile, but not forever. Lady Cynthia's father was an earl, but he'd squandered most of the money, and sold off the lands not under the entail, Cynthia had told me. The Bywaters had a bit of money from Mr. Bywater's job in the City, but they were a penny-pinching family. Lord Rankin, who owned the house in Mount Street, had riches, but he hadn't been above demanding that his young maids entertain him. I'd nearly gotten the sack one night when I'd gone to stop him.

I raised my head. "You know a chap with money," I said to
Mr. Fielding. "Lord Alois Symington, who took you in. Would
he be willing to take in six more? He certainly did well by you."

"No," Mr. Fielding said abruptly. His eyes flashed. "I'd never
give a child over to that bastard."

I blinked, and even Daniel stared in surprise. "But . . . he
sent you to Oxford . . ."

"Oh yes, His Benevolence did." Mr. Fielding's voice took on
sharp bitterness. "I angled for it, because it was the only thing
that would get me out of his house. I became a vicar and finagled the living in Shadwell so I'd never have to see him again."

22

I took in Mr. Fielding's swift breath, his eyes glittering with rage.

"I see," I said quietly. "There is more to that story, then."

"There is." Mr. Fielding sat straight in the seat, every inch of him brittle. "He took me in, all right, but I had to be grateful every day for his charity. He thought the way to bring out the goodness in a boy was to not spare the rod. I was to study hard, go to the school he chose, and make his name. Any transgression was brutally punished. Everyone praised him for his kindheartedness, and was amazed at how well I turned out."

"How well he made them *think* you turned out," I corrected. "I am so sorry, Mr. Fielding."

Daniel removed his cap and ran a hand through his tangled hair. "So, all these years, when you lorded it over me that Symington believed in you enough to take you in while I had to live rough, hasn't been quite true."

"How could I tell you the truth?" Mr. Fielding demanded. "Admit that I'd been snatched from a life in the gutter by a man who beat me, belittled me, and locked me in an attic room night after night? All to release the devil from within me, he said."

"I can't believe you stayed in that room," Daniel said in mild surprise. "You can pick locks faster than anyone I know. Why people bother with locks when they see you coming, I don't know."

"I stayed because he had food," Mr. Fielding answered. "At least, I did at first. He also had a lot of money, and I relieved my torment by scheming ways to take it from him. Persuading him to send me to Balliol was a step. Being granted a living was another step. Getting myself elected to the Foundling Hospital board with all those aristos is yet another. One day, I plan to be in a position to ruin him. I will pound his reputation into the ground, and dance on it."

"I see," I repeated. I did, a number of things. "Now that members of the board might be procurers . . ."

"Never in my wildest dreams did I think they would be." Mr. Fielding scrubbed at his close-cropped beard. "Bloody hypocritical blackguards. I will pull them down as well. To think I toadied to them, when they are just as foul as my bene-factor. It shows, Daniel, that you can trust no one. *No one.* I've always said so."

Daniel, I perceived, was not ready to disagree with him.

"I understand why you wish to ruin your so-called benefac-tor and these swindling, procuring governors," I said. "I agree that you should. But you cannot lower yourself to their level. Embrace hard work, Mr. Fielding. That is what lifts one above the others. Hard work at your profession, being the best you can at what you do. *Then* you can hold your head up, and no one can take that satisfaction from you."

Mr. Fielding stared at me a moment before he let out an incredulous laugh. "You are an amazing lady, Mrs. Holloway." He shook his head, still laughing. "I suppose you sleep very well of nights."

"I do, as a matter of fact." I gave him a quelling frown. "Now, Daniel, you must tell me where we are going. You cannot mean to face Luke on your own."

"Never fear," Daniel said with firmness. "I have a few constables awaiting my orders, as well as McGregor anticipating my every report. I simply needed a direction." He pointed at me. "*You* will remain in the coach."

"*I* know what he looks like," I argued. "But do not worry. I will hang back and let you and the constables wrestle Luke to the ground. I would like to see that man have his comeuppance."

Lewis had no wish to take his carriage into the rookeries around Seven Dials, so we descended at Dudley Street and went on foot. The road the bullies had herded me down was in fact Great White Lion Street, the same road the children directed us to. A few narrow lanes opened from this street, none of which I wanted to enter.

It was afternoon, but shadows were thick here, and always would be, no matter how fair the day. With lowering February skies, it was dark in the rookery, even at this early hour. A noisome stench hovered, reminding me that this had been a place of decay and disease. I supposed things had improved since the time of the Great Plague, but today I could not believe it.

Daniel began to ask those on the street the way to the lodgings of Luke Mahoney. The layabouts stared at Mr. Fielding in his collar and me in my coat and hat, probably concluding we were missionaries. Daniel didn't fit this image, but they were reluctant to speak with any of us. Some, in fact, told us threateningly to clear off.

"This way," I said, taking the lead.

Daniel protested, but I won the battle by simply charging ahead. I made for the tavern where I'd hidden myself, reasoning that perhaps the barmaid or someone else there might know Luke's direction.

As we entered the circle that was Seven Dials itself, I saw, in the thinning crowd, the large head and shoulders of the brute called Luke.

"There." I seized Daniel's arm and pointed.

Before Daniel could start for him, a rumble sounded behind me, a growl of fury that seemed to shake the very stones I stood on. The noise came from Mr. Fielding, who shoved past us and ran at full speed toward the towering Luke.

Luke turned his head, saw Mr. Fielding coming. A look of alarm spread across his face, and he bolted.

"Damnation!" Daniel leapt after him. "Kat—back to the coach," he shouted over his shoulder.

Luke shot out the other side of the circle, heading south. That way led to wider roads, and to the railway station at Charing Cross, which lay near the end of St. Martin's Lane.

I dashed after Daniel, against his orders, but I had never been one for obedience. I had no confidence that I could fight Luke myself, but I might be able to summon help or prevent him from escaping.

Luke ducked into a side street as he ran, likely knowing every bolt-hole in the area. Mr. Fielding was hard on his heels, but Daniel did not follow. Instead, Daniel turned down a lane parallel to the one Luke had taken, in an attempt to cut him off.

I followed Mr. Fielding. I made that choice because I feared Mr. Fielding would kill Luke before we could wring any useful information out of him. Luke might have nothing to do with Nurse Betts, but he did know a great deal about procuring children and could possibly lead us to the lost foundlings.

We ended up in Long Acre, which was heavy with traffic. Bow Street lay to the east of us—with any luck, we'd chase Luke straight to the Bow Street nick, but I doubted he'd let that happen.

Luke knew the area well, diving into side streets and tiny passageways that were cramped and filthy. Unfortunately for him, Mr. Fielding and Daniel, children of the dark side of London, knew it too. I had grown up in streets farther to east, but I did know Covent Garden like the back of my hand, and Luke was racing directly toward the square and the market.

I picked up my skirts, feet flying as I ran after the two men and into the market proper. I supposed Luke meant to lose us in the confusion, but I knew the quickest ways through the stalls.

Vendors cursed as Luke pounded by, pursued hard by Mr. Fielding. Daniel boiled out of an alley behind a hotel that backed onto the market, nearly into Luke's path. The man checked himself and changed direction, but I sprinted through gaps in the stalls, landing directly in front of Luke as he barreled through.

"Stop!" I shouted, my hands up.

I do not know why I thought Luke would obey. He could easily slam me aside, and there wasn't a thing I could do to stop him.

In the next moment, Daniel felled him with a running

tackle. Mr. Fielding burst from the stalls where he'd fallen behind as Daniel and Luke began to fight.

I'd seen Daniel in combat before, but then he'd pretended
to falter and lose, in order to preserve a disguise. This time, he
fought in earnest, his fists flying, boots kicking, not missing a
trick. No rules or gentlemanly behavior for Daniel—he fought
to win.

Mr. Fielding snatched up a loose board and stepped toward
the tumbling mass of Daniel and Luke, ready to strike. The
men moved too fast, however, and Mr. Fielding might hit Daniel instead.

And that is just what Mr. Fielding did. The board came
down, slashing Daniel across the back of the head. Daniel fell
as I cried out, losing his grip on Luke. Daniel landed on his
back, and Luke took advantage and sprang away.

"He's *mine*, damn you." Mr. Fielding glared at Daniel and
dashed after Luke, tossing away the board as he went.

"You bloody fool!" Daniel roared, but Mr. Fielding was
gone.

I helped Daniel to his feet. He pressed his hand to the
back of his head, and his fingers came away red. The vendors
who'd witnessed the fight surged forward to assist, but Daniel
waved them off.

"I'm fine." He took a few steps, but I clung to him.

"Sit down. He's hurt you."

Daniel gently dislodged my grasp. "He's maddened. We
need to stop him."

I agreed, but a blow to the head could be perilous. Daniel,
however, started away, his steps even. I went right after him.

Together we pursued Mr. Fielding and Luke down Southampton Street. If they reached the Strand at the end, Luke

might be lost in the crush of traffic, and again, could reach railway stations that would put him far out of reach.

Daniel smiled as we entered Southampton Street, cracking the sweat and soot on his face. He brought a police whistle out of his pocket and blew it.

More whistles sounded in response, the bobbies of Covent Garden answering Daniel's summons. Constables surged down Southampton Street, and more ran in from the Strand at the other end. They surrounded Luke just as Mr. Fielding caught him.

Mr. Fielding's cry of rage rang through the dimming afternoon. He raised his fist and smashed it into Luke's face, and raised it again.

This time, I saw the glimmer of a knife. I shouted, but Daniel was beside his brother, deftly twisting the weapon from Mr. Fielding's hand.

By the time I reached them, Mr. Fielding was cursing and struggling. Daniel jerked Mr. Fielding's arm behind him and took him down to the ground, holding his brother fast.

"Not yet," I heard Daniel say to him. "We need to hear the man's story first. You'll have your vengeance, my old friend, I promise you that."

Mr. Fielding jerked from Daniel's hold. But instead of regaining his feet to go after the subdued Luke, who was now being placed in handcuffs, he sank into a crouch, put his hands over his face, and began to sob.

Luke was a sorry specimen as he sat in the interrogation room inside Scotland Yard. The constables who'd caught him had wanted to drag him to Bow Street, to lock him away to await the magistrate, but Daniel convinced them to load him into a police van and drive him down the Strand and around to Great Scotland Yard.

Inspector McGregor, who took over as soon as we arrived, was not pleased to see me. He scowled hard from his height and barely allowed me a greeting.

But he knew I'd never be persuaded to leave, so he let me peer through a grilled window into the room where Luke awaited, as I'd done another time he'd questioned a villain.

Luke had his hands cuffed before him, chained to the table. The bluster had gone out of him—he gazed across the table at Inspector McGregor, Daniel, and especially Mr. Fielding with great fear.

I was not certain Mr. Fielding should have been allowed in the room. He ought to be with me, watching through the window, as I couldn't be sure he didn't have more knives on his person.

But Mr. Fielding admittedly had calmed a great deal since Covent Garden, and now his countenance was blank, hiding his raw emotion. His seemingly cool demeanor along with his collar had induced Inspector McGregor to let him take part.

"We've got you dead to rights on procuring," Inspector McGregor said to Luke in his crisp way. He touched a small stack of papers he'd placed on the table. "And charges of assault going back several years. No one's forgotten their beatings by you. You're also here on suspicion of the murder of Miss Nell Betts."

Luke looked confused. "Don't know 'er."

Mr. Fielding moved, but Daniel threw him a cautioning look. "You wouldn't have known her name," Daniel said to Luke. "She found the bawdy house where you took the children, didn't she? You saw her snooping and decided to get rid of her."

"You mean the biddy what was with you today? Yeah, I chased her off. She'd no business down there."

"Not her." McGregor's growl cut in. "A few weeks ago. She was a nurse from the Foundling Hospital."

Luke's brows furrowed then his expression cleared. "You mean the nun? I run her off too. She was knocking at the door, yelling at the ladies inside. It's my job to run people off."

"Where did she go?" Daniel asked. "Did you follow her?"

"You a copper?" Luke looked Daniel up and down. "Ain't fair, is it, when you lot make coppers look like one of us."

"I agree," Daniel said, his voice steady. "Did you chase her?"

Luke reddened. "Had to. She weren't going to leave off. Kept screeching she was going to the police. I had to get her out."

"So you followed her to make sure she didn't come back," Daniel said. "Where did she go?"

"East End."

"A large area," Daniel persisted. "You followed her all the way there?"

"Yeah. She walked. Didn't take no hansom or omnibus. She didn't have no coin, I guess, being a nun."

Mr. Fielding finally opened his mouth. "She was not a nun. A nurse." His voice was hard. "At the Foundling Hospital."

The repetition of who she was did not seem to shake Luke. "I thought she were a nun and would stir up trouble with the Peelers and the reformers. I followed her to Whitechapel. It's a bad place, is Whitechapel. I didn't like to be there."

For a man from St. Giles to describe another part of London as a "bad place" was saying something.

"Where *exactly* did she go?" Daniel prompted.

Luke shuffled his feet under the table, his eyes taking on animallike fear. The odor emanating from him was not pleasant.

"As I say, it's a bad place. Looked to me like she didn't know it well. Started wandering, like she were searching for a turning. She ends up at a church, the one right in Whitechapel High Street, making like she'd go in. Then she changes her mind and marches toward the theatre some ways on. She turns behind that, but I didn't follow. That took her into the territory of Naismith."

I jumped at the name. Naismith was the man whom Daniel blamed for the death of Mr. Carter—he believed Naismith had ordered Mr. Carter and all his cohorts murdered.

Both Daniel and Mr. Fielding went very still, the air crackling with their silence.

Inspector McGregor, always efficient, carried on. "Why do you call it that?"

Luke stared at the inspector as though he were daft. "Everyone knows. Naismith is a hard, hard man, and no one goes to Bethnal Green if they ain't one of his. I turned around and hightailed it home."

"Leaving the young lady there," Inspector McGregor said in a stern voice. "Though you knew it to be very dangerous for her."

"I thought she were a nun. Their lot is always going into slums, trying to save bloody sinners. Ain't ya?" He switched his glare to Mr. Fielding.

Then he faltered. I could not see Mr. Fielding's eyes from where I stood, but whatever was in them made Luke shrink back.

"And this is why you claim you did not assault Nurse

Betts?" McGregor went on remorselessly. "Leaving her with wounds that proved to be mortal?"

Luke's face lost color. "I tell ya, I never touched 'er. Ya can't pin this on me."

"Possibly not. Not if you have witnesses."

His eyes widened. "What witness is going to be running about Naismith's lands? If she went there, looking to bleat about bawdy houses, she probably met his bullies. I didn't want to meet them, not by meself. So I went."

"Very well." Inspector McGregor made a note on the papers before him. "If that is your statement regarding Nurse Betts, I will have it written up, and you will sign it."

Luke slumped in relief, but the inspector straightened his sheets and cleared his throat.

"That leaves the charges of assault, one on Mrs. Holloway, if she wishes to prosecute, and the others on . . ." Inspector McGregor consulted his papers. "Oh, numerous men and women. And the procuring of children for prostitution purposes."

"Only doing what I were told," Luke protested. "'Sides, the lads and lasses weren't doing nothing in Ma Aster's house they weren't doing on the streets already. She likes 'em with experience. She gives 'em a bed and meals. Damned sight better than they'd have in the back lanes."

I expected Mr. Fielding to launch himself at Luke, but he remained still. Daniel too was deathly silent.

"That leaves the question of the children from the Foundling Hospital," McGregor continued. "Where are they, Mahoney?"

Luke again looked bewildered. "I don't know, do I? Never seen any foundlings. I told ya, I only took kiddies from the street what were already on the game. No stealing from foundling homes. What do you take me for?"

A strange world, I thought, when a procurer and a ruffian for hire could hold himself lofty because he only kidnapped children who were already ruined.

Inspector McGregor tapped his papers to the table to straighten them and rose.

"Luke Mahoney, I am charging you with assault, procuring, and helping run a bawdy house. Constables will be along to escort you to your new accommodations. Ma Aster is already enjoying hers. I imagine a few weeks on the treadmill at Coldbath Fields will take a bit of the pride out of you."

Luke's defiance was gone. The man who'd terrified me on the street slumped in his chair, resigned.

I still expected Mr. Fielding to attack Luke now that the interrogation was over, but he rose without doing anything rash and followed Inspector McGregor and Daniel out.

McGregor was chuffed, I could see. He'd brought in a villain who'd long eluded capture, and he was happy. Daniel and Mr. Fielding, however, were both quiet with anger.

"What now, Inspector?" Mr. Fielding asked as soon as the door to the interview room was closed. "Will you put together constables to flush out the thugs in Bethnal Green? Or give up? Mr. Naismith is a powerful and frightening man."

He spoke with great cynicism, and Inspector McGregor sent him an irritated look. "We have plenty of men at Bethnal Green already, some remarkably talented. They'll keep searching until they find whoever killed the poor woman. You have my word on it."

Mr. Fielding remained unconvinced. He said nothing more, however, only led the way out and downstairs, his stride so rapid Daniel and I barely kept up with him.

Lewis waited with the coach, the man leaning on the wheel

and chatting with one of the constables. The horse slumped on one back hoof, eyes closed. When Lewis saw Daniel, he waved a farewell to the constable and sprang up onto the seat, un-looping the reins and holding the now-awake horse steady.

Daniel helped me into the carriage. Mr. Fielding hung back, speaking swiftly and quietly to Daniel. I couldn't make out all he said, but I heard the name "Naismith."

I half climbed down again. "You cannot rush out to find him by yourself, Mr. Fielding. I understand how you feel, but you'd come to grief."

Mr. Fielding's eyes blazed with emotion. "*Do* you understand, Mrs. Holloway? I've just learned that the man who took away the only person who was good to me in my childhood has now taken away the only woman I ever grew fond of. How can you ask me to be sensible about it?"

"He *might* have ordered the men to Mr. Carter; his toughs *might* have waylaid Nurse Betts. You are not to know. If Inspector McGregor says there are good men in that area who will find out, I believe him."

A year ago, I would not have had such confidence in the inspector. But having observed him for this space of time, I had come to understand he truly was an excellent policeman.

"I am to go tamely home, am I?" Mr. Fielding demanded. "Instead of running down murderers and locating the foundling children?"

"Not tamely, but you do need to return home, Mr. Fielding. Remember that the lads and lasses from Ma Aster's house will be there. They need looking after. You must be there when they arrive, or they might believe you've deserted them too."

Mr. Fielding glared at me, a hard rage in a hard man. He might have taken on the dress and mannerisms of a clergyman, but they could not hide the villain he'd once been and likely still was.

Then he deflated. Mr. Fielding pressed the heel of his hand to his eyes, but he did not completely break down as he had in Covent Garden. In a moment, he straightened again, drawing a breath of resignation.

"Damn and blast you, Mrs. H. You know how to ferret out a man's greatest weakness, and then hit him over the head with it." His gaze flicked to Daniel. "How are you enamored of this woman?"

Daniel's smile warmed his face. "If you must ask, you will never understand. Lewis." He called up to the coachman. "Take Mrs. Holloway wherever she wishes. I'll get Errol home in a hansom. Holding him every inch of the way so he doesn't bolt."

While Mr. Fielding glowered at him, Daniel assisted me back into the coach, his hands gentle through rough gloves.

"Bless you, Kat," he whispered, then he slammed the door, and waved Lewis on.

I noticed he took a firm hold of Mr. Fielding's arm as he steered his brother away.

Lewis opened a little hatch in the top of the coach and asked where I wished to go. I told him.

Not long later, I alighted in Cheapside, the coach too large to fit comfortably in the narrow lane where the Millburns' home lay. I ran on alone, my legs trembling, and knocked on the door.

Grace herself flung open the door. "Mum?" she asked in concern. "Where've you been? I was worried."

"I'm here now, my darling." I swept Grace into a long embrace, the wind pushing the door closed behind me.

I breathed the scent of her hair, the wool of her frock, the sweetness of her. I thought of the mite who'd been saved from the bawdy house, young and frail, the two sisters clinging to each other, hardly daring to hope.

Grace hugged me in return, as though sensing I needed this comfort. I took solace in my child, and let my tears come.

23

As much as I hated parting from my daughter, it was refreshing to return to my own kitchen that evening, smell the good things burbling on the stove, and hear Tess sing out her greeting. Mr. Davis sat at the table, chortling over something in the newspaper. Mrs. Redfern swept in, giving me an approving nod, and swept out again, ever efficient in her duties. This was an easy place, I realized, comfortable and without strife, one I'd made my own.

Tess had started a fairly simple supper, as the Bywaters and Cynthia were dining alone tonight. I finished the sauce for the pork roast and potatoes, and Tess had already made a nice salad and peas pudding—mashed boiled peas beaten with butter and eggs, and wrapped in a pudding bag for more boiling. The last of the apple tarts went up for dessert.

After Tess had gone to bed, I sat at the table to make my notes, the kitchen quiet for the night. Daniel did not come, though I hadn't much expected him to.

I'd spent a farthing on another small notebook not long ago, and in it I wrote not about my recipes and menus, but about the puzzles we were solving. I started a new page now, trying to render what we'd discovered into efficient lists.

Nurse Betts: Luke claims to have chased to Whitechapel, but he ran away, fearing Naismith's men, and did not witness her murder.

I tapped my pencil to my lips and added an addendum. *Or so he says.*

I went on.

Mr. Naismith: Who is he in truth? Perhaps speak to Inspector McGregor for clear picture. Did his ruffians kill Nurse Betts? Did he kill Mr. Carter?

I left space for any answers and continued.

Who is skimming money from funds for the Foundling Hospital? All of the board? Or only one or two? Why did Mr. Fielding not know of this?

And the most important question of all.

Where are the children?

I underlined the last three times, then wrote, *Speak again to Bessie.*

I put away the notebook and went wearily to bed. Before I climbed under the covers, I said a prayer for Grace, as I did every night, adding more for the children I'd met today in addition to the missing foundlings. I prayed for Mr. Fielding, that he might find comfort, and asked God to look after Nurse Betts. Then, exhausted, I snuffed out my candle and crawled into bed.

In the morning, I made buttered muffins and plenty of bacon for breakfast. Before Elsie left for her half day after luncheon, I asked her to find Bessie and tell her I wanted a word.

Elsie looked surprised I'd want to speak to Bessie, but she promised to deliver the message.

Today, I would remain in my kitchen and cook. No dashing among the rookeries after villains, no breaking my heart over those London swallowed. I let my thoughts be absorbed in each dish, shutting out the horrors of the world by focusing on my tasks of cookery.

Miss Townsend had called me an artist. I supposed I was, painting with raspberry puree and lemon curd, sculpting with dough and marzipan.

And what the devil had become of Miss Townsend? I was growing quite concerned.

I decided that afternoon to teach Tess how to make tarts called maids of honor. I had prepared a puff pastry dough in the morning, a long hour of rolling and folding, placing butter between the folds, rolling again.

Tess and I cut the finished dough to fill small tart pans, and I added a good helping of raspberry jam to each. We filled the rest with a mixture of butter, almond flour, and curd cheese, with a dusting of mace. More tart dough covered the tops, and in they went to the oven, fueled by Charlie.

Thinking of the children yesterday, I gave the boy an impulsive hug, promising he'd always have a home here. Charlie gave me the puckered frown of a ten-year-old not understanding what an adult was on about, but tolerated the hug. He knew I did daft things from time to time.

Tess ran a finger through the empty filling bowl, scooping up the remnants of cheesy custard and popping them into her mouth. I pretended I didn't see her but assigned her the washing up, as Elsie was out.

I kept several of the tarts back for us when I sent up the

evening meal. Elsie returned after the February night had fallen, and I lit the lamps.

"She wants to see you, Mrs. Holloway," Elsie said as she tied on her apron to make a start on the supper dishes. "Bessie, I mean. She's worried about something but wouldn't talk to me."

"Thank you," I said to Elsie. "I will arrange something. Any more word on the children?"

"No." Elsie pumped water into a tub and carried it to the stove to heat. "But no one seems alarmed. It's very strange."

"It is indeed."

I would simply have to speak to Bessie, and soon, though I could invent only so many excuses for wandering about London. I pondered what to do the brief time I lay in bed before I fell into deep slumber, and the next morning, I decided to recruit help.

Mrs. Bywater had sent down instructions with Mrs. Redfern that I was to prepare a special tea for her gathering of female friends this afternoon. Mrs. Bywater had enjoyed the maids of honor at supper last night, and wanted more of those, plus petits fours, scones, sandwiches, and the like. It was a long list. I'd be preparing the feast all day.

I dropped word with Sara, the upstairs maid, to ask Lady Cynthia to step down to the kitchen whenever she had a moment. Not a quarter of an hour later, Cynthia strode into the kitchen in all eagerness.

"What is it, Mrs. H.?" she asked. "Thanos told me all sorts, and so did McAdam when he stopped at the pub on Bedford Square yesterday." The pub had an upstairs room where writers and scholars, many of whom studied at the nearby British Museum and library, gathered to talk about art, history, poetry, and novels. Bluestockings were welcome, and Cynthia could meet Mr. Thanos there without courting scandal.

"I wondered if you'd be willing to go to the Foundling Hospital today," I said as I continued rolling my new batch of puff pastry for the maids of honor. "Bessie wishes to speak to me—I thought perhaps you could bring her back here. Oh, and a housekeeper called Mrs. Shaw. She might know things without realizing."

"Right ho." Cynthia grinned. "I'll dress up and play Lady Bountiful. Maybe take Thanos with me to lend credence. Perhaps the matrons will believe we want to reward the two ladies for services to the Hospital."

"Don't embellish too much." I patted more butter into the dough and carefully folded it. "Let Bessie know she's coming to see me, and she'll likely find a way to leave. She's clever."

Cynthia's eyes twinkled. "Never worry, Mrs. H. I'll be a model of discretion."

"You are kind to do this," I said with sincerity. "I would not ask if there was another way."

"Don't be silly. I'm interested in this too, and happy to help."

Before she could race away, I asked her, "Do you know what's become of Miss Townsend?"

Cynthia's cheerful mood evaporated. "No, indeed. We're growing rather worried. She usually sends word."

I hoped, I sincerely hoped, she'd not come to harm because of her assistance to us. Miss Townsend was a resourceful young woman, but danger did not always care. Nurse Betts had been resourceful as well.

"Let us keep a lookout for her," I said.

Cynthia gave me a nod and skimmed out as quickly as she'd come in.

Tess and I continued preparations for the tea. To keep myself from fretting during the wait, I mixed and baked a large cake and covered it with buttercream and glacé fruit. It was a complicated endeavor, and the hours passed quickly. By the time I sent up all the tea things, arranged daintily on porcelain plates, Cynthia returned.

Behind her came Bessie, a scowl on her face, and Mrs. Shaw. I saw Mr. Thanos's boots above, but he disappeared from view.

"Thanos was invited in to the ladies' tea," Cynthia said, an impish look on her face. "Auntie is taken with him now that he has a sponsor. I suppose I'd better go up and make certain he isn't overwhelmed by Auntie's dithering friends."

Cynthia looked very pretty this afternoon in a tea gown of deep blue trimmed with pink. She'd put a fur cape over this for her trip to the Foundling Hospital, and looked every inch the Lady Bountiful she'd purported to be.

Mrs. Shaw and Bessie both greeted Elsie warmly, but Mrs. Shaw did not look best pleased to learn we were to have our tea below stairs. "I thought when her ladyship invited us out, we'd be sitting upstairs in the parlor. Not shunted off to the servants' hall."

"It's nice here," Bessie told her defiantly. "Warm. Cozy even."

I gave Bessie a grateful nod. "Thank you both for coming. I do have a nice meal ready for us."

I'd made extra plates of the scones and sandwiches, tarts and petits fours. While I'd sent the whole cake upstairs to sit on the sideboard, I'd used part of the cake batter and buttercream to make miniature versions, each with a slice of glazed fruit on top.

I carried the tray into the servants' hall, and Tess, told beforehand what I was about, agreed to serve us. She dived too much into the role, however, asking in what she thought was a posh voice, if I, "moodam," wanted more sugar in my tea.

Once Mrs. Shaw, softened by the beautiful treats before her, began to tuck in, Tess went quiet. She would not leave the room, too interested in the problem at hand, but she did close the door, shutting us in, as I'd instructed.

"Now then, Bessie," I said. "Can you tell me what has been worrying you?"

Bessie cast an uncertain glance at Mrs. Shaw, then shrugged. "Don't matter if I get the sack. I'm right sick of a place that loses children. What's worrying me is *her*."

She pointed a finger, dusted with icing sugar, at Mrs. Shaw.

Mrs. Shaw coughed. She gulped down the large bite of tart and quickly wiped jam from her mouth.

"What do you mean, girl?" Mrs. Shaw demanded. "I came with you today to keep an eye on you. With your young man banged up, you're not to be trusted."

I raised my hands to restore peace. "Please. Let us discuss things calmly. Bessie, what do you mean? No, Mrs. Shaw—*let her speak*."

Mrs. Shaw went quite red but subsided at my stern look.

Bessie scowled. "She knows where those kids have gone, I'm sure. I heard her a-whispering with another maid, and I think she said she'd nab some more."

"I did no such thing!" Mrs. Shaw gaped in shock. "You are a wicked, wicked young woman."

She raised her hand as though to deliver Bessie a blow, and I caught it. Tess darted forward and rescued the three-tiered serving tray before it was knocked to the floor.

"Mrs. Shaw." I cut through her rage. "I think you had better tell me. All of it. You know the governor who is doing this, don't you? And you know exactly where he is taking the children."

24

In fact, I knew no such thing. I was guessing.

Mrs. Compton had told me that Mrs. Shaw was "sweet" on one of the governors, who would be far above her in station. Not that misalliances did not happen, but I doubted a governor of the Foundling Hospital, who would be a rather lofty gentleman, would risk a dalliance with a housekeeper.

But if Mrs. Shaw had been seen conversing with the governor, glancing about furtively, her actions might be taken as a woman who was having, or wanted to have, an affaire de coeur. They could also be the actions of a woman colluding with one of the governors to remove the children in order to ask for more funding, as Mr. Thanos said had been done.

Mrs. Shaw drew a sharp breath. "I were only looking out for the Hospital. No one wants the poor creatures, but it costs so much to care for them. If pretending they're fostered out or adopted away by kind people makes the crown or private donors give us more money, where's the harm?"

She spoke in all sincerity and innocence. Perhaps she was innocent. Perhaps the governor presented it to her as a scheme to provide more for the children—Mrs. Shaw did seem to like them. I remembered how kind she'd been to Grace, but I now shivered.

"Where's the *'arm*?" Bessie demanded in a near shout. "Ye get poor tykes kidnapped and put God knows where, and you say where's the 'arm? They trust ya—they ain't got no choice. And ye spirits them away. Where to, eh?"

"A good question," I said severely. "Let us have it, Mrs. Shaw. Who did you give the children to, and how can we find them?"

Mrs. Shaw gazed at our unyielding faces. Tess had set down the tray, but she remained solidly by me, no mercy in her.

"What are you all imagining?" Mrs. Shaw asked in astonishment. "I'd never hurt our lads and lasses, not a hair on their heads."

"Then where are they?" Bessie asked before I could.

"In the country." Mrs. Shaw's defiance began to turn to nervousness. "There's a nice big farm where some of the boys and girls are apprenticed. They're there, enjoying the outdoors and not being cooped up in the Hospital."

"It's a bit cold this time of year," I said. "Like as not, they're working hard, and in the rain."

"No, no." Mrs. Shaw gave me a pleading look. "He said it was all for the best."

"Who did?" I leaned to her. "Which of the governors has wrapped you around his finger? Or are all of them in on it?"

Mrs. Shaw stared at me a long moment, then she dissolved into sudden tears. "You're wrong. He's a kind man. Only wants more money for the Hospital, for more teachers and warm blankets."

"No, he is skimming the extra money for his own use," I

said in a hard voice. "I have seen the account books." I hadn't understood a line of the account books, in truth, but I trusted Mr. Thanos.

Mrs. Shaw looked up in stunned disbelief. "What you mean? Not His Grace. He'd never do that."

My hands tightened to fists, my patience at an end. "A *duke* has done this? Which?" Several were on the board, Mr. Fielding had said. In theory, great men and generous benefactors.

"Duke?" Mrs. Shaw looked confused again. "No, I mean Bishop Exley. He's a kindly gentleman. Said it was the only way to convince others to pay more attention to the Hospital."

"Bishop Exley?" I remembered the gray-haired gentleman with spectacles balanced on his nose who had been with Lord Russell the day we'd fetched the ledgers. He'd seemed puzzled and confused by our accusations, but of course he'd pretend to be so. He'd not stopped Daniel taking away the ledgers, but he couldn't very well prevent him without arousing our suspicions. Exley must have believed we'd never decipher them, but he did not know Mr. Thanos, a genius with numbers.

"Think, Mrs. Shaw," I said. "If he wants good for the children, why take only you into his confidence? Why worry everyone else? Wouldn't it be better that no one reported the children missing? Which is what happened."

Tears trickled down Mrs. Shaw's cheeks and dropped into the pastry cream on her plate. "He said it would be best no one knew. So he could provide without glorifying himself."

"Mrs. Shaw." I rose, unable to keep still. "Nurse Betts *died* because she was looking for those children. She searched in the wrong place, alarmed the wrong people, ran the wrong direction. She'd have remained safely at home and be all right if you had simply told her the truth."

"Oh, my good God." Mrs. Shaw also climbed to her feet, but

very slowly, as though pulled up by invisible strings. "That can't be right."

"It can. You were proud that this man confided in you, weren't you? You alone. And you never smelled a rat." I clenched my fists, understanding how Mr. Fielding had felt in the room at Scotland Yard, wishing he could strike down Luke. "How did you get the children out?"

Mrs. Shaw began to shake. "I packed up their things and woke 'em early. Took them out through the church gate to a hired coach. And off they went."

"And where is this farm?" I asked. "We had better discover whether they are truly there."

At last Mrs. Shaw began to see the enormity of it. She fell to her seat, rocking back and forth. "I didn't mean ... I thought ... I'm sorry . . ." Her weeping increased, threatening to become hysteria.

I swiftly exited the room, making my way to Mr. Davis's pantry, to which I had the keys. I poured out a glass of brandy and carried it hastily back to the servants' hall.

My legs were trembling with both relief and more anxiety. If Mrs. Shaw was right, then the children hadn't been taken by procurers after all. Perhaps they were safe. But I would make certain of it.

I made Mrs. Shaw drink the brandy, which quieted her. I gave it to her not out of compassion, but so she wouldn't bring the maids, footmen, Mrs. Redfern, or Mr. Davis down to inquire what was the matter.

It did bring Elsie, and I regarded her calmly. "Elsie, will you accompany Mrs. Shaw back to the Foundling Hospital? You will find James there—tell him to run for Mr. McAdam. And Bessie, will you please find out where this farm is, if Mrs. Shaw does not know?"

Mrs. Shaw continued to weep. She'd been the perfect dupe.

"I'll just finish me scone and all this clotted cream," Bessie said, lifting the half-eaten thing to shove into her mouth. "Haven't had a treat like this in . . . ooh, never have, I don't think."

"I will wrap up the rest for you," I said, feeling generous toward the young woman. "Thank you, Bessie. You have been of enormous help."

I sent Mrs. Shaw, Bessie, and Elsie—and a basket packed with tarts, scones, and cakes—off in a hansom to the Foundling Hospital. I knew Elsie would fetch James, who would fetch Daniel, who would be willing to run to the ends of the earth to discover the truth.

"Well," Tess said as she helped me clear up. "What a silly old fool."

I had to agree. "I daresay this man knew exactly how to flatter Mrs. Shaw. I only hope she hasn't caused more harm with her thoughtlessness. Poor Nurse Betts."

"Why'd Miss Betts run to Whitechapel?" Tess carried plates to the sink, beginning to wash up without being asked. "Why not run back to the Foundling Hospital?"

"She was looking for Mr. Fielding," I said, knowing in my heart I was right. "But she wasn't certain of the direction of his church. She wanted to tell him what she'd found, and that she'd feared the children had been sold to the bawdy house. She and Mr. Fielding had become friends, perhaps more than that, and he was one of the governors himself. He'd know what to do."

My heart ached for her and Mr. Fielding both. The lady might have been good for him, softening what was hard in him. I wondered if Mr. Fielding would ever let himself care so much again.

As I began to take out pots to begin the next meal, Mr. Davis arrived. "They're asking for you above stairs," he said. "You are much in demand, Mrs. H." He said it good-naturedly, and not in surprise.

I sighed and untied my apron. "Nothing for it, I suppose."

I walked upstairs with Mr. Davis, who returned to supervise the serving, steeling myself to face a crowd. At least Cynthia and Mr. Thanos would be there, and I could take comfort in their presence through the scrutiny.

When Mr. Davis opened the drawing room door, I stopped in astonishment. Miss Townsend sat resplendent near the window, given the best chair in the room.

She rose gracefully. "Good afternoon, Mrs. Holloway. Once again, I bow to your prowess. You do have a divine cook, Mrs. Bywater."

Mrs. Bywater, flattered, simpered. "She does well. Follows instructions quite nicely."

I held my tongue and curtsied, as was polite, but my knees had gone weak in relief at the sight of Miss Townsend. I'd feared the worst for her, worried she'd gone to investigate as Nurse Betts had done and come to the same fate.

"She's been painting like fury," Cynthia said, with an admonishing look at her. "Never letting her friends know she'd shut herself up, living on bread and water, working away like a demon."

Miss Townsend gave me her beautiful smile. "I forget the passing days when I paint. Bread and water is a bit of exaggeration though, Cynthia. I do take a moment for a cup of tea."

Mrs. Bywater's friends laughed, finding Miss Townsend incredibly witty. Cynthia joined them.

Mr. Thanos, who'd risen politely at my entrance, gave me a nod. "It really is a splendid tea, Mrs. Holloway. You have outdone yourself."

I gave him another curtsy, pleased. "Only a bit of plain cooking, sir. As I do every day."

Mr. Thanos began a protest, but I managed to retreat. No one had offered me a coin this time either, but today, I really didn't mind.

The next morning was my full day out, and I rose early, anxious to begin it. I hadn't heard a word from Daniel, but Elsie, upon her return last night, assured me that she'd given the message to James to find him.

When Bessie, in Elsie's hearing, had demanded Mrs. Shaw make inquiries about the location of the farm, James had declared before that lady could answer—"Oh, I know where it is," and raced away, presumably in search of Daniel

I had no doubt James knew exactly where the farm lay, though he might not have understood the significance of this knowledge. He was good at ferreting out things with no one being the wiser, which was precisely why Daniel had put him in place at the Hospital. I hadn't approved, fearing danger to James, but I had to admit Daniel had been wise to let him nose about.

Tess and I prepared breakfast, and then I changed my frock, putting on my brown dress and hat I'd managed to repair. I wanted to look my best for Grace. Today would be hers.

When I reached the top of the outside stairs, I found Daniel, in his working clothes, lounging against the railing. His face lit with his smile when he saw me.

"I've come to steal you away, Kat. A jaunt to Shadwell, and

then I'll take you to Grace. I thought you'd like to look in on the children Errol took in."

I did wish to, and had planned to later this afternoon. But Daniel had provided a coach once more, as I found when he walked me around the corner to South Audley Street, the faithful Lewis to drive it. I decided not to turn down the opportunity for a comfortable ride.

Daniel handed me in and sat beside me as the carriage bumped slowly through traffic toward Oxford Street.

"I found them, Kat," he said.

I exhaled. "I hadn't wanted to ask. Too afraid of the answer."

"James knew exactly where the farm lay—I have not asked him how he found out, because I'm certain it's best not to know. I rounded up several men from the board, including Bishop Exley, and off we went. They were reluctant at first, but Lord Russell is horrified by this affair and insisted. All five children are safe and sound. The farm is a place—one of several—where they take babies who are gravely ill when their mothers leave them at the Hospital's gates. They are fostered there until they can be nursed back to health. It's a safe place, and would not be suspicious if the older children were found there. Two of the children couldn't wait to return to London, but the other three begged to be allowed to stay at the farm. They enjoyed working with the animals and having fresh air, as cold as it was." Daniel put his hand on mine. "So . . . All's well that ends well."

"What about Bishop Exley?" I asked, my heart warm with relief. "He instigated this plot. I hope it won't end well for *him*."

"Lord Russell has raked him over the coals already. Exley will have to give over the amount he managed to gain from rather gullible donors and be reprimanded and shamed. If he has already spent the money on luxuries for himself—well, that is his misfortune. He'll have to come up with the sum in any case. He's clergy, and has connections in the aristocracy, so he might not be arrested and prosecuted for fraud, but he'll never be trusted again. And he'll be retired from running a parish, Lord Russell vows, as well as dismissed from the Foundling Hospital board."

"A pity." I frowned. "It seems too easy for him. He ought to answer for Nurse Betts's death. As should Luke."

"I made certain Exley knew what happened to her and why. He was guilt-stricken, I am happy to say, and I hope it haunts him. Inspector McGregor was not kind to him, but as I say, an arrest won't stick. Though he'll be watched."

I sank back. "I am glad the children are all right. More than glad. I was sick at heart for them." I closed my eyes, basking in the realization that all was truly well. When the coach rounded the corner and started for High Holborn, I opened my eyes again. "Miss Townsend is safe too, I am pleased to relate."

"Yes, Thanos told me. I brought him in to explain to Lord Russell and McGregor about the swindle. Thanos said Miss Townsend had returned home and he is eager to see what she's painted. He also went on and on about the tea he'd been invited to yesterday with Mrs. Bywater. He's quite taken with your cooking."

"Hardly surprising. The poor man does not eat well." I slid my hand from Daniel's. Hardly proper for him to hold it.

"There is more," Daniel went on. "Inspector McGregor's faith in the police of Bethnal Green was not misplaced. They did find the men who struck the blows that killed Nurse Betts. They're well known in the area as great brutes, and McGregor made certain they were taken in. *Those* arrests will certainly stick."

I sat up. "I am glad. Though it won't help Nurse Betts. Or your brother."

"Justice will be meted," Daniel said, going quiet. "According to the men brought in, Naismith knew exactly who Nurse Betts was—that is, he knew she was connected with Errol, and dear to him. Which means he knows who Errol is and his connection with Carter."

"Oh." I went cold. Mr. Naismith, Daniel had told me before, had wanted to murder everyone connected with Mr. Carter. He'd not realized, apparently, that Daniel had survived, or even who Daniel was. But if he'd discovered Mr. Fielding's identity, he might know about Daniel.

"Exactly," Daniel said grimly. "He was sending a message to Errol, a warning. Not that my brother will heed that warning."

"Do you think Mr. Naismith knows who you are?"

Daniel rubbed his forehead. "I have no idea, Kat. I've tried to evade him for years, at first fearing he'd recognize me as one of Carter's associates, and then wanting to remain in the shadows while I plotted my revenge." He let out a breath. "That may be all for nothing now."

"Have a care, please." I reached for his hand again, propriety vanishing with my worry. "I would not like this dangerous man to decide to come after you."

"Nor would I." Daniel squeezed my fingers. "Or send me a message by harming *you*. Promise me you'll stay indoors as much as you can, Kat."

"I can hardly bring home the comestibles I need by hiding in my kitchen. Nor will I give up my days out with Grace."

"True, but you can send someone for ingredients or take along a burly footman to protect you when you go to the market. Likewise you can remain at the Millburns the entirety of your day and half out. It's cold these days. I'm certain it's cozy."

I gave him a disparaging look. "The simple solution is to tell Inspector McGregor what a bad man Mr. Naismith is, and have him arrested."

"I have told him. McGregor is eager to go after him, but it is not easy. There must be evidence that he ordered Nurse Betts to be killed, not simply a thug's word." Daniel gave me a quiet nod. "But McGregor is thorough. He will push for the harshest conviction for her killers. Naismith will receive the message that he is not untouchable."

"Good." I was not bloodthirsty by nature, but Nurse Betts had been innocent, a good woman.

We lapsed into silence as the coach made its slow way through the City and out to Whitechapel and then Shadwell. Bells were chiming the hour when we arrived at All Saints, sweet and clear, out of place in the darkness of the slums.

The first thing we heard upon knocking at the vicarage door was Mr. Fielding's housekeeper, Mrs. Hodder, shouting. The door was wrenched open, but instead of the housekeeper, the tall young man, the oldest of the children rescued from the bawdy house, glared out at us.

"Yeah? What you want?" His belligerence subsided when he realized who we were. "Oh. You again."

"Devil take it." Mr. Fielding's growl sounded behind him. The boy rolled his eyes but moved off, and Mr. Fielding appeared in his place. "Ah. It's you," he echoed the lad. "You'd better come in."

Mr. Fielding was in shirtsleeves, and his collar hung by one button on the back of his neck. "Go after that little wretch Michael," he called to the retreating youth. "He's nearly up the chimney again."

The young man made an exasperated noise and dived into the dining room.

Mr. Fielding led us into a sitting room, now littered with piles of clothes, blankets, and pillows. He moved a stack of blankets from a chair and waved me to it.

"I'm going through the poor boxes to salvage clothing for the tykes. And extra bedding. I have rooms enough for them, yes, but not sheets." Mr. Fielding's hair was mussed, his look distracted. "I cannot imagine why men long for fatherhood. They have to be mad."

"They have wives and servants to look after the children," I informed him, "and so aren't bothered by them. I quite admire you for taking them in."

"Of course you do. I was trying to be admirable." Mr. Fielding softened his tone. "And the devil I'd let them go to a workhouse."

While he was harried, I could see Mr. Fielding was less grief-stricken, more pulled into the present than lingering in the past. Nurse Betts, I imagined, would approve.

Daniel moved another box and took a seat. Mrs. Hodder appeared, eyes wide, but Mr. Fielding waved her off. "We don't require refreshment," Mr. Fielding told her. "I have put upon you enough as it is."

She apparently agreed, as she moved out of sight with barely a nod.

"She'll give notice with all this chaos," Mr. Fielding said mournfully. "She's a wonderful housekeeper, but I have asked too much, I think."

"I am pleased to hear the children are lively," I said. "It means they are not broken."

Mr. Fielding sobered. "They are up and down. Like normal children one moment—that is to say, hellions—the next, they take fright and will barely speak. Will be like that for a while,

I wager. Their lives will never be the same, but perhaps they won't be lost entirely."

"*You* managed." I gestured at the comfortable room. "Here you are."

Mr. Fielding sent me a wry look. "Only because I became a ferocious little devil. Fought like hell for everything." He paused. "But yes, here I am."

Daniel waited until we were finished. "We came with news," he said lightly. "Do you want to hear it?"

"Don't be heartless, old cock," Mr. Fielding said in a hard voice. "Of course I want to hear it."

Daniel proceeded to tell him that the foundling children were safe and well, and of the culprit on the board of governors. When he mentioned the name Bishop Exley, Mr. Fielding stared in incredulity, then exploded with laughter.

"That sanctimonious old weasel. A confidence man, is he?" Mr. Fielding's laughter ended in a cough. "Well, well. This means a place for a suffragan bishop might be dangling for the taking. Hmm."

A suffragan was an assistant, if I remembered aright. "Do you believe you could have a chance at it?" I asked.

"Of course, dear lady." Mr. Fielding gave me a sly wink. "Where do you think Exley's demesne lay?" He spread his hands. "The East End."

He chuckled again, then caught sight of Daniel's quiet eye on him, and his laughter died. "You have more to say."

Daniel nodded and related the tale of McGregor arresting the villains who'd killed Nurse Betts. Mr. Fielding listened stoically, and when Daniel finished, he collapsed back into his chair.

"Damn the bastards," he muttered. "Damn them straight to

hell. If they're not hanged until they're black in the face, I hope every evil man they're banged up with tears them apart. If they don't, I will."

I flinched at the vicious words, but I could not condemn him for them. Nurse Betts had not deserved to die, wretched and in pain. Likely the bullies had hurt many more besides her.

"I told you we should go after Naismith," Mr. Fielding went on. "That chap I told you about, his enemy, is willing. He very much wants you to join us."

"And then we'd be in thrall to a man as bad as Naismith or worse," Daniel pointed out.

"We'll cross that bridge when we come to it."

Daniel scowled at him. "This man wants *me* in his fold, does he? Have you asked yourself why?"

"Because you're in thick with the police," Mr. Fielding answered easily. "Of course I deduced that."

"He'd pump me for knowledge I am reluctant to give," Daniel said. "Then where would we be? Dead, probably."

Mr. Fielding shrugged, the movement too nonchalant. "You disappoint me, dear brother. But you are no doubt right." He seemed to dismiss the matter, but I had the feeling Daniel and I hadn't heard the last about this man who wanted to go after Mr. Naismith.

Mr. Fielding became somber once more. "The hell of it is," he said softly, "Nell was killed not because of the reprobate me, but because of the reformed me. She believed in me, the vicar who worried so much for the foundling children. If she'd known the rogue I truly was, she'd never have tried to find me to help her that day." He rested his head on the back of the chair, gazing at the ceiling, hiding what was in his eyes.

"You are better than you know," I said gently. "If you'd truly been the rogue, she would have seen it. You are not as good at hiding it as you think. She knew, and saw the good man beneath."

Mr. Fielding snorted a laugh, lifting his head and wiping his cheeks with the heel of his hand. "Is she truly so naive?" he asked Daniel.

"Mrs. Holloway is a wise woman," Daniel said. He lifted a blanket and absently began to fold it.

"And Daniel is a facetious man," I countered. "*You* went to divinity studies to become a vicar," I said to Mr. Fielding. "Learned scriptures. Some of that must have rubbed off on you—you cannot have been exposed to so much goodness without it seeping in."

Mr. Fielding continued to laugh quietly. "You do know that much of history is littered with blood-churning wars in the name of God, Christ, and good works?"

"I do. But these are more civilized times."

"Ha. Read a newspaper more often, dear lady. You will learn much that is shocking."

"Be that as it may, I will continue with my assertion that you are a good man, and can bring forth that goodness when you wish. A shoot does not grow on rocky soil."

Mr. Fielding grinned at me, his good humor restored for now, which was what I had intended. "Don't preach the parables to me, dear lady—I know them by heart."

"I am pleased to hear it, Mr. Fielding."

I reached into my coat pocket and withdrew the photograph Daniel had given me of Nurse Betts and the children in her charge. I held it out to Mr. Fielding. "You keep that. Something to remember her by."

Mr. Fielding went perfectly still as he took the photograph and gazed down at it. His hand shook once, and he swallowed.

I left the room before he could say anything to me, and

when I turned back, his attention was still on the picture. Daniel sat in silent compassion, and I left them alone.

I went upstairs in Mr. Fielding's house before we departed it, to visit the children. They seemed to be settling in, and the littlest girl, I saw with some relief, had lost her terrified blankness. The older two girls were looking after her.

The three lasses shared a large bedroom, which they looked upon as a great luxury. The two youngest boys shared another room, and the oldest lad had his own, next to Mr. Fielding's. He was an unhappy young man, snarling at me that this cozy arrangement would not last. Mr. Fielding had no money, the youth said, and Mr. Fielding's parish would force him to throw them out.

I had other ideas about that.

I attempted to hug the youngest girl, but she went very stiff when I touched her, and I backed away. Perhaps she'd come to trust again, but I could not imagine it would be soon.

Daniel and I took our leave as Mr. Fielding was explaining to the youngest lad why climbing the chimney was a bad idea, and Lewis drove us back toward the City.

"I'm sorry for Mr. Fielding," I said as we rode. "But I believed what I said, you know. That your brother has a good heart. Deep down."

"No, the good heart is yours." Daniel took my hand, his fingers caressing through my gloves. "I've always known that."

While his words and his touch comforted me, I could not let that be the end of it. "He will come around. Perhaps caring for the children will be the making of him. He can repay what Mr. Carter did for you both."

"Possibly." Daniel's tone was cautious, and I had to concede he knew Mr. Fielding far better than I did.

When we arrived at Cheapside, and I prepared to leap down and walk to the Millburns, Daniel asked Lewis to wait, and he accompanied me to the house.

I had told my friend Joanna about Daniel, of course. She looked him over dubiously as he grinned at her, which I understood. Daniel was in his laborer's clothes, and with his unruly hair and worn cap, he did not appear the heroic figure I'd made him out to be.

Grace, however, was delighted to see him. "Good day, Mr. McAdam." She shook his hand with pretty manners. "I am glad you've come to visit me."

"I've done one better," Daniel said, giving Joanna his most charming smile. "I'm here to take you on a treat, you and your mum both. A visit to an artist, who has done a painting of your mother."

Joanna's brow puckered. "Oh?"

"I explained about that," I said quickly. "Miss Townsend sketched me cooking. Nothing untoward. I am pleased to hear she has finished."

"Not quite finished," Daniel said. "But the picture is complete enough that she wouldn't mind you having a look. As I know you're longing to."

I was. When Miss Townsend had announced she'd finished the painting, a great curiosity to see it had surged through me. But of course, the picture was in her private studio, and it would not be dignified or proper for me to beg to be admitted.

Daniel must have arranged it. He always knew how to turn me up sweet.

25

Miss Townsend's studio was in Mayfair, in a narrow house in Upper Brook Street, near Hyde Park. She'd hired the house and put her studio on the top floor, where the light was best.

Lady Cynthia, Mr. Thanos, and Bobby were in the studio when we arrived. They greeted Grace with pleasure, as did Miss Townsend when she was introduced.

Miss Townsend, who did not seem surprised I had a daughter—Bobby had likely told her—gave me a penetrating look, one filled with understanding.

"This is where I've been rusticating," Miss Townsend said, indicating the studio with a wave. "I apologize, Mrs. Holloway, for not sending word. I had no idea anyone would be so worried about me. I tend to forget the time when I'm hard at it."

"I'll say," Bobby growled.

The rooms at the top of the house had been knocked together to form one great loft, six windows letting in light. It was a bit chilly, though a stove had been fitted to the chimney, trying its best to cut the cold.

Miss Townsend had been working on several canvases. Three large ones dominated standing easels, and one painting, more complete than the others, leaned against the wall under the windows.

"I'm not finished by a long way," Miss Townsend said. "But I wanted your opinion. Have I got it right?"

I stood back and gazed at the four paintings. She'd put the figures of a cook and her assistant in each, and tables, dishes, and some of the food, but not the background.

I'd worried about being recognized in a painting, but I needn't have bothered. While the cook had my shape and my style of cook's dress and apron, the face was a sort of blur with the merest line of jaw and nose. In one, the cook was looking down, her eyes not visible. A curl of dark hair laced from her cap to droop down her neck, exactly as mine did when I was hot and hurried.

In spite of its odd nature, the painting amazed me. In simple lines, with nothing sharp, Miss Townsend had conveyed the portrait of a cook hard at work, capturing the *movement*. A cook was never still, always chopping, peeling, stirring, basting, and scurrying to and fro.

In another painting, the cook was at the stove, her back to the room, and again, I could imagine her shaking the pan or flipping frying sausages. The assistant, having the slim figure of Tess, her unruly hair, and often askew cap, vigorously chopped a carrot.

The food was more recognizable than the two people—with a glimpse of a scullery maid in the far room washing dishes. A bowl of cooked potatoes sprinkled with parsley gently steamed. Mushrooms, dark and fresh, overflowed a basket.

Bright fruit lay both cut and uncut, and in another painting, the table held cakes and tarts, a loaf of sugar waiting to be pounded into usable chunks.

I stared in awe, my hands coming together in delight, as Miss Townsend watched me carefully.

Grace came to stand beside me. "Is that you, Mum?" she asked with childish frankness. "You're all blurry."

Laughter around me loosened my tongue. "It is me," I told her. "And yet, it's *every* cook. And every cook's assistant. They are beautiful."

Miss Townsend relaxed. "I'm pleased you approve." Her words were light, but I heard gratification in them.

"Will people truly buy these?" I asked.

"Oh yes," Cynthia assured me. "Judith sells all sorts of canvases. She has people lined up for her next ones."

"Good," I said. "These should be seen."

"You are a lovely woman, Mrs. Holloway," Miss Townsend said. "I will pour wine, and we will celebrate. Lemonade for your daughter."

She had servants downstairs apparently, though I'd seen not a sign of any—Miss Townsend had admitted us to the house herself. She summoned one, not by a bell but through a speaking tube, to my and Grace's intense interest.

An elderly butler, who pretended not to notice that a cook, her daughter, and a common deliveryman had come to visit his mistress, arrived with a tray of glasses and a bottle of wine, a carafe of lemonade for Grace. He served with an air of one who'd rather be elsewhere, but I imagined he was used to Miss Townsend and her eccentric guests.

After the butler departed, Daniel told the company all that had transpired, and to lighten the mood, I related the tale of visiting Mr. Fielding and the children staying with him today.

Much merriment was had at Mr. Fielding's expense, the man now finding himself in the middle of a crèche.

As our friends sipped wine—which was exceedingly good; I'd have to ask what it was for Mr. Davis's benefit—I managed to step to a solitary corner with Miss Townsend.

"I hope you will not take offense at my lack of delicacy," I began, "but I was thinking through who I knew with wealth. And yours was the only name that leapt to mind."

Miss Townsend regarded me calmly, if a trifle coolly. "Oh?"

"To be blunt, Mr. Fielding—while he might *possibly* have a fortune stashed away from ill-gotten gains—likely has very little. Not enough to keep six children of varying ages in his house, anyway. He has promised not to send them to a workhouse, but without a benefactor, they might have little choice in what happens to them."

Miss Townsend's brows arched. "I see. And you wish me to be their benefactor?"

"Not necessarily. But you move in prestigious circles, and I've seen that you can encourage people to do as you please. Do not protest—you enthralled Mrs. Bywater as easy as anything, and I know you've done the same to me. But these are unfortunate children, and I will put aside my pride and ask you to help."

Her coolness vanished. "Of course, Mrs. Holloway. Could you doubt that I would be happy to assist? The fact that you let me into your kitchen, your sanctum, and allowed me to sketch you in spite of the inconvenience of it, shows that you have a kindness in you. I will be their benefactor, have no fear. I won't bother canvassing my friends and clients, who, I am afraid to say, can be a bit closefisted."

I held up my hands in protest. "Truly, I did not intend to have you do it single-handedly."

"Nonsense. I know how to set up a trust. Who knows, I may extend it to help still more unfortunate children. I have no intention of marrying and having children of my own, so why not help those who have nothing?"

"You are very kind."

"No, I am conceited. But pleased to help for your sake. I have been watching you, Mrs. Holloway, and I know you have a goodness in you with extraordinary depth."

I had said much the same thing about Mr. Fielding. No wonder he'd brushed my observation aside. It was a bit embarrassing.

D aniel saw me and Grace back to the coach, telling Lewis to return us to the Millburns. He would not accompany us, he said, explaining he had business to take care of, but promised he'd speak to me later.

As he often said this upon departing from me, I did not hold myself tight in anticipation as to when the later would be. He might come tonight, or I might not see him for days.

I enjoyed the ride to Cheapside with Grace, the two of us admiring houses and public gardens we passed, or counting church steeples. When we reached the Millburns', I helped Joanna serve tea, and we had a fine time.

I returned home, ready to work again, but looking forward to Monday afternoon.

I described Miss Townsend's pictures to Tess, in as much detail as I could. Miss Townsend had extended the invitation to Tess to visit her studio on *her* day out, and Tess expressed eagerness to see the paintings.

"Funny she did them all fuzzy," Tess said. "I didn't necessarily want to show me face, but what if people think the paints ran in the rain?"

"She works in the style of the French artists," I said, suppressing my laughter. "Like Monsieur Renoir and Mary Cassatt, as Cynthia told us."

"Ah well," Tess said. "They're a funny lot, ain't they, painters?"

"I suppose," I said. "So are cooks. Let us get on, shall we?"

Daniel did come that night as I sat alone in the quiet darkness in the kitchen, a single candle on the table for company. Dying coals hissed in the stove, the occasional droplet of water thudded from the pump in the sink, and boards creaked as the house settled.

The knock at the door roused me from my thoughts, and I hurried to open it to Daniel.

"I made tea," I said as he sat down, brushing water out of his hair. A fine rain had begun to fall. "The last of Mr. Li's."

"You are good to share it with me, Kat."

"Of course. It is better with a friend."

I measured the tea into a pot and after it steeped, I poured out. We drank it without sugar or cream, the tea so smooth and fine it needed no embellishment. We sipped in contented silence for a moment, I thinking of Mr. Li and hoping he was well and happy in China with his family.

"Ah, I almost forgot." Daniel set down his empty cup. "I've brought you a token."

He reached into his pocket and withdrew an envelope, a plain one, with no writing on it. I eyed it in curiosity.

"I know you are proud," Daniel said, "and might throw it back in my face, but you helped me—and my brother, and many others—with your time you have so little of, and at your own expense. I came to you, and you did not turn me away."

"Why should I?" I asked. "Children in peril are nothing to walk away from."

Daniel placed the envelope in front of me. "Please keep this as a gesture of my appreciation."

Mystified, I lifted the envelope and peered inside. It held banknotes.

"Daniel . . ."

Daniel broke in quickly. "I pay Thanos for lending me his mathematical brain. I pay Lewis to drive me where I wish. I pay James to run hither and yon for me, and a few other scamps to keep an eye out when I need it. Why should I not give you your share?"

I was not the mathematical genius Mr. Thanos was, but I could swiftly count money.

"Daniel, there is ten quid here." I took out the notes, large and ruffling. "I cannot accept so much. A few bob, possibly, but never this."

"You can, and I hope you will. You do much for everyone." Daniel gave me his melting smile. "Put it aside for Grace and the tea shop you plan to open."

He knew exactly how to get around me, did this man. I slid the money into the envelope and laid it on the table. "It is far too extravagant. You do not have to pay me. I am not a shop-keeper."

Daniel sighed in resignation and reached for the envelope. "Ah, well. It was a faint hope."

I pressed my hand to it. "On the other hand, it *is* ten quid."

Daniel laughed and withdrew. I plucked up the envelope and closed it into my notebook.

He was right, such funds would be handy for Grace. When I had my tea shop, I'd pay him back from the proceeds.

"Now that we have settled that, I have a question." I lifted the teapot, determined to savor every last drop. "When the explosion happened at Coldbath Fields, I saw you there."

Daniel held out his cup for more of the dark amber liquid. "I know you did. Wherever there is trouble . . ."

"That man with you," I said before he could make a joke of it. "Who was he? Is *he* who you work for?"

I did not expect a straight answer. Therefore, I was surprised when Daniel sent me a quiet nod. "He is. I can't tell you his name. But yes."

I recalled the tall, spare man with the spectacles, who gazed about him with such derision. I shivered. "He has cold eyes."

"And a cold heart." Daniel traced the handle of his teacup. "But he is brilliant, and he has the respect of the Yard. Or the terror of it—I'm not certain. One reason we discovered and captured the villains who killed Nurse Betts, without Naismith being able to stop us, was because of him."

"I see." I felt a chill. A man that criminals as nasty as Naismith feared was not a man to run afoul of. "And you work for him? Why?"

"Not a thing I chose." Daniel kept his eyes on the steaming tea. "It was chosen for me." He paused a long moment. "And there is the rub."

I gave him a perplexed look as I filled my own cup. "Why do you say that? I thought you liked chasing villains. You are so very good at it."

"I do, and I am." Daniel's grin shone briefly then faded. "He has told me I must go away again. I can't tell you where." He let out a breath and finally looked at me. "I have refused."

I grew more bewildered. "You just said you had no choice."

"Well, we shall see if he accepts my refusal. But I am reluctant to leave London these days. I have more reason not to throw myself headlong into danger. I admit I enjoyed it when I was younger—needed it. Now . . ."

"Now you have James," I said, thinking of Grace. "Children change a person."

"James, yes." Daniel slid his hand across the table to me. "And you."

The breath I drew was ragged. Daniel teased me often, but his declarations were few. Perhaps because I put him off, or teased him in return.

"Me," I said in a near whisper.

"Yes. God help me." Daniel's fingers tightened on mine. "How can I leave, when the damn fool things he has me do might mean I never see you again?"

Again I sat in silence, unsure what this new awareness would mean.

"If you have made a pledge to him . . ." My voice was faint.

"Not so much a pledge, but it is something I can't break. I was a bad 'un, Kat. As bad as my brother, I'm sorry to say. This is my penance."

"Oh." I still did not understand completely, but I was edging closer. Daniel traveled to Scotland or Ireland or the Continent, chased Fenians who'd cheerfully kill him at any instant, and ran after terrible villains, because he had no choice. The bespectacled man had him in a stranglehold.

"For how long?" I asked.

"Until I convince them I've paid." Daniel released me. "I still can't tell you the entire story. But I will, in time—swearing you to secrecy, of course. Once I'm finished."

My eyes stung. "You might be dead before then."

"I might be, yes."

I studied him for a long moment, while the tea gave up its

heat to the chilly room. Without word, I rose and moved to his side of the table. Daniel watched me come, his expression guarded as I sat down beside him.

"Then we must make the most of our time, my dear friend," I said.

I clasped his hands in mine, leaned forward, and softly kissed him on the mouth.

Acknowledgments

Thanks go to my editor, Kate Seaver, who loves Kat Holloway as much as I do. Also to my dear husband, who puts up with the quirks and inconveniences of living with an author.

Don't miss the next book in the
Below Stairs Mysteries.
Coming soon from
Berkley Prime Crime!

Photo by Silvio Portrait Design

Jennifer Ashley is the *New York Times* and *USA Today* bestselling author of the Below Stairs Mysteries, including *Scandal Above Stairs* and *Death Below Stairs*. She also writes as national bestselling and award-winning author Allyson James and bestselling author Ashley Gardner. She lives in the Southwest with her husband and cats, and spends most of her time in the wonderful worlds of her stories.

CONNECT ONLINE

JenniferAshley.com
🄵 JenniferAshleyAllysonJamesAshleyGardner
🐦 JennAllyson

Ready to find
your next great read?

Let us help.

Visit prh.com/nextread

Penguin
Random
House